this story!

Christy R. Diachenko

Psalm 40:2

Christy R. Diachenko

Broken Promise

Christy R. Diachenko

Christy R. Diachenko

Cover Art Designed by: **Val Muller**
Cover Photo by: **Christy Diachenko**

Copyright Christy Diachenko ©2014
All rights reserved
ISBN 13: 978-0692340301
ISBN 10: 0692340300

Broken Promise

Christy R. Diachenko

Christy R. Diachenko

ALL RIGHTS RESERVED

Publisher's Note:

This is a work of fiction. All names, characters, places, and events are the work of the author's imagination. Any resemblance to real persons, places, or events is coincidental.

Cover Art Designed by: **Val Muller**
Cover Photo by: **Christy Diachenko**

ISBN 13: 978-0692340301
ISBN 10: 0692340300

DWB PUBLISHING
www.dancingwithbearpublishing.com

From The Author

My most sincere, heartfelt thanks to:
My Lord and Savior Jesus Christ. Because He is my every-
thing.
Willie Thompson. For encouraging me years ago during our
WMUU days, to go ahead and write the story that was ram-
bling around in my head.
Marie McGaha. For taking me under your wing and giving a
newcomer a chance.
My precious Mom and Dad. For being there to love and pro-
tect me during my darkest hour.
Joelle Lanfear. For proof reading and helping me think in
some different directions. Your thoughts and insights were
incredibly helpful.
Lisa Garris, Debbie Parrish, and Janine Shamey. For reading
my story and giving me honest critiques.
Jeff McCall. For your law enforcement input.
My co-workers. You know who you are. The Lord has used
you all in an amazing way as instruments of His healing.
Each of you are so special to me. Your support, your kindness, your love - God has used them all to get me where I
am today. I couldn't have done it without you.

*"I waited patiently for the Lord to help me, and he turned
to me and heard my cry. He lifted me out of the pit of despair, out of the mud and the mire. He set my feet on solid
ground and steadied me as I walked along. He has given me
a new song to sing, a hymn of praise to our God. Many will
see what he has done and be amazed. They will put their
trust in the Lord (Psalms 40: 1-3, NLT)."*

Christy R. Diachenko

~ *Prologue* ~

The child's lower lip trembled. The covers were tucked in around him ready for nap time, but he looked at his mother with sad eyes. "Momma, teacher said in Sunday School that everybody's a sinner. She said we all do bad things that make Jesus sad. She said if we 'cept Jesus to be our savior, we'll go to Heaven." He balled his tiny fingers into a fist and rubbed at the tears forming in his eyes.

"Yes, honey. That's true."

"But Momma, I don't know how to 'cept Jesus." The tears began to flow down his cheeks. "I wanna but I don't know how."

"Would you like me to help you?"

Five-year-old Christopher hiccupped, sniffled, and looked at her expectantly. "Yes, Momma. I love Jesus and I want to go to Heaven."

"Honey, when God created the world, everything was perfect just like in Heaven. There were no sinners and the people He created lived in a beautiful garden. But one day, Satan came and tempted the people to disobey God.

"God gave them all kinds of wonderful things in their garden, but they decided to disobey God and do the one thing He told them not to do. Because of their sin, they could not live in the beautiful garden anymore. Ever since then, all people born are sinners, even little boys like you and grownups like your daddy and me."

She reached to smooth a stray hair from his forehead. "God could not let sin into Heaven because Heaven is a perfect place."

"Like the garden?" he asked.

"Yes, honey, like the garden. But you know what? God still loved the people He created, even though they chose to disobey Him and ruin the perfect plan He had for them.

"Their sin had to be punished. But God didn't want His people to be punished forever, so he sent Jesus, God's only son, to take the punishment for them. Jesus was perfect and never sinned, so He was the only one who could take the punishment. Jesus died for you and for me so that we could live with Him in Heaven someday."

"What's 'died,' Momma?" he asked.

"Remember when your hamster died?"

"Yeah. We dug a hole and put him in the ground, and I couldn't play with him anymore." Christopher looked puzzled. "Did Jesus get put in a hole?"

"He was buried in a tomb," his mother said. "Kind of like a cave. But guess what?"

"What, Momma?" he asked, looking at her intently.

"Jesus didn't stay in that tomb."

"How did He get out of there?"

"God brought him back to life. Jesus lives in Heaven now and He loves us so much. He wants us to be His children. He wants us to believe that He loves us and died for our sins so we could live with Him one day. He wants to live in our hearts, and He knows the very best way for us to live on this earth. If we obey Him, we will have peace and joy."

"How can I be His children, Momma?" Christopher asked. "I wanna belong to Jesus. I want Him in my heart."

"All you have to do is talk to Him, sweetheart. Tell Him you know you're a sinner and that you're sorry for your sin. Tell Him you accept Him to be your Savior and that you want Him to live in your heart and guide your life." She smiled and gently put a hand on his blonde head. "Do you want to pray now, honey? Do you understand?" She prayed inwardly that her young son would remember the truths he had been taught since he was born, and that God would open his heart to believe.

Christopher sat up in the bed and paused for a moment, his brow furrowed while his mind processed what he had heard. In a moment he said, "Yes, Momma. I wanna be Jesus' child."

His expression was very serious, and his eyes began to fill with tears once more. "But Momma, I don't wanna stop being *your* little boy."

"Oh, sweetheart, you won't. Mommy and Daddy will always be your mommy and daddy, and Jesus will be your Heavenly Father." She pulled him into her lap and hugged him close.

"Can I talk to Jesus now, Momma?" he asked, cuddling against her.

"Yes, honey. Go ahead."

Christopher folded his small hands together and bowed his head. "Hi, Jesus. It's me, Christopher Gordon. I'm sorry sometimes I sin. Thank You for dying for me and I'm glad You're not still dead like my hamster. Please save me from my sins. I want You to be my Heaven Father forever and ever. I want You to live in my heart and I want to obey You, Jesus. Amen."

Mary Gordon shared the good news of Christopher's decision with her husband and daughter when they returned home that afternoon. They rejoiced together that God had spoken to Christopher's heart at such an early age. That night, Matt and Mary tip toed into Christopher's room, looking at him while he slept.

"Watch over him, Father," Matt prayed in a whisper. "Let his life bring glory and honor to You, Lord Jesus. Guide and direct his steps, protect him, and help him to be sensitive to Your leading."

"Lead him to the right spouse someday, Lord," Mary said. "Help him to remain pure and upright in all his relationships, no matter what the temptations. Help him not to settle for less than your best for his life."

The loving parents finished their prayer by dedicating their son to God. They each leaned over and kissed his cheek gently.

"Our precious boy," Mary whispered when a tear trickled down her cheek. "Use him, Father. Use him in a mighty way to share Your love."

~ * ~

Ten years later

"Mom," Mickey Sterling flounced into the room. "I am nearly fifteen years old. Why can't I go to the party?"
Anne Sterling sighed deeply. "Mickey, honey, I don't have a good feeling about some of those kids. They surely do not appear to be interested in Godly things, or in living lives that are pleasing to the Lord."

"Mom, I can't believe you call yourself a Christian when you're always judging and condemning. Angela and the kids in her neighborhood are so nice, and they want me to be part of their group. I feel like a baby when you say I can't hang out with them. What am I supposed to tell them? 'My mom won't let me come to your house?'" She sighed the sigh of an aggrieved teenager.

"I've made my decision, Mickey. I'm sorry you feel the way you do but like it or not, my job is to protect you. I cannot allow you to participate in something when I feel a warning in my spirit. I love you, honey. I know you don't believe me right now, but the fact remains. You are my precious girl, and I will do whatever I have to do to keep you safe."

Mickey burst into tears. "I'll bet if Dad hadn't been killed, *he* would have let me go. If Dad was still here, you wouldn't be so mean."

She ran upstairs and slammed her bedroom door. She stood for a moment, staring furiously in the direction she had come. *Why is she like this?* Mickey thought angrily. *It's not like I'm a child. She's always pushing religion and the Bible down my throat. I don't need God and I don't need her.*

She walked aimlessly to her closet to look at her favorite clothes, pouting and thinking of all the reasons why she didn't like her mother. She conveniently forgot how hard her mother worked to provide those garments for her.

Her thoughts tumbled over in her mind and her attitude continued to sour while the evening progressed. Finally, she gave up and went to bed, tears of self-pity trickling down her face.

A knock on her door awakened her at 6:00 am. "Mickey, honey, are you awake?" her mother asked.

Remembering her anger of the night before, Mickey flipped back the covers, jumped out of bed, and swept open the door. "I am now, Mom. Thanks a lot."

"Mickey, I need to tell you something."

Her serious tone and heartbroken look gave Mickey pause and she sat down on the bed. "Okay, Mom. What?"

Anne sat beside her. "Honey, I don't know how to tell you this, so I'm going to just say it. Angela and two of her friends were killed last night."

Mickey felt like a jolt of electricity just coursed through her veins. "Mom, you're not serious. You're just saying that."

Anne's sob caught in her throat and the tears began to flow. "Oh, honey, it's true. She was driving her parents' car without their knowledge or permission. Apparently, the girls had been drinking and decided to drive up into the mountains. They crashed into a tree after losing control on a curve. They were killed instantly."

Mickey's shoulders began to shake uncontrollably, and tears coursed down her cheeks. "Oh, Mom, no!" She clung to her mother for comfort while the shock and horror of what happened sank in. She sobbed in anguish feeling she could never stop. The reality of the tragic event continued to wash over her like waves, making her feel she would be ill.

~ * ~

A very subdued Mickey waited at the door when her mother returned from her job at Publix that evening. "Mom, can we talk?"

"Of course, honey." Anne put her purse on the kitchen table. "Let's sit in the living room. My feet are killing me. I was on the register all day."

Once her mother was seated comfortably on the couch, Mickey stood before her and began awkwardly. "Mom, I'm sorry. I was so hateful to you." She began to cry softly. "I didn't mean what I said. I love you, Mom."

"Come here, honey. Come here." She patted the seat beside her. Mickey sat and wrapped her arms tightly around her mother. Anne hugged her back and let her cry.

When her sobs abated, Mickey sat back. "Mom, I'm so scared. If I had been with Angela, I'd probably be dead right now." She grabbed a tissue from the box on the end table and dabbed at her eyes.

"I would have gone to Hell, Mom. I know you've tried to teach me about accepting Jesus as my Savior, but I thought I was okay on my own. I thought religion was just for old people. No offense, Mom."

Anne smiled. "None taken."

Mickey stared out the window. "I can't believe Angela, Cynthia, and Sharae are gone. Gone. Just like that. I'll never see them again."

She sighed deeply. "Mom, I want Jesus in my life." She began to weep again, her heart and her pride broken.

12

"I can't handle this, and I can't handle life. I see now how badly I need God."

Inwardly, Anne Sterling rejoiced. *Oh Father, thank You! I've prayed for my baby girl for so long. And her father prayed for her before she was even born. Thank You for showing her the way.*

With gentle loving words, Anne made sure Mickey knew what accepting Jesus entailed. Assuring her mother of her desire to commit her life to God, Mickey prayed and asked Jesus to forgive her sins, come into her heart, and be her Savior.

After supper, Anne and Mickey took a walk in the field behind the house. They looked up at the star-studded sky and Anne took Mickey's hand. "Honey, I think your daddy is looking down on us right now. He loved you so much. Did you know he prayed for you when we found out I was pregnant?"

"He did, Mom?" Mickey felt the prickle of tears again. The thought of her father's love wrapped over her like a warm blanket. "What did he pray for?"

"He always prayed first that you would find Jesus and give your life to Him. But the second prayer was that you would find a Godly man to be your husband someday. A man who would treat you kindly and gently and love you more than life itself."

Mickey stopped and took a deep breath. "Wow, Mom. Just, wow." She looked up at the sky again. "Thanks, Daddy. I found Jesus tonight. I don't know about that husband you prayed for, but we'll see what happens."

With smiling faces wet with happy tears, mother and daughter made their way back to the house.

Christy R. Diachenko

~ *One* ~

College
Freshman Year

"**M**ickey, I love you." Christopher looked across the table, his emotions starkly revealed on his handsome face.

Mickey looked irritated and put her fork down forcefully on the dessert plate. "Chris, I told you before, I just don't feel that way." She lowered her voice when the nearby diners looked at her. "I wish I loved you like that but I cannot help that I don't."

Mickey toyed with the corner of her napkin, then crushed the piece of cloth into her lap and took a deep breath.

"Christopher, I need you to make me a promise." She looked at him, her blue eyes intense. "I need you to promise you'll never talk about this again, or we won't be able to continue this friendship. I really like you, Chris. I mean you're like family and you're my best friend. We have so much fun together and I'm comfortable with you. But I can't be a true friend if I'm constantly afraid I'll have to hurt you by having this conversation over and over."

She squared her shoulders and looked at her empty plate. "I need your promise, Chris."

Shock, rejection, and hurt rolled over Christopher like waves crashing against the shore. Mickey told him before that she did not have romantic feelings for him, but he was sure in time she would come around. He could not believe what she asked of him.

"Mickey." His square jaw set tense with anger. "I don't think I can do that, and I don't think it's fair for you to ask. I guess we can't be friends. I wonder now if we ever

15

really were. I think you've just been toying with me since we met that day between classes. I've been foolish to allow myself to follow a path leading nowhere."

Christopher asked the waitress for the bill and got up after leaving payment on the table. In awkward silence they left the restaurant and walked to his car. He dropped Mickey off at her dorm without a word, revved the engine sharply, and drove off, stewing in his anger and hurt.

Mickey went to her room in tears. *I wish I could love him*, she thought miserably. *But you can't manufacture feelings that aren't there. I can't help it. I do love him as a friend but not in the way he wants me to love him. I just don't feel all warm and fuzzy.*

She climbed onto her top bunk and sobbed, grieving for the loss of her dear friend and over the fact that she hurt him so deeply.

Several long weeks went by, during which Mickey and Christopher neither spoke to nor saw each other. Mickey's roommates were aghast when they found out what had happened.

"You're crazy, girl," said Joelle. "He's such an awesome guy. I'd marry him in a minute."

"Yeah," put in Janine while she took hot rollers out of her hair. "Christopher Gordon is a fantastic guy. He's a strong Christian, a complete gentleman, he's fun, and he's totally gorgeous. How can you *not* love him?"

Sophomore Faith looked up from her book with a look of worldly-wise arrogance. "You're just a freshman. I guess you're not mature enough to know a good man when you see one."

Mickey tried to explain. There was just no chemistry, no feelings beyond that of friendship but they simply could not understand. Finally, she gave up and told the girls she did not want to discuss the subject anymore.

~ * ~

Christopher sat on his bunk Friday evening several weeks later, misery written all over his face. He regretted his angry outburst the day Mickey demanded the promise in addition to his actions during the following week.

Sure, he could live without Mickey just fine, he recklessly asked every girl he knew well out on a date. But his plan backfired because he ended up comparing each girl to Mickey. Not one could measure up.

That's it, he thought, jumping off the bed, grabbing his cell phone. *I'd rather she be only a friend than not be with her at all. Besides, maybe someday things will change.*

He called and Mickey asked if she would meet him at the snack bar. She agreed and said she would see him at eight o'clock that night.

Christopher waited only a few minutes when he glanced up to see Mickey tentatively approaching the corner table. She looked elegant and sophisticated in her tan linen slacks, heels, and purple silk shirt accented with a gold chain, earrings, and watch. Her dark hair was drawn back and clasped into a pony-tail with a lavender cloth bow. Wispy bangs fell casually across her forehead.

She's so cute and petite. I just want to protect her and love her for the rest of our lives, he thought. Then he inwardly shook his head. *You'd better stop that, man. That kind of thinking is going to get you into trouble. Your decision is to be 'just friends'. Don't forget that.*

Christopher got up and pulled out her chair. They ordered ice-cream sundaes and after the waitress left, he began. "I'm so sorry I was harsh and unkind before, Mickey." His voice cracked with emotion. "I was tremendously hurt but that was no excuse to take out my anger on you. I did not act like a Christian, or a gentleman, and I apologize." His eyes begged her to understand.

17

After a moment, he sighed deeply. "I realize you can't force feelings that aren't there." He stared at his reflection in the napkin holder.

"I've missed you so much these last few weeks," he said softly. He looked up and waited until her eyes met his. "I will make you the promise you asked for, Mickey. I do love you with all my heart, but I promise I will not talk to you about those feelings anymore. I do want to make another promise to you, though. I'll always be here for you. I'll always be your friend."

Tears of relief welled up in her eyes, so he handed her a napkin. "Thank you, Chris. I don't know if you really understand but I appreciate your just accepting that this is how I need things to be."

The waitress brought their orders, and they began to eat.

"I missed you, too, you know," Mickey said in a lighter tone. "I went out with the girls a couple of times and even dated but it just wasn't the same."

Christopher smiled. "Me, too. You want to go to the game when we're done?"

"Sure," she replied happily, feeling a huge burden had been lifted from her shoulders. All was once again right with her world.

~ Two ~

Eight years later

The Sunday sky was overcast, and rain fell gently. Mickey stood alone in the graveyard, her mind numb with grief. "What will I ever do without you, Mom?" She sobbed and clutched her umbrella tightly. "I know you're with the Lord and I'm so glad your pain is finally over but now I don't have anyone."

She leaned down to place a bouquet of pink and white carnations and roses on the grave. She straightened and automatically reached a hand to tuck a stray curl behind her ear. "Oh, Mom," she said helplessly. "Where am I going to go? What am I going to do?"

Once again, the pain of her loss struck Mickey like a physical blow. Three months earlier her precious mother passed from this world to rest in the arms of her Heavenly Father.

Anne Sterling's fight with cancer proved painful and difficult. In the end, thanks to continuous pain medication, she died peacefully at home with Mickey by her side. Her body now rested next to her husband in the small church cemetery.

The parishioners lovingly contributed their talents to make the graveyard a place of beauty and solitude, where people could go to grieve and reminisce in peace. Large oak trees spread their shading branches over the area and a stone fence, covered with ivy, circled the perimeter.

Small circular flower beds were scattered here and there along the pebbled path that meandered throughout. Carefully planned varieties of plants provided color year around. The magnificent peaks of the Blue Ridge Mountains rose in the distance, illustrating to God's people His power and strength.

The May rain dripped steadily, adding to Mickey's gloom and despair. Thoughts and memories swirled through her mind. The mother she adored, who had not only been her parent but her best friend, was now gone. She considered her beloved home where she felt safe and secure.

Her heart clenched when she thought of her horses, her cat, and her dog who unfailingly offered unconditional love. The precious animals made their furry shoulders available for her to cry on at any time day or night.

Mickey stared at the grave thinking of the day her mother's dreaded diagnosis had been pronounced. Life went from smooth, secure, and uneventful to uncertain at every turn. She insisted on caring for Anne herself whenever possible and treasured every moment with her.

I should have been able to handle the whole thing, she thought, remembering those last months when balancing work, home duties, and her mother's care became nearly impossible. *I know Mom insisted I get help and so did all my friends, but I should have taken care of her myself. I feel like a total failure. I shouldn't have had to hire that nurse.*

She remembered her plan to sell her horses to help. Her mother's insurance was cancelled several years earlier due to new government regulations and the small amount of money Anne put aside over her lifetime was eaten up quickly by doctor visits and cancer treatments. But Anne adamantly refused to allow her to part with her animals.

"God will provide, honey," Anne had said. "I don't want you to sell them. I just don't have peace about that. I know how much you love those horses. Yes, my insurance was cancelled but I also know God has a plan."

Tears pricked Mickey's eyes again when she remembered their dog, Kip, searching the house for Anne, his expression both confused and mournful. During those harrowing days following Anne's death, Mickey could literally feel God's grace holding her up like a giant hand. The comfort she sought to extend to Kip in his sorrow was an extension of God's comfort to her.

Now a huge test of her faith loomed before her. Medical bills and funeral expenses equaled a staggering sum. Mickey felt like she received a kick in the gut. Reality loomed before her. Not only could she no longer afford to keep her horses, and she would have to sell the family home and property. With affordable housing non-existent in Misty Cove, she would have to leave the historic town in which she grew up to find a new place to call home.

With a heavy sigh, Mickey left the grave and walked forlornly to a nearby cement bench. She sat on the damp surface and tugged the raincoat closer around her small frame.

"Lord, I feel so alone," she whispered. "No parents. No family. Christopher is in Maine now and I hardly ever hear from him. He didn't even respond to my text about Mom."

She stared at a bright yellow daffodil thinking absently that the flower looked far too happy on this miserable day. "My animals are all I have left. Oh, dear Father, I don't want to lose them, too. I know Mom said You would provide but I'm just not seeing any answers. I feel like even You are so far away, God."

The umbrella fell and she buried her head in her hands. Rain fell softly on her curly dark hair, and she began to pour her heart out to her Lord, begging for His nearness and comfort.

Pastor Thompson's message that morning assured God's children that He was always there, even during times of darkness. Desperately Mickey pleaded with her Savior for the strength to get through this painful season of her life. Her prayer absorbed her so that she did not notice a person open the wrought iron gate, enter the graveyard, and approach.

The broad-shouldered man wore a tan colored raincoat and held a black umbrella. He stood watching Mickey for a few minutes, then cleared his throat. She jerked her head up, self-conscious, and embarrassed that someone should catch her crying. She stared in amazement.

The thought flitted through her mind that he had become even more handsome than when she last saw him. His sandy blonde hair had darkened a bit and his frame filled out nicely. His dark brown eyes still emanated the same warmth but reflected her pain.

"Christopher!" she exclaimed. "Where did you come from?"

"I just got the text about your mom a few days ago. I've been up near Clayton Lake for the past few months shooting Moose. There was no cell service up there. If I had known, I'd have come sooner."

His voice was deep and gentle. "I went by the house and when I didn't see your car, I figured you might be here. I knew church must have let out by now." He sat down beside her, sheltering her with his large umbrella. "How are you, Mickey?"

"Oh, I'm doing ok," she said, a little too brightly. Christopher put his arm around her. "Mickey, it's me. You don't have to put on an act. I understand. I remember how I felt when my parents were killed." His kindness melted her defenses and she wept openly, unable to hold back the tears.

"Oh, Chris, I don't know what I'm going to do," she choked between sobs. "I'm going to have to sell our place and the horses. That's all I have left now, besides Kip and

Snippit. That property has been in my family for five generations."

She hiccupped, sniffled, and continued, "I've tried to crunch the numbers every way I can think of but I just can't find any other way to pay the debts. I don't want to have to move but I don't think I'm going to have any choice."

She glanced miserably over at the grave. "And my mom. I know she's been gone for almost three months now, but I still miss her so much. It hurts so badly. She was my best friend. I thought I'd start to feel better by now. My whole life has fallen apart. First, I lost her, and now I'm losing everything else."

~ Three ~

Christopher gently held the woman he loved, letting her cry out her grief. Though he didn't catch every word of her emotional story, he understood the gist of her situation. He sheltered her with his umbrella and wished for the millionth time that he could hold her forever.

Over the years Christopher tried to start a relationship with one girl or another but to no avail. He felt deceitful when he knew full well there would never be a future with them. He finally decided that his heart would forever belong to only one. Seeing Mickey again reinforced that truth.

When Mickey's tears abated, she slowly sat back. "I'm sorry to soak you even more than the rain," she said, again embarrassed by her loss of control. She noticed a black smudge on his coat. "Oh, no," she groaned. "I got makeup on your coat."

"Hey, don't you worry about that. It's not often I get to hold a weeping woman in my arms," he said, gently teasing. *Not that I'd want to hold anyone but you.*

Mickey smiled. Christopher was such a dear. He knew her so well. Any awkwardness between them melted away, even though they had seen each other in person only a few times since they graduated from college.

"You always could make me smile, even when I'm sad," she said, trying to wipe the tear stains and streaked mascara from her face with the handkerchief he gave her. "Why don't we go back to the house? We can talk there where we can be dry."

"Sounds good," replied Christopher, rising to his feet.

They shared his umbrella and headed for their cars in the church parking lot. Mickey thought fleetingly that sharing an umbrella was so easy with him. She always felt very uncomfortable around men who were much taller than she. Christopher stood just a few comfortable inches taller than her own five-foot-six frame.

Christopher prayed while he drove toward Mickey's house. *Lord, I want to help her. I think she really needs me now – more than she ever has before. Please show me the way and help me to be the friend she needs.*

He sat at a red light watching an old green Volkswagen beetle sputter by, when the thought came to him. *Marry her.*

"What?" he said aloud. "No way. She'd never do that. And besides, I promised never to talk to her about that kind of thing again."

But he could not shake the thought. The story of Hosea came to mind. *Guess I'm not the only man You've asked to willingly take on a difficult situation, Lord,* he thought. Gradually a plan began to form.

Lord, he prayed while he turned into the gravel drive that led to Mickey's house, *is this truly of You? I surely do not want to make a mistake about something of this magnitude. And I don't want to somehow think I'm seeing this coming from You if my own desires and emotions are doing the talking. I don't want to rationalize this into being Your will. This kind of seems like a crazy answer and I really can't imagine her going for it.*

A quiet assurance and peace filled Christopher's heart that the idea was truly from God. He felt absolutely certain that one day, his beloved Mickey would grow to love him in return. That would be worth the wait, no matter how long, no matter how hard.

Lord, please show her if this is Your will for us.

Please lead her to accept my proposal.

Christopher and Mickey climbed from their cars and, dodging raindrops, ran for the porch of the brick two story house. The wind began to blow and the tall oak trees in the front yard swayed slowly. Ominous thunder rumbled overhead, promising heavier rain to come. Mickey quickly opened the door and they walked into the kitchen.

"Whew!" she said, taking his umbrella and shaking it out the door. "What a mess."

"Yeah." Christopher removed his damp raincoat. "You really know how to roll out the welcome mat around here."

She smiled and draped his coat over a chair. "We only bring out the storms for the really special people," she said, winking at him.

A small sable colored Sheltie bounded into the room. His tail waved furiously, and he barked sharply at the top of his voice.

"Kip!" Christopher greeted the dog, kneeling to the floor and taking his head gently in his hands. "How are you, boy?" Kip squirmed happily and licked Christopher's hand. "You've really grown into a beautiful dog. The last time I was here, you were just a pup."

Mickey stooped to pat Kip's silky head. Then she rose and stood by the sink, her back rigid. *I will not give up Kip,* she thought. The tears pricked at her eyes again. *He's been with me since he was old enough to leave his mother. He wouldn't understand. I can't do that to him. He's family. And Mom loved him so much. He was like her guardian angel while she was sick.*

She imagined the look of hurt and abandonment in those intelligent brown eyes if the worst were to come true. *But what if I can't afford to care for Kip and Snippit? What if I can't afford a pet friendly apartment?* The prick of tears became drops that began to roll down her cheeks.

Christopher looked up and gazed at her for a moment. He rose, gave Kip one final pat, and went to her. He put his hand lightly on her shoulder. "Let's go sit and talk, Mickey." She turned and they headed for the living room.

"I don't know what to do," Mickey said hopelessly. She sank down on the couch. "I've tried to consider every angle but there's just no way to hold onto this house and property."

She sighed. "My neighbor, Mrs. Watson, offered to let me board with her for free, if I would take care of the housework."

Mickey grabbed a couch pillow and hugged the cushion to her, staring at the mahogany curio cabinet across the room. "Mrs. Watson isn't an easy person to be around, so I'm not real excited about having to live in the same house with her," she explained, grimacing at the thought of having to stay in such close proximity to the ill-tempered, impossible to please woman.

Mickey continued sadly. "But she's the only person in this town who can take on a boarder. I know some of my friends at church would want to help but I also know none of them have room. Mrs. Watson also made it very clear she didn't want a dog around, no matter how nice and well-behaved it was, and she's allergic to cats. And of course, she doesn't have the property to keep horses and I could never afford to board them.

"Seems my only choices are to live with her or move to a city where I can find an affordable apartment. You know how I hate city life. Either choice means saying good-bye to the horses." She sighed deeply and shrugged. "But I have to pay off the debt. I can't afford to keep this property."

She noticed Christopher's puzzled expression when she mentioned cats and a brief smile lit her face. "You haven't met Snippit, have you?"

He shook his head. She pointed to the beautiful gray tabby who emerged from under the sofa right on cue.

"She's gorgeous, Mickey." He offered his hand for the cat's inspection. Snippit regarded him solemnly with her large green eyes, then daintily stepped toward him. She sniffed his hand thoroughly and began to rub her head on his fingers.

"She likes you," Mickey said, smiling while she reached over to stroke the cat. "She's very sweet. I got her last year." To prove her affection, Snippit leaped lightly onto Christopher's lap and curled up, purring and kneading her paws in delight.

"Oh, and over there is Bilbo," Mickey commented, pointing to a lush planted five-gallon aquarium with a beautiful Betta fish swimming elegantly along. "My dream is to one day have a huge marine set up. You know, a two- or three-hundred-gallon tank with fish and all manner of corals. The works."

Christopher looked at her with one brow raised. "Wow, you don't go for cheap and easy, do you?"

"Hey, a girl can dream, right?"

"Absolutely." He gently stroked the cat in his lap.

Mickey admired how comfortable he seemed. *Not all men like cats*, she thought. *I'm glad he like my Snip.*

Christopher drew a deep breath, looked up, and began. "Okay, I have an idea but first let me give you a little info. Thankfully, I didn't have much debt coming out of college. The Lord really blessed my photography business, so I've been able to put away quite a bit in savings and investments."

He looked a bit sheepish. "What I'm trying to say is, I'm doing well financially, and I'd like to suggest we go into business together."

Mickey looked at him. "Doing what?" she asked, a curious but doubtful expression on her face. "Sounds like you don't need any help from me to succeed."

"Here's the thing," he said. "For a long time now I've been wanting to invest in a place with a lot of acreage, so I'd be able to shoot on my own land and not have to travel twenty-four seven."

He let out a frustrated sigh. "Besides, everybody wants a piece of the pie these days and getting photography permits can be a real hassle and expense, especially when people find out I'm a professional.

"I'd like to find a place of my own out West somewhere, like Montana or Wyoming. I've been out there several times now. There are so many amazingly beautiful areas. Plus, there are national forests and parks everywhere with all kinds of wildlife. I'd never run out of material."

Mickey looked puzzled. "Ok. I can understand that. But where do I fit in here? I love wildlife and gorgeous landscapes as much as the next person but how exactly would we work together? I don't know beans about professional photography. I pretty much just stick with my iPhone and Instagram."

Christopher paused for a moment to scratch Snippit's chin, then continued. "You know how I love photography but what you may not know is that I've always had this secret dream of owning horses. The problem is, being out on shoots for days or weeks at a time and taking regular care of animals just doesn't mix.

"I know you've always talked about wishing you could raise and train horses, so a ranch out West would be perfect. We could work together when I'm free and you could handle things whenever I have a project that takes me away."

"But Christopher, what about the living arrangements? I mean, we can't just..." Mickey fell silent while she searched for a tactful way to convey her thoughts. Finally, she blurted out, "We can't just live together. We're both Christians. You know that wouldn't be right, Chris. I know everybody and their brother shacks up these days, but I don't want people thinking I live like that."

"Of course not. That's not what I was suggesting." He looked at her carefully. "I was thinking we could get married."

Mickey inhaled sharply and alarm spiraled though her. A cautious look filled her eyes. "Christopher," she said. "You promised."

He put up his hands. "I know how you feel, and I haven't forgotten my promise. We wouldn't have a traditional marriage. Don't worry, I'm not going to pressure you about a romantic relationship. We'd sort of be like roommates and business partners who just happen to be married. Then we can live in the same house together without damaging our testimony or dishonoring the Lord."

Mickey looked at him in astonishment. *What an absurd idea*, she thought. *That is just crazy! I can't marry someone I don't love.*

"What you're suggesting is a marriage of convenience, right? Seriously? Chris, isn't that just a bit cliché? I mean really, this isn't the dark ages."

Then her tone softened a bit when she saw the hurt in his eyes. "Chris, what if you meet the right woman some day? Then you'll either be sorry you're tied down or we end up divorcing." She shook her head. "Besides, I'm not like a charity case or something. You don't have to sacrifice your whole life and future for me."

Christopher shook his head, while inwardly thinking he would gladly give up anything for her. "You don't understand, Mick," he said. "I'm not feeling sorry for you. I really think we'd make a great team, I know the whole 'marriage of convenience' thing isn't done much anymore, in this country anyway, but I really think we could make the situation work. That is," he paused when the thought struck him. "Unless you're involved with someone."

The tick-tock of the grandfather clock in the corner seemed exceptionally loud. Christopher agonized in the awkward moment while he waited for her response. He was grateful the cat in his lap gave him something to do with his hands.

Mickey stared for several minutes at the multicolored braided rug on the floor, her thoughts a wild jumble of confusion.

"There's no one in my life, Chris." *And there hasn't been anyone since Lee, thank goodness*, the sarcastic thought invaded her mind. *I won't ever go looking for romance again.* She felt the familiar surge of pain, bitterness, and fear that came every time she remembered her one and only boyfriend and their months of dating in college. Mickey sighed and paused for a moment to collect her thoughts, trying to push the dark memories away.

Finally, she spoke. "I don't know what to say, Chris. I'll have to think this through and pray about it. I just..." She looked at him blankly and shrugged. "I just don't know."

"Of course." He nodded. "I understand. I know this idea sounds kind of off the wall and probably a little scary, but I think marriage might just be the way to go. I know you have to feel peace about it, too, though. And please know this; for me, we would be making a lifetime commitment."

Mickey nodded, her face solemn. Christopher wanted desperately to take her hand but sensed that now was not the time for physical contact.

He rose slowly placing Snippit gently on the floor. "I think I'll head back to the motel before that storm really gets going. I know you're kind of overwhelmed right now but just remember we've always been such good friends, almost like brother and sister. We could always talk and really connect. I think working together all the time and living in the same house would be great. I believe we'd have a fantastic life."

The brother and sister phrase relieved Mickey a great deal. She looked at him and smiled. "You're right. I never have stopped missing you since we graduated. You're like family to me."

Christopher smiled. "Same here." They walked back to the kitchen, and he retrieved his coat. He shrugged his way into the garment and grabbed his umbrella. He grinned when he glanced at the stacks of cookies on the counter. "What's this? Trying to be the next great baker?"

Mickey blushed. "Baking is relaxing for me. I'm taking these to church for a bake sale to benefit the youth group."

"Great!" Christopher said with a smile in his voice. "They won't need any other contributions with all these." Then he looked at Mickey piteously. "Do you suppose you might be able to spare a few for a lonely, tired, out of town visitor?"

Mickey chuckled. "Oh, you do go on." Laughing again felt so good. She quickly put together a plate of cookies and covered them with plastic wrap. "Here you go, you poor, pitiful thing."

Christopher accepted the plate. "Mmm...." he said in anticipation. Then he gave Mickey a gentle smile. "I'll be

32

back tomorrow so we can talk. How about we grab some dinner after you get off work?"

"Sounds good. I'll be ready around six, okay?"

"I'll be here." With a grin and a wave, Christopher sloshed his way to his rental.

He prayed fervently on the way back to the Mountain Rest Motel. He spent most of the evening reading *Hosea*, and other Bible passages, seeking the Lord's direction while munching on the chocolate chip Heath Bar cookies.

He also placed a few calls to friends at home to whom he often went for counsel. They all agreed that, if the Lord gave him peace about the plan, proceeding seemed the wise course of action.

~ * ~

Mickey paced the floor until almost midnight. Her thoughts ran the gamut from thinking '*no way, this is insane*' to '*that's the perfect solution*'. Kip tried to comfort her but finally gave up and retired with Snippit to the couch. He rested his nose on his paws and looked at her with soulful eyes.

Finally, Mickey decided pacing accomplished nothing. She went upstairs and got ready for bed. After washing her face, brushing her teeth, and putting on her sleep shirt and sweats, she crawled into bed and propped the pillow up against the headboard.

She retrieved her Bible from the drawer of the bedside table, feeling the need to hold the book tonight instead of reading from her iPad. She rested her hands on the beloved copy of God's word given to her by her mother on her twentieth birthday. She began to talk to her Lord.

"I don't know if this is right or not," she prayed. "Part of me feels like if I do this, I'll never have a chance at the love I've always dreamed might come along. But then, I know I'll never have that anyway. I haven't even felt attracted to anyone since Lee."

Her heart again grimaced with pain. *If that's what romance and love leads to, then forget it,* she thought. She got a grip on her wayward emotions and continued with her prayer.

"Lord, I'd rather be in a marriage of convenience with Chris on a ranch, than have to live out the rest of my days alone in some city apartment. But to be married to someone I don't love..."

Her voice broke and she reached to grab a tissue to dab at the tears beginning to prick in her eyes. "It seems like there ought to be love." Her tone was bewildered at first but then her eyes hardened. *I know better than that. Love is a stupid myth.*

Suddenly a phrase from Matthew 7:7 came to her mind. *Ask and it shall be given unto you.*

"I won't," Mickey said. "I won't ask for love. That's what got me into trouble the last time." Again, the verse flooded her mind. *Ask and it shall be given unto you. Seek and ye shall find. Knock and it shall be opened unto you.*

"Hmph! Yeah, right. I learned my lesson long ago. Asking for love gets you nothing but abuse and pain."

Memories of that horrible year in college flooded through her mind. She recalled with chagrin how self-satisfied and proud she had been the day she told Christopher about Lee.

She entered the snack bar that day, her face flushed with excitement and wonder. She and Christopher had fourth hour free every Thursday, so they ate lunch together. Mickey plopped down at their regular table where Christopher was already seated and clasped her hands together.

"Oh, Chris, you're not going to believe this. I think I've finally met 'the one.'" She smiled widely. "I met him the first day of Financial Management. His name is Lee Davidson."

Unbeknownst to Mickey, Christopher searched his mind frantically for something to say. His heart plummeted to his toes at her words. *I thought I really saw her like just a friend, but I guess nothing has changed. I still love her.* The thought of her with someone else caused him something akin to physical pain.

He tried to look pleased. "Wow, Mickey, that's great," he said. "What's he like?" He was sure his tone was unconvincing.

"He's really good looking," she said with a giggle, seeming not to notice his mood. She reached a hand to push her hair back behind one ear. "He's kind of quiet sometimes but he's a real take charge kind of guy, a strong decision maker."

Mickey stared blissfully out the window. "I can't believe a guy that amazing likes me. He's already brought me flowers and candy five times and we've only been out a few dates. He's so sweet and caring. He calls my cell all the time just wanting to be sure I'm all right and to find out what I'm doing."

"I'm happy for you, Mick." Christopher forced himself to look at her, thinking that he should be glad for anything that made her happy but feeling a bit alarmed at how fast the guy was moving.

"I'm definitely in love," Mickey said with a wide grin. "Took me 'til my junior year but finally I'm in love. I feel like I've waited and prayed forever. When I met Lee, I said, 'Lord, I want him no matter what'! Now the Lord has said my prayer and given me just what I wanted."

She paused a moment, and a slight frown clouded her face. "I guess I won't be able to talk to you much anymore, Chris. Lee said he wanted me with him all the time.

He was angry when he found out we were friends. I don't want to do anything that makes him upset like that.

"He said that if we're going to be a couple then I can't be having friendships with other guys. He got really ticked the other day when I let some random guy hold the door for me. But he was right. I should have been more thoughtful of his feelings."

"Okay," Christopher said, while thinking, *What? Angry about a gentleman holding a door? Seriously?* He picked up his sandwich, unable to look at her any longer. "We'd better eat, or we'll be late for English Lit."

~ * ~

Mickey shook her head, bringing her thoughts back to the present. *Nope, I won't. I will never ask for love again. I demanded love once and I received pain in return. I will not ask again.* Stubbornly she opened her Bible but comprehended little from the words she read.

As she laid the book aside, she remembered again her mother's insistence that the Lord would provide. *She always believed that,* thought Mickey. She pulled the covers up around her shoulders. *She was so sure. Like she heard directly from God about it. I wonder if Chris' idea could be God's provision.* She sighed deeply and tried to sleep.

After a very restless night, Mickey finally gave up and rose early. "I need to know Your will, Lord," she pleaded while she prayed over breakfast. "I want to do what's right here. Please give me direction."

She finished her cereal and toast, drank the final swallow of orange juice in her glass, and stuffed the dishes into the dishwasher. After stepping into the rubber boots she kept by the door, she headed out to feed the horses and turn them out for the day. The overnight rain refreshed everything. The air smelled clean, and the plants and spring flowers looked a shade brighter.

Fili and Kili nickered eagerly, sticking their heads over the stall doors when she came into the barn. She patted each gelding while she walked by. *I'm so lucky to have these guys*, she thought. *It's going to tear my heart out to lose them.*

She raised the two horses from the time they were only four months old. When word reached her six years ago about the rescue of two Friesian cross foals from a horrific situation, she immediately applied online to adopt them and made the trip to the rescue farm in Arizona.

When she arrived and saw the youngsters, her heart went out to them. Though weanlings, they were quite small for their age. Their thin sides, scraggly hair, and sunken eyes spoke of their lack of care and nutrition.

The rescue organization's director said the foal's owner apparently left town. The weanlings and their dams were abandoned in a small corral with no food and only what rainwater collected in a large bathtub.

Mickey's application was approved, and she adopted the two youngsters. After months of tender loving care, they blossomed into beautiful adult horses. Fili a dark bay with no markings, and Kili, jet black with one white hind foot and a white star on his forehead. Both animals had long, thick, wavy manes and tails.

Mickey named them based on characters from her favorite books and movies *The Hobbit* and *The Lord of the Rings*. She guessed their heritage probably contained a mix of Friesian and Thoroughbred but breeding really did not matter. She loved them deeply.

Mickey gave each horse a measure of oats, then climbed the ladder and threw down two flakes of hay from the loft. She breathed in the delicious scent of summer fields and sunshine and began to imagine the ranch she and Christopher might own. Her pulse quickened. In that quiet moment she felt a rush of excitement at the realization of the positive elements of Christopher's proposed partnership.

Even if I'm not in love with him, having a ranch would be so incredible, she thought. *He's such a wonderful friend and I've always dreamed of having a big spread where the horses would have more room. Now my dream could actually come true.* She grinned, picturing lots of land and herself raising horses and riding in the mountains whenever she wished.

But the fingers of disquieting conviction gripped her soul. *Marriage is supposed to be a picture of Christ and the Church,* a part of her cried. *Marriage should be the union of two people who truly love each other as husband and wife, the way Christ loves us.*

But really, I do love him, Lord, she rationalized. *I love him because he's my dearest friend. Loving him that way is still a kind of love. I will not risk a repeat of what happened with Lee.*

Tears stung at the back of her eyes and she straightened. *I will not. Besides, this way I can have the best of everything: a ranch, horses, a dear friend, and security without the pain and abuse. Surely, we can serve the Lord together through our friendship.*

Ask and ye shall receive. The words echoed again "No," she said, pushing the thought away. "I won't. I'll never ask God for love again. I learned the consequences last time. I'll never make that mistake again. Being with Christopher will be safe, actually. I'll never run the risk of being tempted to ask for love again because I'll be married and unavailable."

Mickey felt a bit unsettled but she climbed down the ladder, opened the stall doors to let out the horses, and headed back to the house. Though she sensed something still amiss in her spirit, she did feel definite peace about

Christopher's proposal. She concentrated on filling her mind with thoughts of the exciting days to come.

~ Four ~

Despite her lack of sleep the night before, Mickey's day at the bank proved surprisingly pleasant. All the transactions went smoothly, and her boss complimented her several times on her efficient work. By the end of the day, Mickey felt a lift in her spirit which had not been present since the day her mother received the cancer diagnosis.

She stopped by the church on her way home to drop off the cookies for the bake sale. Pastor Thompson was just leaving and stopped to talk for a few moments. He assured her of their continued prayers on her behalf.

Warmed by his kind support, Mickey traveled home with a smile on her face. She quickly changed into a pair of trouser jeans, a lavender tank top, a purple animal print cardigan, and Birkis sandals, then waited for Christopher to arrive.

She heard his car enter the drive at six on the dot. He waited at the door while she gathered her purse and said goodbye to Kip.

"All ready?" he said amiably.

"Yep." She came out onto the porch and caught her breath. He looked dashingly handsome in black jeans and a hunter green polo shirt that showed off his toned arms and broad shoulders.

Mickey felt a moment of discomfort. The thought ran through her mind about what damage those strong arms could do. She nervously reached a hand to tuck a curl behind one ear. When she glanced again at Christopher, he gave her his usual warm smile and the look in his eyes made her feel safe and secure once more.

He may have turned into one gorgeous piece of eye candy but he's still the same old Chris, Mickey thought with relief. *He's still my best friend and he would never hurt me.*

"I hope we're going someplace good," she commented while they walked down the steps. "I'm starved."

"Only the best for you, madam," Christopher said with an exaggerated British accent while he gallantly opened the car door for her with a flourish. Then he looked at her thoughtfully. "Actually, unless things have changed since I was here last, we really don't have a lot of options," he added, thinking of the limited number of eateries in the small town. Mickey chuckled in agreement.

Ten minutes later they entered *Mist on the Water*, Misty Cove's only upscale, sit-down restaurant, and took a booth in the corner. After ordering, Christopher looked at Mickey expectantly. "So, Mick, have you had a chance to give my idea any thought?"

"That's the biggest understatement of the year," she said with a laugh. "All I could do last night was think and pray about your proposal. And I've come to a decision." She took a sip of water, then looked him in the eye.
"I will. I'll agree to marry you."

She watched Christopher's face light up and his lips curved into a smile. His heart began to pound. *I can't believe it! She'll finally be mine*, he thought. *All mine and no one can ever take her away.*

"Now, Chris," she said. Tendrils of nervousness began to grip her. "This has to be the way you talked about last night. I mean, you know how I feel, or rather how I don't feel, and I don't want—"

"Hey, whoa there, sista!" Christopher patted her hand gently, reigning in his racing thoughts immediately. "I promised, remember? I'm just happy because I know we'll make a wonderful team. We've always had so much fun together. We're like family and I know our life together is going to be great." He spoke with such conviction that Mickey began again to feel excited at the prospect.

"Besides," he said with a wink. "I always did fancy having the most beautiful woman on earth at my side. Have I told you how fantastic your hair looks like that?"

Mickey had allowed her thick brunette hair grow to shoulder length. Her natural curls spiraled around her delicate face while bangs wisped softly across her forehead. The restaurant's cozy lighting caught the beautiful auburn highlights. She looked like she just stepped out of a magazine ad.

A slight blush crept over Mickey's face, and she smiled. "One of the girls at the bank introduced me to an amazing hair product. I used to always straighten my hair but after using Wen," she put on an exaggerated southern accent, "I was able to fully embrace my natural curls without dealing with a tangled, frizzy, disgusting mess."

"You look amazing!" Christopher exclaimed. "Your natural style suits you to a tee."

Feeling uncomfortable, Mickey changed the subject. "Have you found a place out West yet?" she inquired. "Or do you still have to look around?"

"I think the perfect place is a ranch I found out in Montana," he said, his eyes shining with boyish excitement. "The place sits about ninety miles southwest of Great Falls. There are a little more than two thousand acres. And get this; part of it borders Glacier National Park.

"Oh my word, Chris! Glacier National Park? Are you serious? Do you know how long I've wanted to go there? Have you seen the ranch?" Mickey asked in one excited breath.

Christopher grinned. "Yes, I went out there last month. Here are some pictures I took." He reached for his iPhone and tapped into the photos before handing the unit to Mickey.

"The present owners are Mildred and Malcolm Mac-Gregor," he explained. "The land has been in their family for generations. They've been cattle ranchers most of their lives but recently retired. They want something smaller and more manageable since none of their kids have any interest in taking over the ranch.

The waitress brought their orders. They paused to thank the Lord for the food. Christopher also prayed for wisdom in the decisions that faced them and for blessings on the road ahead.

As he prayed, Mickey felt complete peace chase away any remaining doubts, though something still bothered her slightly about her motives. She put her thoughts aside and focused on Christopher's words while he finished his prayer, adding her soft "amen" after his.

As they started on their salad, Mickey studied the first photo. "That's the front of the house," Christopher said. "It's a two-story log home with four bedrooms, three bathrooms and of course a kitchen, dining room, den, and living room. There's also a fantastic attic, a big semi-finished basement, and a two-car garage. Oh and the living room has a great river stone fireplace. There's a rustic lodge feel to the house but with all the modern conveniences. In fact, they remodeled a lot of the house a few years back in anticipation of selling."

Mickey grinned. "I love the wraparound porch. I can already see us sitting on that swing, watching the sun go down."

Mickey swiped to the second picture. "That one is the view from the kitchen window," he said. He watched her face, knowing she would be enraptured.

"Oh, Chris, how beautiful!"

Just a few miles from the house, majestic mountains rose up, a panorama of splendor as far as the eye could see. In the foreground lay a beautifully landscaped lawn. Beyond the one-acre yard and across the road, a lush green meadow grew with a small stream meandering through the grasses.

Mickey looked at the remaining photographs which featured a large old barn with dark rustic siding, a large pasture on the north side of the property, and the view of the house from the back.

"I'm convinced," she said in a rush. "Let's make an offer!"

"Whoa now!" he said, putting his hands in the air. "Are you sure you don't want to go see for yourself? I mean, I wouldn't expect you to make a decision based just on my pictures."

His grin faded. "I'm serious, Mick. This is where we'll be living and working long term, Lord willing. I would hate for you to get out there and find out you don't like the place. Do you want to fly out and look things over in person?"

Mickey considered his words. *I don't really have much choice, now do I?* she thought.

"I know you probably don't think you have many options but there's no reason we have to rush," Christopher said and Mickey wondered if he was telepathic. "Those debts of yours aren't going anywhere. You don't have to pay them off tomorrow, so if you find you don't really like this place, we'll find another that we can both agree on."

Mickey looked thoughtfully at him, part of her wondering if he really meant what he said. "You know, I think I'd like to do that," she said. "This will be my life, too, after all."

Christopher nodded, refusing to be baited by her tone. "I'll call tonight and arrange a ticket for you," he said easily. "When do you want to leave and how long do you want to stay?"

Mickey drummed her fingers on the table. "I'll need to let them know at work that I'll be taking some annual leave." After a moment, she felt silly for her negative spirit and defensive tone.

"May I see the pictures again?"

"Sure," he said. "But let me run out to the car and get my iPad so you can see them a little larger."

He returned in a moment and handed her the device. "There's a couple short videos on here also."

Mickey looked at each picture again and watched the videos. She felt complete peace about the property and the beautiful house.

"Actually, I don't think I really need to go out there. Pictures don't lie. That is unless you've *Photo Shopped* them," she said with a grin, trying to make up for her earlier unpleasantness. "This place is everything I've ever dreamed of and is absolutely beautiful. I think we should go for it." She smiled. "I guess I just wanted to be sure I was an equal partner here."

Christopher smiled and nodded. "I understand completely," he said, then reached for a bite of lasagna. "If I ever make you feel you're not, please tell me."

They finished the meal while discussing how and when to make the move. "I'll call the real estate agent tonight and tell her we want to make an offer," Christopher said with growing excitement in his voice. "I don't think there will be any issues when we have the inspection. I checked everything pretty thoroughly when I was out there."

Mickey grinned. "That's a relief. Sounds like the house move in ready. I'll start packing right away. I think my boss at the bank is interested in my house. He's hinted at it several times. I'm pretty sure he'll buy."

"Fantastic," Christopher said. "A quick sale on both ends would be great."

Mickey smiled, anticipation beginning to color her face and her tone. "I'm getting really excited about this! Now I can't wait to get out there. I love my home here, but I know God is in this change. I think you're right. We'll make a good team, partner. I just wish I had more cash to bring into the deal."

"Oh, no." Christopher looked deeply into her blue eyes. "Don't even go there. I planned to make this type of purchase anyway. Please do not give that another thought. Besides, you may be surprised at what you have left once your place is sold and the debts are paid off."

Mickey stared at him closely and saw a look in his eyes that brooked no argument. She nodded slightly and reached to gather her purse. They left the restaurant talking excitedly about the ranch and all the possibilities.

Christopher dropped Mickey off at her house, promising to call her after he talked with Joanna. He drove back to the motel with a great sense of satisfaction, certain that somehow this situation would work out better than he could ever dream. He spent much time in prayer before retiring.

Mickey crawled into bed that night with a mixture of conflicting feelings. She was sure this change in her life was of the Lord, but she also felt that something still was not quite right. She sighed, turned out the light, and snuggled down under the covers.

I just need to rest, that's all. I'm just tired.
Ask and ye shall receive. The verse echoed.
No, I'm just tired. I need to sleep.

~ Five ~

When Mickey turned in her resignation a week later, her co-workers were shocked. However, when she explained she was getting married, there were squeals of delight. They immediately began to pepper her with questions and insisted on treating her to lunch. Though the attention was fun, Mickey still felt vaguely uncomfortable. Knowing the reality of her situation, but not feeling at liberty to explain, left her a bit ill at ease. After they returned from the local cafe, Mickey headed for the bank president's office.

"Come in, Mickey, come in." David Spears stood behind the mahogany antique desk and offered his hand, which Mickey shook warmly.

This kind man had been a wonderful influence in her life. He took over Misty Cove Savings Bank when his father retired. All her life, Mickey could remember her mother telling her about the Spears family.

Anne Sterling loved and respected them a great deal. Though David lived and commuted from a larger city, he and his wife took great interest in the little community of Misty Cove. They were dedicated Christians who enjoyed using their prosperity to help others.

"I understand congratulations are in order," David said, his eyes warm and smiling.

"Yes, thank you." Mickey smiled, again feeling a bit uncomfortable. She knew people expected her to act like a giddy teenager in love, but that ship had sailed long ago.

She seated herself in the burgundy leather covered chair opposite her boss's desk and smiled again. "I'm really excited about all of this," she said, but felt a prick of conscience. *I am*, she thought. *I can't wait to see the ranch. I am excited.*

"My fiancée and I are going to be moving, though," she continued. "We're going to buy a ranch out in Montana, so I'll be putting my house up for sale. I thought you might be interested."

David immediately made an offer which was at least fifteen thousand dollars more than Mickey intended to ask. Her jaw dropped in shock, and she started to protest, knowing that the place would never appraise for that much.

But David put up his hand and smiled. "I've had my eye on that property for a long time," he said, looking at her over the glasses perched on his nose. "You know how hard finding a place in Misty Cove can be; nobody ever leaves! My wife fell in love with your house during that Christmas party a few years back. We're both tired of townhouse living and commuting."

The bank president removed his glasses and leaned back, putting his hands behind his head. "I'll also take care of the closing costs and drawing up all the papers, if you're agreeable, that is. You've done an excellent job here, Mickey. Consider anything over the appraisal a wedding gift."

David rubbed his hands together happily, looking just like a little boy at Christmas. "You're really giving us the gift, you know. We're going to have a great time. I'll be retiring in a couple years and having a place with some land will be wonderful. I know the grandkids will have a lot more fun there than in that townhouse."

Mickey smiled. "The property and the house are definitely great for kids."

David stood and extended his hand once more. "I wish you and your finance all the best," he said, his voice a bit husky. "We're going to miss you."

Mickey felt tears forming while she thanked him and headed back to her office. He had been a surrogate father during the years she worked for the bank. *Thank you, Lord. You're proving to me that I made the right decision. Everything seems to be falling into place.*

Again, she felt a prick of conscience, telling her to surrender all to the Lord but a rush of fear overshadowed that still small voice. Her stomach lurched and she forced the thoughts away. With trembling hands, she began to sort through the papers in her 'in' basket.

~ * ~

During the weeks that followed, Mickey's days were full of packing, training her replacement at work, and getting details of selling the house finalized. Christopher returned to Maine to pack and finalize things there.

Mickey called him after the closing and told him about the extra money. He suggested she take whatever was left after paying off the bills to try to find a good truck and horse trailer. Touched at his thoughtfulness, Mickey agreed wholeheartedly.

The old trailer she refurbished years ago was in pretty bad shape and her rattletrap old truck was not much better. She wondered how the vehicles would make the long trip west without falling apart. She immediately went to her computer to begin a search.

On her last day, Mickey's co-workers threw her a lavish party. Christopher returned and dropped by the bank late that afternoon. Mickey had to admit she enjoyed watching the envious looks. He carried himself with the strength and character of a marine, yet emanated a demeanor of kindness and gentleness that made him approachable.

David pulled Mickey off to the side and whispered, "He's a good man, Mickey. I feel better now, having met him. I'm sure he'll do right by you."

He looked at Mickey with a twinkle in his eye. "And he passed the background check with flying colors. I was so relieved." Mickey laughed out loud, and David gave her a fatherly hug. "I'm so happy for you, little girl."

Mickey broke the news of her marriage and the move to her church friends that Sunday. She waited until the last minute so she wouldn't have to go into too much detail. *They just won't understand why I'm doing this*, she thought firmly.

Explanations were still not easy. She told Pastor Thompson she and Christopher had been friends since college but he still looked at her with concern. He seemed to sense something was amiss. He told her not to hesitate to call if she ever needed anything and assured her of his prayers for them.

The ladies who had watched Mickey grow from an infant to a beautiful young woman were thoroughly disappointed at not being able to finally give her a bridal shower and go to her wedding. Mickey assured them she understood but said there just wasn't time for anything fancy. Tearfully, they wished her well and promised to mail gifts to her new home.

~ *Six* ~

Mickey awoke with a peculiar uneasy feeling in the pit of her stomach. For a moment she lay still, staring at the ceiling. Then she remembered. *This is Monday. Two weeks ago, I quit my job. This is my wedding day.*

Slowly crawling off the mattress onto the floor, she rose, and looked around the nearly empty room. Most of her belongings were already neatly packed and the boxes and furniture moved down to the living room.

She walked to the window and stood thinking while she gazed out over the land her family used to own. Despite her excitement of the week before, she now felt nervous with a touch of nostalgia. After this day, her life would be forever changed.

Heavily, she sighed. *Oh Mom, I wish you were here to give me some counsel. I don't know anything about living in the same house with a man. I don't want to do things that will make him angry like I did with Lee.* A tear ran down her cheek while she resolutely turned to head for the shower.

Mickey took some extra time under the hot pulsing water, hoping the warmth would help drain some of the nervousness and tension from her body. She dressed carefully, putting on an elegant white suit and fixed herself up for the occasion. By 9:00 she was ready and went downstairs to wait for Christopher to arrive.

As the minutes ticked by, she began obsessing that he might be angry. She told him the night before that she did not feel comfortable with their wearing wedding rings.

I hope he's not ticked off about that, she thought anxiously, wringing her hands together.

Just then, she heard his knock on the door. Christopher looked very distinguished in his blue pinstripe shirt, navy suit, maroon tie, and wingtip shoes. Mickey gave him a wobbly smile.

"My, my. You look like some kind of Wall Street executive, not a rancher."

"Oh, we ranchers do throw on the fancy duds every now and again," he said in a phony southern drawl. His eyes twinkled and he gave her a jaunty grin. "C'mon honey bunch, let's go get hitched."

Mickey felt relief at his teasing. He clearly was not angry with her.

The county probate court was twenty miles away, but they passed the time listening to comedy and enjoying the laughs. Christopher seemed to sense her need to downplay the day, so he played some of his favorite comedy routines to lighten the mood.

They arrived at the court in good humor but while they sat in the outside office waiting to enter the judge's chambers, Christopher looked at Mickey with a somber expression. "You might want that lip someday you know," he said looking at her. "And why didn't you ever tell me you could tap dance?"

Mickey jerked her head around and looked at him with fire in her eyes, ready to defend herself. Then she realized her heels were tapping the tile floor and she had been biting her lip. She began to chuckle when she realized how her nervousness showed.

"Sorry, I guess I'm just a little antsy."

"Hey, there's nothing to be scared of. We both agreed that this was the right thing to do. We've both sought the Lord and both of us have peace about this, right?"

She nodded and reached a hand to tuck a curl behind her ear.

"All right, then. Everything will be okay."

Christopher went on, talking about how they would pack the moving van, the specifics of the trip, and various other mundane everyday things. Mickey began to feel better and appreciated his effort to calm her nerves.

After a brief ceremony that pronounced them husband and wife, Christopher and Mickey stopped for a light lunch before beginning the drive home. Upon arrival, Christopher announced he planned to return to the motel to pack his things but that he wanted to get some pictures first.

"We'll only have one wedding day," he said firmly when Mickey protested. "Even for a marriage like ours. This is our only chance to capture the memories. C'mon, I'm a photographer. Humor me."

Mickey slowly smiled and reluctantly agreed. She stood under the large oak tree in the front yard while Christopher mounted the camera on a tripod. He zoomed in, focused, and fiddled with the speed and aperture settings.

He took several test shots and when he was satisfied that everything was just right, he hit the timer button. He raced to stand beside her, and they put on their best smiles. After taking dozens of photographs of various poses, he put his equipment back into the Jeep® and headed for the motel.

Christopher returned an hour later with the moving van following him. In the back rode several strong men from Mickey's church who volunteered to help with the heavy lifting.

They spent the afternoon loading furniture and boxes. By late evening their belongings were finally all stowed despite the tight squeeze. Christopher thanked the men for their help and drove them back to town.

The newlyweds slept in sleeping bags on the floor that night, Mickey upstairs and Christopher in the living room. He lay there in the empty room thinking wryly that this was not exactly the way he had envisioned his wedding night.

Help me to be patient, Lord. I know I'll just have to wait until Mickey comes to love me. He turned over on his side. *I just hope she does come to love me one day. At least now she's mine forever and I'll never have to be without her again,* he thought while he drifted off to sleep.

~ * ~

Christopher awakened before dawn the next morning. He placed the packed cooler filled with sandwiches, snacks, and bottles of water in the pick-up. Mickey found the late model Silverado in a dealership in Greenville for an extremely good price. He smiled when he remembered her comment about the look on the salesman's face when she paid cash for the vehicle.

Christopher looked at the sky. Not a cloud could be seen and the forecast called for dry weather for the rest of the week. Thankful they wouldn't have to start out driving in rough weather, he got into the truck and started the engine.

Mickey came sleepily outside a few moments later while he was hooking the horse trailer to the truck. She carried an overnight bag, in which she packed the last of her personal items, and a suitcase containing several changes of clothes. She put the bag and the suitcase on the floor of the passenger side of the truck.

Christopher saw her when he turned around and his heart pounded. *My wife,* he thought proudly. *She's really my wife. I never thought this day would come.*

She looked adorable dressed down in her faded comfortable jeans, purple tee shirt, and lavender seersucker Birkis sandals. Her hair was drawn back into a pony tail and the auburn highlights shone in the early morning sun. The longing to go and gather her in his arms nearly overpowered him.

 Stifling his feelings, he said, "Good morning. Did you sleep well?"

"Yep," Mickey said and walked to the trailer to help him. "I hope you did, too."

Christopher nodded with a smile. When they were satisfied the trailer was secure, they hitched Christopher's Jeep to the back of the moving van, then went back to the house to eat a quick breakfast. They used up the last of the cereal and milk and tossed the empty containers into a bag to place in the outside trash can.

Christopher patted Kip's head fondly. The bewildered dog stuck to Mickey like glue. He had not the faintest idea what was going on but was sure all their things disappearing out the door did not bode well.

Kip licked Christopher's hand and looked up, his expressive brown eyes imploring him to make things right. Christopher gently petted the dog for a moment, murmuring soft words of comfort. Then, fastening a leash to Kip's collar, he led him outside and helped him up into the cab.

Mickey searched the entire house for Snippit. She began to seriously worry that the cat might have made a frightened get away when they were taking boxes and furniture out to the van. She finally found her hiding in a far corner of the closet in the bedroom.

With a sigh of relief, she slowly inched her way toward the terrified feline. "Poor baby, are you scared out of your mind?" She gently scratched Snippit in her favorite spot under her chin. "It's all right, we're just going to a new home. And I'll be right there with you."

Gently Mickey pulled the cat out and cuddled her in her arms. She spent several moments trying to calm her be-

fore proceeding downstairs and putting her in a large carrier.

Mickey did her best to make Snippit's traveling arrangements comfortable. A soft, thick blanket lined the entire carrier. A small box of litter pellets fit in the back and
containers of food and water were attached to the cage's
heavy wire door. She placed the carrier on the passenger
seat beside Kip.

Christopher haltered Fili and Kili and led them to the
back of the trailer. Mickey helped him load the horses, then
put some hay in their nets and ensured the water buckets
were full. They made a final check of the trailer gate to
ensure a secure latch.

"I'm so glad we found this trailer," Mickey said with
heartfelt thanks. "I would have been a nervous wreck trying to haul them cross country in that old one. And this one
has a few more comforts, thankfully."

Mickey sighed deeply and looked around, feeling
suddenly tearful. "I guess that's everything. I'll just make
one last trip to the bathroom and then I'll be ready to go."

"Righto," Christopher said, walking toward the van.
"Take your time." He watched her climb the steps and dis-
appear into the house, knowing she needed this one last
look around her old home.

Mickey slowly walked through every room, her footsteps echoing in the emptiness. Now that all her belongings
were gone, the house no longer felt like home. *I guess it
really is people and things together that make a house a
home*, she thought while she climbed the stairs.

When she came back down, she felt ready to begin
the trek ahead of them. Before opening the truck door, she
paused for one last look at her childhood home. Her gaze
took in the house, barn, and the beautiful mountains beyond. She sighed softly while tears welled up in her eyes.

Slowly she turned and climbed into the driver's seat. "We're in for a long drive, Kip," she said, giving him a pat. She started the engine and waited for Christopher to move out. "Don't let me fall asleep now."

~ *Seven* ~

Mickey awoke Saturday morning feeling disorient-
ed. Sleepily she sat up. When she went to swing her legs
out of the bed, she hit her heels hard. "Ouch! Oh, brother." She forgot she was in a sleeping bag on the floor.

She sat for a moment hugging her legs to her, looking
at the boxes piled high all around her new bedroom. *I don't
even know where my makeup is*, she thought sourly while
she rose and walked into the bathroom. *Or my shower gel,
or my Wen, or my brush.*

Mickey flipped on the light and saw her overnight
bag on the counter. *Oh yeah,* she thought, feeling a bit
guilty for being so negative. *I put that in here last night
before I collapsed. Thank goodness. I'm so glad we're finally here.*

With the horses in tow, the usual three-day trip
stretched into four because they stopped often to attend to
the needs of the animals. Mickey yawned and wished she
could crawl back into the sleeping bag. *Must be the time
change*, she thought ruefully. *And it's a lot colder here
than I thought it would be.*

Hoping to wake and warm herself up, she proceeded
to shower. While she stood enjoying the feel of the hot water washing away the travel dirt and grime, she recalled
their arrival the evening before.

They pulled in at the ranch around 6:00 pm but still
needed to settle the horses in the barn and get some of
Mickey's boxes up to her room. Several men were there to
meet them, so all the heavy furniture had to be brought in
also.

The clock said 1:20 am by the time they finished,
and Mickey's exhaustion overwhelmed her. All she could

think about was sleep, so she didn't bother with supper or a bath.

As she showered, she remembered her first impressions of the ranch. Nearly a mile long, the driveway curved from the road to the house. The entire drive was lined with aspens, their new spring leaves tipping the branches.

Closer to the house the trees angled away, and one could see a fenced area to the left which encompassed the barn. The drive curved around and ended in a wide semicircle at the garage entrance.

Two pebble paths bordered with large stones led out of the parking area, one to the kitchen door in the back and one to the entry way in the front. A worn dirt path went down to the barnyard gate on the left side. Through the gate the path continued to the barn.

Mickey stepped reluctantly from the shower, dried off, and dressed. When she finished drying her hair and putting her curls back into a ponytail, she looked at her make up.

I'm going to be unpacking and getting all hot and dirty today. She picked up the tube of foundation. *Why bother?* At once a memory transported her back in time.

~ * ~

As Mickey prepared to go play tennis with Lee, she glanced in the mirror. She decided since they would be playing out in the heat, she wouldn't bother with makeup. Her roommates assured her she looked fine, so Mickey happily skipped downstairs to the lobby of the dorm.

I'm so lucky to have him, she thought. *I still can't believe he wanted to go out with me. He's my tall, dark, and handsome dream come true.*

As she approached, she noticed how fine he looked in his royal blue polo shirt and tan shorts. She grinned at him with a tender expression in her eyes.

"I do not believe you." He looked down at her, his icy blue eyes cold and his tone disdainful. He put a hand on his hip.

"What?" Mickey's happy smile began to fade. *What have I done now?* she thought, genuinely confused. You expect me to be seen with you with your face like that?"

His voice was low and angry. "Good grief, Mickey. You look like an old bat. Get back up there and make yourself presentable. I can't believe you did this to me. You know the old saying 'If the barn needs painting, paint it?' My dear, I think you need at least two coats."

Lee slammed his tennis racquet down on the floor and shoved his hands in his pockets. He turned his back to her and went to stare out the window, his jaw clenched. The dorm monitor looked at them in shock.

Mickey turned slowly, almost dropping her tennis racquet. Numbly she returned to her room to do his bidding.

~ * ~

Mickey clutched the tube so hard the lid shot off and foundation squirted on the mirror. A tear slipped unbidden down her cheek while her mind returned to the present. She wiped at her eyes angrily, suppressing a sob. *I'm not taking any chances*, she thought, pulling out a foundation brush and salvaging what liquid she could.

After she finished, Mickey went to the barn to feed the horses, then headed back to the kitchen. She poked around looking for something to eat for breakfast, when Christopher sleepily stumbled into the room. Hair disheveled and his red tee shirt and gray sweatpants rumpled, he stretched, yawned, and went to get a glass of water.

"Oh man, we don't even have the glasses out yet," he moaned. He rubbed his hand over the stubble on his chin. "I wonder where my razor is. Moving is really a pain. Hopefully this will be the last time."

"Amen to that," Mickey said fervently.

She found some cups and a package of Pop Tarts® in a bag and they sat cross-legged on the floor to eat. Kip, who would not let Mickey out of his sight, wagged his tail gently. He whined slightly and extended his paw. Mickey laughed and broke off a small bite for him.

"All right, I'll humor you, Kipster." The dog accepted the piece politely but then gulped the morsel down. "You didn't even taste it!" Mickey exclaimed with another laugh. "I'll find your food so you can have breakfast, too, don't worry."

She looked around the unkempt kitchen. "I'm really looking forward to having everything unpacked and in place."

"Me too," Christopher said.

After finishing off two Pop Tarts®, Christopher looked at her. "You didn't have to get all gussied up today, Mick," he said. "We're going to probably be a mess by the end of the day what with unpacking and all."

"Oh, Chris," she said lightly, trying to mask her fear. "I didn't want to make you sick on our first day here."

"Whoa, girl," he said, grabbing her hand when she tried to get up and forcing her to remain seated. "Make me sick? Are you kidding?"

Christopher rose then and pulled her up, wrapping his arms firmly around her to impede any escape attempts. "You get fixed up whenever you want to but you're beautiful no matter what." He pulled back and looked deeply into her troubled eyes, puzzled by the fear reflected in the blue depths. "Do you understand?"

"I think so," Mickey said, a bit breathless at his nearness and wondering why. "But..."

"No buts about it, my friend." Though he did not want to, he gently released her. "Don't you give those buts another thought."

"Okay, I won't." She stepped back feeling the need
to get away. "I'm going to go up and get started in my
room." Never had she wanted to just relax in his arms
and be held and the feeling scared her.

Christopher began to snicker.

"What?" Mickey asked, a bit put out that he was
laughing.

"Uh, Mick," he said, still chuckling. "All the rooms
are yours."

Slowly, Mickey got the joke and laughed with him.
"Yes, I guess they are! So, to rephrase that, I would like to
get started on my *bed*room."

"As you wish, madam," he said gallantly. "Let's get
your bed set up first," he suggested. "Then we can put the
boxes on the bed so we'll have more room to maneuver. I
think all the furniture you wanted in there is in the hall."

"Sounds good. You know, we'd better position things
like my old bedroom if possible. That might help Snippit to
adjust a bit more easily."

"Yeah, poor thing. She did look kinda lost. Did she
ever come out of her crate?"

"Not yet," Mickey said with a grin. "But she'll be all
right when things settle down."

Mickey thoroughly enjoyed fixing up her new bedroom. Christopher insisted she take the master and the
room was a good bit larger than the one in her old house.
The large bay window across from the door looked out on
the south pasture and the majestic mountains beyond.

The window featured a cozy seat which, Mickey decided, with a nice pad and a few comfortable pillows would
make a perfect place to pray. A large walk-in closet opened
to the right and a nice sized bathroom to the left. They positioned the bed at the center of the doorway wall and the

antique oak roll-top desk that had been her father's next to the window.

"Now I can look out and be soothed by those gorgeous mountains when I get sick of paperwork." She smiled with pleasure.

"I don't think I'll ever get tired of the scenery around here. We've got to get out for a ride tomorrow. I can't wait to start exploring our land." Christopher gazed out the window with pride. "I love it, Mickey. *Our* land."

"I wish I could have helped you with the money, Chris." A frown clouded her face when she again thought of the expenses involved with the move. "I feel like a freeloader. I haven't contributed anything except the truck and trailer."

"*You* are your contribution," Christopher said, laying his hand on her shoulder firmly. "Your being here is worth more to me than any amount of money. The Lord has allowed me to be very successful, so I had plenty of money put away. I like having some invested in property."

He gently took her chin in his hand and looked at her, the sincerity in his warm brown eyes reassuring her. "Please, don't ever, ever think you owe me. I mean it when I say your being here is enough. Your talents, your company, and your friendship will make my life richer than I ever dreamed. I just hope you will be happy with your life because I know I'll be with mine."

Though Christopher tried to speak from a friend's perspective, his face betrayed him. Mickey felt something she could not define rush through her at his touch.

What's wrong with me? she thought frantically. *I must be losing it.* She searched her mind for an explanation but decided her discomfort must be due to the newness of their situation and the fact that she knew they were now 'married'.

Gently but firmly, she pushed his hand away. "Okay then," she said in a lightly and turned to grab a dust cloth. "I won't worry about it anymore. And Chris, thanks," she added, not wanting to hurt his feelings. "You are one of the most generous people I know. This house and this land have fulfilled just about every one of my dreams. I'm glad you're my friend."

Christopher thought, *and your husband,* but said nothing. He took pride in knowing Mickey was his wife but knew time would be required before she would feel comfortable using the terms husband and wife given their situation.

~ * ~

By mid-afternoon they had gotten most of the kitchen appliances, cookware, and other odds and ends unpacked and put away. Mickey and Christopher were both tremendously happy with the large kitchen, since both loved to cook.

The room featured an updated stove and oven combination, a dishwasher, a relatively new refrigerator-freezer which the MacGregors left, and lots of cupboards and counter space including a nice sized island. A separate pantry gave plenty of room for food storage.

The open concept design allowed for a formal dining area on one end and breakfast nook on the other. A door opened to a flight of stairs that led down to the basement and another flight leading upstairs.

Mickey and Christopher moved to the living room to start unpacking the boxes there. Mickey sighed while she gazed out the large picture window. "I think the view is going to be fabulous from every window. That front yard is great."

"Landscaping was Mrs. MacGregor's hobby, Christopher said. "She really made that lawn a work of art."

They gazed at the huge fir tree in the center of the yard. The surrounding thick lush green grass looked soft like carpet. Along the perimeter a long yard wide strip of hardwood mulch made a bed for clumps of beautiful flowers. The area was bordered by gray flat stones on the inside and a short white picket fence to outline the yard on the outside.

"I'm definitely going to do my best to keep that lawn up," Mickey said firmly. "I love working with plants and flowers."

"I'll help whenever I can. We'll have to get a riding mower, though. That is a lot of lawn!" Christopher turned. "We'd better get a move on if we want to finish unpacking."

"Right. Let's git 'er done!" Mickey said with a smile.

~ * ~

They worked steadily for the rest of the day, arranging the living and dining rooms, and even taking their exercise equipment down to the basement. Kip followed them from room to room acting personally responsible for overseeing their progress. By early evening, most of the rooms were in some semblance of order.

Tired but happy, Christopher and Mickey sat down to a late supper, the last of the turkey and cheese sandwiches from the cooler, sweet tea, and chips.

"Thank you, Lord, for a good day," Christopher prayed before they ate. "Thank You for getting us here safely and thank You for all that we were able to accomplish today.

"Thank You for seeing fit to bless us with this beautiful place to live and work. Help us always to honor and glorify You with our successes and our failures. I pray that You would bless our life together and help us to always put You first. Amen".

"Amen," Mickey said softly, feeling completely at peace about her new situation.

As they began to eat, Christopher looked up suddenly. "Hey, tomorrow is Sunday. I've completely lost track of the week."

Mickey put down her sandwich. "You're right. You know I was thinking on the way out here that I'm really going to miss my old church."

"I know what you mean. Let's ask around in town this week and see if we can find a good church nearby."

Mickey nodded. "Meanwhile, why don't we just have our own little service here?"

"Great idea, Mick," Christopher said eagerly. "I really miss getting to worship with others. Hey, how would you feel about reading some scripture and praying together every evening after supper?"

"That would be fantastic. There's just something amazing about praising God with another believer."

They put their plan into action immediately and their time of fellowship and worship together left both feeling satisfied and closer to their Lord. Christopher closed in prayer and when they rose, he noticed Mickey suddenly grab the back of the recliner. She stood completely still, squinting slightly.

"Mick, are you okay?" he asked, his voice laced with concern.

"Oh, I'm fine," she said with a small laugh but her shaking voice and the strange look in her eyes gave her away.

Christopher took her hand and felt her fingers trembling. He searched her face intently. "You're getting a migraine, aren't you?" Ever since he had known her, Mickey suffered the debilitating headaches, and he learned long ago to recognize the signs.

Mickey slumped with relief at the kindness in his voice and the fact that he knew instantly what was wrong. "I think so," she said with chagrin. "All of the sudden I feel shaky all over and I'm seeing all kinds of bright zigzag lines."

He squeezed her hand in reassurance. "I'm not surprised you're getting one what with all the upheaval during the last few days. Let's get you to bed," he said firmly.

With no further warning, Christopher scooped her up and carried her to her bedroom. Carefully he laid her on the soft bed and put a pillow under her head. "Do you have any of those pills you were telling me about the other day?"

Mickey nodded. "I think I have a few somewhere but I don't remember exactly where I put them. They're probably in the bathroom."

"I'll try to find one," he said. "Maybe we can ward that headache off before the pain gets too bad."

Mickey lay still, feeling completely overwhelmed at his tender care of her in her current state of vulnerability. Things with Lee had been completely different. She closed her eyes, remembering.

~ * ~

The week of mid-terms was incredibly hectic. By Friday, Mickey's exhaustion threatened to overwhelm her. She had a date with Lee to go to the football game that night but while she walked toward her dorm, she felt the aura of an impending migraine.

I just can't endure a game tonight, she thought, wincing at the thought of all the noise and the bright spotlights. *I'm going to just call and explain things to him.*

But Lee was completely unsympathetic and quite disgusted. "What kind of weakling are you anyway?" he said angrily. "Don't you know the Proverbs thirty-one woman was strong? Besides, you know full well I can't be seen at that game alone. Why don't you stop thinking of yourself for a change? And for crying out loud, you're only twenty years old. You act like an old woman with all these aches and pains. Get over it."

Mickey went with him. All through the game the throbbing in her head increased. The thumping continuous beat of the pep band and the cheering shouting crowd finally forced her to excuse herself.

She quickly made her way to the restroom and was sick. Still nauseated with head pounding, Mickey left the stadium facilities and made her way back to her dorm. She went to bed immediately, but the pain did not abate until well into the night time hours.

Lee ignored her soundly for days afterward. She called him every night and said she was sorry. Finally, she went to him in desperation, apologized again, and begged him to understand.

At first, he was quite cool and aloof but while she went on apologizing for her weakness, a benevolent smile slowly crossed his face.

"Okay, Mickey, I'll forgive you. Dear, I know thinking of others is hard sometimes, but we just have to learn not to be selfish. We have to learn to ignore our own pain, real or imagined."

Always ready to assist her in finding solutions to her spiritual shortcomings, Lee continued. "You've been single for a long time and all you've thought about most of your life is yourself. If you want to be in a relationship, you have to start thinking about someone else."

He continued in this vein for nearly fifteen minutes, then said, "I have a great book you really should read, Mickey. Maybe that would help you work out some of these sinful areas you have so much trouble with. I think it would teach you how to be the right kind of Christian woman."

Mickey dutifully read the book, giving insisted upon daily reports to Lee of what she had read and how the words had pointed out failures in her life and character. She never again said anything to Lee if she had a migraine or physical ailment. Even in her greatest pain, she did her best to put on an act so Lee would not have cause to condemn.

~ * ~

Her unpleasant memories were interrupted when Christopher returned with the medicine and a glass of water. Gently he held the back of her head while she swallowed the pill. "Now just lie back and rest so that medicine can work," he whispered, easing her head back onto the pillow.

He stayed at her side, gently stroking her hair until he was sure she was asleep. He moved to the easy chair in the corner and dozed. In about an hour, Mickey awoke and sat up carefully.

Christopher jumped up, immediately alert. "Mick, are you okay? How is the pain?"

Mickey climbed from the bed and moved about slowly. "Gone, I think," she said with a wobbly smile. "Thank goodness for that medicine. The way it gets rid of a migraine really is remarkable."

She paused and looked at him. "Thanks, Chris, for being so kind. You'll never know how much it means to have someone be understanding when one of those headaches hit."

Christopher smiled and rose. He touched her face gently, then turned. "You'd better get back into bed. You need to rest so that headache won't come back."

~ Eight ~

The next week was filled with activity while Mickey and Christopher finished settling in and arranging the house. Wednesday, they decided to spend the day on horseback, exploring part of their land. They dressed warmly because the early June temperatures were still a bit chilly.

As they crossed the North pasture, they let the horses break into a canter.

"You really handle horses well for someone who never owned one," Mickey commented, pulling Kili to a slow trot when they neared the far gate.

Christopher smiled and patted Fili's neck. "I had a friend up in Maine who had several horses. We formed kind of an informal riding club."

He maneuvered Fili so he could reach down and unlatch the gate. "A bunch of us guys loved to ride but weren't home enough to keep our own animals," he said while they rode through. "Tom let us come out whenever we had time. He's the one who taught me to ride." "I'm impressed. You ride like a natural born horseman." Mickey smiled at him admiringly.

"Why thank you, my dear. You are too kind." He turned slightly sideways in the saddle and made a comical bow. Fili took advantage of the moment of distraction to reach down and grab a mouthful of grass.

Mickey giggled and clucked to Kili, who took off into a smooth canter. Seeing he was about to be left behind, Fili jerked his head up, gave a sharp whinny, then followed briskly.

After a short distance the tall grass gave way to forest. They began making their way through the trees and up the mountain. Christopher pointed to the ground.

"Look, Mick. Cougar tracks."

Pulling Kili to a halt, Mickey leaned over and eyed the paw prints thoughtfully. "Wow," she commented at last. "That's kind of scary to think of them being so close. Do you think they'll bother the horses?"

"I don't know. I hope not." Christopher frowned slightly. "We'll probably be all right if we keep them in at night. That's when the cats are most actively hunting, I think.

That's a good idea," Mickey said, sounding relieved. "I would be horrified if something happened to them."

"Me, too." Christopher nudged Fili with his heel. They rode on in companionable silence, enjoying the woods and the gentle sound of clopping hooves on the forest floor. Soon they came to a shallow stream. Bright yellow buttercups dotted the bank, and the water made a gurgling sound.

"I'll bet this is the same stream that runs through the pasture," Christopher said thoughtfully.

He guided Fili into the water and the horse slowly picked his way across. Mickey followed on Kili. She glanced downstream and smiled. A small raccoon was sitting on a rock calmly watching them while he washed something over and over in the cool water. He drew his paws from the stream and inspected his dinner carefully, then popped the fish into his mouth.

How cute, thought Mickey, while Kili splashed his way out of the water on the other side. *I love all the wildlife around here. Chris certainly won't run out of subjects to photograph.*

They were near the top of the mountain when they emerged into a large meadow. Wildflowers were scattered here and there, providing bright dots of pink, blue, yellow, and purple in the tall grass. On the far edge of the field, they could see a large outcropping of rock.

"Race you to the rock," shouted Mickey and gave Kili the cue. He took off galloping with delight, kicking up the dirt behind him.

"Hey, no fair!" Christopher said with a snort. He and Fili took off after them and arrived just half a length behind. "Good race there, Mick." He was laughing while he jumped down. He strode over and pulled her out of the saddle. "Really fair."

She smiled and put on a superior air. "Now, Christopher, everybody knows you have to be prepared for anything out here. That's the mark of a true mountain man."

"Right. How could I have forgotten about the old 'sudden unexpected race' trick?" Christopher said, tapping his head. "And after all that training. I guess I'm still just a tenderfoot after all."

They laughed together while they climbed up and sat on the huge rock. "Oh, Chris, look at that view," breathed Mickey in awe. She hugged her legs to her chest and rested her chin on her knee, gazing at the scenic beauty.

The valley stretched out before them and the mountains beyond reached up, providing a sharp contrast to the bright blue sky. Snow-capped peaks in the distance glistened in the sun like they had been sprinkled with thousands of diamonds.

"There's our house." Christopher shaded his eyes with one hand and pointed to the left.

Mickey squinted and finally spotted the tiny building. "Sure enough. Everything looks like a doll furniture from here."

"I've got to get some pictures," Christopher said, reaching into his backpack for his camera.

He meandered here and there taking dozens of shots. Mickey sighed deeply with pleasure when he returned to sit beside her. "This place is awesome. I never thought I'd have my own mountain."

Christopher was silent for several minutes while he stared at the landscape. Suddenly he turned to her. "Mickey, I want to ask you to promise me something," he said earnestly.

She looked at him with an inquisitive smile and a question in her eyes but then sobered when she saw that he was serious. "I will if I can," she said.

"Please Mickey, don't ride up here, or on any of these mountains, by yourself." Concern furrowed his brow. "I know you're a capable woman and it's not that I think you can't handle things. But with wildcats up here, things could be dangerous. I'm sure there are grizzlies, too."

He looked into her eyes, silently begging her not to be angry. "Besides you know trail riding alone is never wise. You don't know what might happen."

Mickey gazed back at him, searching his face for a moment, then dropped her eyes. "That makes sense," she said slowly. "I knew a lady once who was badly hurt trail riding alone. Then she had to load the horse and drive the truck and trailer back home even though she was injured." She reached up a hand to tuck a curl behind one ear and looked at him once more. "I promise. I won't ride up here alone."

"Thank you." Christopher reached over and gave her hand a squeeze. "That will be a big load off my mind. I couldn't bear the pain if something happened to you. I know I can't be with you every moment, but I intend to protect you to the best of my ability. Without smothering you, that is."

His eyes twinkled. "Oh and be sure you always have your phone and an extra charger, too. You may not always have service but—"

"Ahem, I believe you said, without smothering? Now you're beginning to sound like my mother," Mickey said wryly, with a smirk on her face.

"Right. Got it," Christopher shook his head and laughed. "I will cease and desist with the smothering and mothering."

Mickey felt oddly comforted and secure. She watched a chickadee nearby pecking at seeds in a crack of the rock, using the bird for an excuse to glance over at Christopher's handsome profile.

I could have done worse, she thought with a measure of satisfaction. *This just might be an easier situation than I thought. After all, I can appreciate beautiful scenery in landscapes and in people.* She nearly giggled out loud at the thought.

But she was tremendously relieved to see that, though he obviously cared about her and would take care of her, he intended to keep his promise of long ago.

No worries, she thought. A prick of conscience smote her. *Ask and ye shall receive.* But she refused to comply and pushed the thought aside.

They sat for a few moments more, enjoying the beautiful spring day.

"I guess we'd better get back," Christopher said, glancing at his watch and stretching while he got up. "It's getting late. We don't want to lose the light."

"Agreed. Let's ride."

Christopher hopped down from the rock and reached up to help her. Mickey reached to take his hand, but he grabbed her around the waist and easily lifted her down to the grass. Her heart pounded so hard at his touch that she feared he would hear.

He gazed at her and suddenly with no warning, his lips descended to hers in a gentle kiss. For a moment she was still with shock and before she could think, he lifted his head.

"Aww, I'm sorry, Mick," he whispered hoarsely. "I shouldn't have done that."

Mickey stared at him, then pulled away feeling frightened, ill at ease, confused, and somewhat betrayed. Her heart raced and she suddenly felt like a trapped animal. She willed herself to calm down and act normal.

Her reaction shook Christopher to the core. Seeing her fright, he realized that he must not lose control again. He turned and they mounted the horses in silence.

Slowly they rode across the meadow and reentered the woods. About halfway back down the mountain when the silence between them became almost unbearable, Mickey suddenly pulled Kili to a halt.

"Chris, look," she whispered.

He stopped Fili and turned. Mickey pointed to a nearby thicket. Through the leafy green wall, they could see a beautiful doe and her spotted fawn. Christopher and Mickey hardly dared to breathe while they sat watching.

The doe looked cautiously out at them but apparently decided they would not harm her. Gracefully she stepped out and quickly crossed the path, her small baby sticking by her side like he was attached with Velcro.
Quickly they disappeared into the forest.

"Wow," Christopher said, letting his breath out with a puff. "I've never been that close to a White Tail before. I've gotten good shots with my 500-millimeter lens, but I've never actually gotten within a few yards of them. Oh, man! Why didn't I have my camera ready?"

"Too bad. But if we had moved or even breathed, she would never have come this way. That was so incredible," Mickey said with wonder while they continued down the path. "I felt like I could just reach out and touch them." Somehow the sight of the beautiful animals soothed Mickey's frightened spirit.

The heaviness in Christopher's heart lifted. Though his control slipped there on the mountain top, apparently Mickey decided not to hold his mistake against him. He determined once again to honor his promise and silently asked the Lord for strength.

As they neared the north pasture, the barn came into view and Christopher remarked, "You know, all the ranches around here have names. We should find one of our own for this place. We can't keep using the MacGregor's name."

"Why not the C&M?" Mickey asked. They rode through the gate, and she turned back to pull the gate shut.

"The C&M," he said slowly, trying out the name. "Yeah, I like that."

"C&M it is then." Mickey smiled, thankful he had not said anything about the kiss. She whirled Kili around and touched his sides with her heels. The horse immediately launched into a graceful canter and Fili followed close behind. The horses raced across the pasture toward home, their riders enjoying the feel of the wind in their faces and the powerful animals beneath them.

~ Nine ~

Friday night after supper, Christopher headed out to the barn and came back with his toolbox. "I'm going to go work on the basement," he said, heading down the stairs.

"Okay," Mickey said from the recliner in the living room.

Snippit jumped up and curled herself on her lap. Mickey picked up a stack of mail and began to sort through the letters and catalogs. "Oh hey, Chris," she called. "Wait a minute."

He trotted back up the stairs and plopped down on the couch. "Whatcha need?"

"Any chance you could get my treadmill or elliptical set up? I've already missed way too many workouts. If I don't get back to exercising soon, I'm going to be the size of the barn."

"Fat chance," exploded Christopher, disbelief on his face. "There's no way."

Mickey went into gales of laughter. Christopher thought for a moment and then realized what he said.

"No pun intended," he said with a chuckle, his brown eyes twinkling. He went on without thinking. "Besides, it wouldn't matter what you looked like, I'd still lo..." he trailed off awkwardly, realizing just in time that he very nearly broken his promise again.

Mickey's smile faded. She froze for a moment, then fastened her gaze on the cat.

Christopher cleared his throat and stood. "I've got some ideas for our exercise stuff the basement," he said with a light tone, trying to ease the tension. "Give me a couple days and then you can see. I want it to be a surprise." He quickly exited the room.

As he descended the stairs, he mentally kicked himself for being so careless so soon after the kiss episode. The look of fright and horror on her face confused him but he remembered that he *had* promised.

At least she finally asked for my help, he thought. *She'd perfectly capable of getting that gear set up but she's going to let me help her. I guess that's some progress.*

Upstairs Mickey went back to reading the mail, much of which was still addressed to the MacGregors. She set aside the letters to be forwarded and a packet of photos addressed to Christopher. While she looked through the rest of the stack, one of the catalogs caught her eye. She slowly began to leaf through the pages.

Featured were various pictures, statues, mugs, and other paraphernalia, all with different landscape scenes or wildlife on them. Mickey was especially drawn to one print which captured a beautiful buck poised beside a mountain lake. Snow covered the ground and moonlight covered the scene with a ghostly light.

Moonlight Stag, *by Christopher Gordon, award-winning wildlife photographer.*

She let her head fall back against the chair with a thump after reading the credit. *I had no idea,* she thought in amazement. *I know he said he was successful but wow. How did I not know about this? I guess I just had so much going on in my own life that I didn't keep up.* She looked down at the catalog again, then began looking at each picture's credit. Eight of Christopher's prints were featured.

She grabbed her phone from the end table and texted, "Could U come up here 4 a min?" to Chris.

"B right there," came his prompt reply.

She got up and went to the kitchen. Within minutes she heard his footsteps on the stairs.

"What's up?" he asked when he came into the room.

She showed him the catalog. "Look what I found, Chris. A picture by award winning photographer Christopher Gordon." She grinned at him. "I know you said you did all right, but this is awesome. I am so proud of you."

His face warmed and he blushed slightly. "The Lord has been good. I began to be successful soon after I started my photography business. I know there are lots of people out there who are talented. I was just blessed to have the right people notice my work."

Mickey smiled. "I think this is great. You are amazing. I just wanted you to know."

Christopher looked searchingly at her for a moment. "Thanks, Mick," he said after a moment. "That means a lot."

"Oh, by the way, this packet came for you." Mickey went to the living room and brought back the mailer.

"These are the pictures I took before we left South Carolina," Christopher said with excitement. He carefully avoided saying anything about their being wedding photos.

"I uploaded the entire memory card to have prints made before we left. I didn't have time to go through them and I knew we wouldn't have our computers and satellite service set up here for a few weeks."

He tore open the envelope and looked critically at each picture. "Not bad for a timer shot," he said, handing the stack to Mickey. "Some of those others are of the place I was renting in Maine."

Mickey glanced through, noticing there were doubles of each picture. "Could I have some of these extras?" she asked, feeling a bit shy about asking.

"Oh sure, that's why I ordered two of each," he said casually. "Just take whatever you want. I'm going back downstairs."

Mickey went through the wedding photos slowly after he was gone. Finally, she took her copies up to her bedroom, leaving the others on the table for Christopher. Without really knowing why, she rummaged through her closet until she located a box of old frames. She inserted one of the close-ups of the two of them and placed the framed photo on her desk.

~ * ~

Over the next few days Mickey heard Christopher pounding away in the basement every time he had a spare moment. Finally, by mid-afternoon that Saturday, he announced that the place was ready for her inspection. Mickey went down the stairs, feeling like a kid opening yet another wonderful present.

Mickey and Christopher both owned nice entertainment systems but they opted to keep his upstairs since the components had more features. He set Mickey's system up along one wall of the basement and positioned all their exercise equipment in a semicircle facing the television. Between the two of them they had a treadmill, a stationary bike, a ski machine, a weight bench, and elliptical.

The roll of antique blue carpet that was formerly propped up in one corner now graced the floor and he had painted the concrete walls white. A mirror Chris discovered in the attic was attached to one side, making the room appear even larger. A ceiling fan set up directly over the exercise machines finished the look. The spacious airy cool space made a perfect workout room.

Three smaller rooms were opposite the long exercise room. One held the washer, dryer, and an upright freezer. Chris had repainted the walls white and installed the same blue carpet to the floor. He built a rack on which to hang clothes and turned Mickey's stand-alone ironing board into a wall mount. The deep sink on the opposite wall was scrubbed clean. Cabinets graced each side of the sink, providing storage for various items.

The middle room was already a half-bath, so he just cleaned up a bit.

"Wow," Mickey said, looking around in delight. "I hope you took before shot! This is amazing! Working out and doing laundry won't be half bad now. Shoot, we could sell memberships and turn this into an official gym."

Christopher smiled with satisfaction at her genuine pleasure. "I couldn't think what we might need the other room for since we already have a room for our office upstairs, so I just painted and left the floors bare. I'm sure we'll come up with something."

Mickey eyed the room thoughtfully. A large window right at ground level graced one wall, offering wonderful light. She knew exactly how she would make use of that room. She smiled while she and Christopher headed back upstairs.

~ * ~

After supper, Christopher and Mickey went up to the guest bedroom to unpack some of the last boxes. Christopher carefully opened a box of Mickey's labeled 'Pictures'. He pulled out a medium-sized framed oil painting and gazed at the scene. A mountain stream was featured surrounded by snowy woods. Small animals peeked out here and there and hidden in the shadows was the faint hint of a deer. He was surprised at how similar the painting was to his photo in the catalog.

"Mickey, this is beautiful," he said in admiration. "Where did you get it?"

She came over to look and blushed. "Ah, um," she said awkwardly, looking down. "Actually, I did it. And I promise, I'd never seen your picture before either." Christopher looked at her in amazement. "I didn't think you had. That's remarkable." He held the picture out at arm's length and studied the work intently. "I never knew you could paint."

Mickey felt silly. She painted solely for her own enjoyment and pleasure and did not know quite how to react. Finally, she said, "I was watching one of those painting shows on TV one day and I remarked that I wished I could paint like that. My mom said, 'Why don't you try?' So, I did."

Mickey peeked up at him. "Painting is fun but really, I do it just for me. I've always loved the look of oils."
"I think you're being very selfish keeping your talent to yourself," Christopher said sternly but with that engaging twinkle in his eye letting her know he was teasing. "But seriously," he continued earnestly. "Your work is outstanding. You truly to have real talent. Is there more?"

Mickey sorted through the box and pulled out several more examples of her work. Christopher examined each one thoroughly but was especially drawn to one of the larger pieces. The painting reminded him of their own land. She had painted the far-off snow-capped mountains in their rugged splendor and a summer meadow with an abundance of wildflowers. Horses grazed in the field and a barn could be seen at a distance.

Seeing how he kept coming back to that one, Mickey smiled. *Now is my chance to do something for him*, she thought with pleasure.

She picked up the framed canvas and handed the painting to him. "Chris, I want you to have this one."
"But Mickey, it's yours." He shook his head and put his hands up while backing away. "I can't take it from you. That's the best one."

"I absolutely insist," she said firmly. She ran her hand through her thick dark curls, pushing them back from her face. "I've been wishing I could give you something special and this is perfect."

She turned, holding the picture in front of her, and started for the door. "Now, let's go hang this in your bedroom."

Her tone brooked no argument, so he followed, deeply touched at her generosity. When they began measuring, Christopher suddenly turned with excitement in his eyes. "Mick! You should use that extra room downstairs -"

"For a studio?" she said with a laugh.

"Yes! It's perfect!"

"My dear, you read my mind. That's exactly what I thought when I saw all the light."

Christopher smiled smugly. "Great minds. We're good, Mick. I'm just sayin'."

"Oh, yeah we are," she said, nodding.

"Let me know if you need me to do anything else in that room. Oh, and we should fix up that half bath a little. Can't have our resident artist living with anything but the best."

Mickey put on a superior air. "But of course, daahling. I must be free to create in the utmost luxury and comfort. Nothing less will do."

They laughed together comfortably while they finished hanging the picture, then went to the office to get their computers up and running.

~ Ten ~

After two weeks at the ranch, supplies for both animals and people were running low. Friday afternoon Christopher and Mickey prepared to set out for the small town of Aspen Ridge located twenty-eight miles north of the C&M. Just when they opened the door to leave, Mickey's cell phone rang.

"Hello?" she said and paused for a moment. "Yes. My husband and I just moved in two weeks ago." She paused again. "Why thank you! We were just headed for town. We'll be needing to stock up on feed, so we'll see you for sure. I'm Mickey Sterling and my husband's name is Christopher Gordon."

After a chuckle and another thank you, she tapped end. "How nice," she said, smiling. "That was Sam from the feed store in town. He's been away and just wanted to say howdy to the new folks. He got my number from the realtor. He seemed really nice. Said to tell you welcome to the area."

Christopher smiled and remarked how kind the gesture was but inside he was rejoicing. Though Mickey preferred to keep her maiden name, she used the term 'husband' with ease. The word came naturally. He thanked the Lord inwardly for this answer to prayer.

Christopher and Mickey returned from their trip stocked with enough supplies to last the ranch a month. They thoroughly enjoyed the time spent together shopping and meeting people. They were much impressed with the friendliness of everyone they met in Aspen Ridge.

Sunday morning, Mickey and Christopher sat together in the sanctuary of Aspen Ridge Community Church. At the feed store, Sam told them about the small ministry established several years earlier. The sanctuary sat ten miles from the town on land donated by area ranchers. Fortunately for them, the church was ten miles in their direction, making for an easy drive except in the winter.

Christopher and Mickey immediately fell in love with the little white building, reminiscent of a one room schoolhouse. A handsome bell swung in a tower on the roof and colorful flowers grew in carefully manicured beds around the perimeter of the building. A small tasteful cemetery sat at the back of the property. The whole thing reminded Mickey of her church back in South Carolina.

As they sang "Amazing Grace", Mickey felt a warmth creep over her heart. She felt quite at home in this small congregation that numbered only thirty-five, including the children. She smiled while she remembered the moments before the service started, when people welcomed them wholeheartedly and seemed genuinely friendly and interested.

Mickey even met the MacGregors who just could not leave their beloved state after so many years. They ended up settling on a small Christmas tree farm a few miles out from town. Mickey immediately fell in love with Mrs. MacGregor. A small round woman with snowy white hair drawn back into a bun, her gray eyes were kind but sparkled with enthusiasm.

Christopher and Mickey were both impressed with the pastor's sermon. He presented the scripture in a forthright manner and didn't mince words but the kindness and compassion in his voice showed his love for people of all walks of life.

He really cares, Mickey thought during the final benediction when the pastor earnestly asked God's protection on them. He continued to pray that they would have the opportunity that week to share God's love with someone in need.

As people began milling about, the pastor came over to introduce himself. "I'm Greg Norris and this is my wife, Lorrie." He looked down at the very pregnant redhead beside him.

"Glad to meet you," Christopher said, shaking his hand. "We really enjoyed our time here today. I'm Christopher Gordon and this is my wife, Mickey Sterling."

He watched carefully to see how she would react to the term. She seemed to take no notice, for she smiled widely and held out her hand. He was greatly relieved that his public use of the term 'wife' did not bother her. She appeared to have adjusted to their new relationship.

Lorrie smiled warmly. "We're so glad you've come. Mickey, I'd love to have you over for lunch once you get settled."

"That would be great," Mickey said, already feeling like she found a friend.

"Good! I'll give you a call in a couple weeks, unless of course..." Lorrie patted her round tummy.

Mickey laughed. "Right. I'll look forward to it."

As the pastor and his wife moved on and Christopher and Mickey made their way outside, a small pain stabbed through her heart. She loved children but with this unusual marriage would never have any of her own. She felt tears threaten but took a deep breath and quickly turned her thoughts back to the friendly folks around her.

A tall blonde came walking over. "Hi," she said warmly. "I'm Jennifer Austin."

"I'm glad to meet you, Jennifer," Mickey said, reaching to shake her hand. "I'm Mickey Sterling. My husband Christopher Gordon is over there. We moved into the MacGregor's place a couple weeks ago. I'm from South Carolina and Chris came from Maine."

"Welcome to the area," Jennifer said, shading her eyes with her hand. "I thought I detected a hint of a southern accent." She grinned. "I like it! What made you choose Montana?"

"Chris is a wildlife photographer, and he wanted his own land. Plus, all the national forests and parks around here provide endless subject matter for him. I've always dreamed of owning a ranch and even though I love the south, I don't know any place more beautiful than northwestern Montana. We're both in our element."

Jennifer nodded. "I know what you mean. I love this part of the country. I'm finishing up my college degree right now and I hate being away from home so much. I spend the week in Great Falls at school and then come home on weekends."

"What's your major?" Mickey asked.

A shadow crossed the tall girl's face before she named her Business Administration major. Quickly she changed the subject. "Mickey, do you have horses?"

"You bet," Mickey said with a grin. "I have two Friesian crosses named Fili and Kili."

"Oh, I love it!" Jennifer said with delight. "A fellow Hobbit© and Lord of the Rings© fan! I have a fantastic little Quarter Horse named, guess what?"

Mickey paused thoughtfully. "Hmm.... I'm guessing Gimli or Sam," she said with a grin.

"You're good, my friend! Gimli it is." Jennifer laughed.

Out of the corner of her eye, Mickey noticed Christopher walking toward the Jeep®. "Jen, looks like I'd better get a move on or I'll be walking home. I'm so glad I met you. Maybe we can get together and ride sometime."

Jennifer smiled again. "I'd love that," she said, her eyes shining. "My mom and I don't have much land but

I'd love to bring Gimli out to your place."

"Sure," Mickey said warmly. "We've certainly got plenty of room to ride. Just give me a call. I'll be starting a new job soon but I'm working from home, so I'll have a pretty flexible schedule."

"Will, do. Bye, Mickey. Great meeting you."

As they drove home, Mickey shared with Christopher the wonderful job opportunity she had accepted. "This is the perfect job, Chris. I've always loved writing and editing. I don't know if you remember but I minored in Creative Writing. And I did a little writing and editing on the side a few years ago.

"Before we moved a Christian publisher approached me about editing for them. They were fine with having me work from home. I just have to let them know when I can start."

Mickey paused for breath. "We need to get the satellite set up soon. I don't want to miss out on this opportunity."

Christopher smiled at her enthusiasm. "I called them Friday. They'll be coming out one day this week."

"Fantastic!" Mickey said.

"You continually surprise me with hidden talents," Christopher said warmly. "I'm so proud of you!"

Mickey blushed slightly and murmured a quiet, "Thank you."

Her heart soaked in his words and his genuine appreciation of her. How different things had been with Lee, who resented her, and was threatened by anything she could do well.

Always there was a lecture on 'balance' whenever she spent any time doing something she enjoyed. Of course, balance to him meant spending all her time focused on him. Mickey shook off the memories and determined to enjoy her day.

Broken Promise

~ * ~

As they entered the kitchen, the mouth-watering aroma of roast beef filled their nostrils, indicating the timer on the oven worked perfectly.

"Mmm," murmured Christopher. "That smell is fantastic. I haven't eaten a real Sunday dinner in ages."

"Me, either," Mickey said. "After Mom got sick, she never wanted much to eat, and I never did a lot of cooking when I was just fixing food for myself. Except for cookies, of course." She tried to grin while she put a pot of raw cubed potatoes on the stove to heat, then quickly headed to her room to change.

She shed a few quiet tears while the pain of her mother's death stabbed her heart again.

I wish you could have seen this place, Mom, she thought while she carefully hung her dress in the closet. *You'd have loved this part of the country.* Then she smiled tenderly to herself. *Nope. She would not have budged from her Blue Ridge Mountains. Not for anybody.*

A few moments later, Mickey returned to the kitchen composed and dressed in jeans and a red tee shirt. She grabbed a couple of potholders and pulled the roast from the oven. She placed the meat on a platter and began to prepare gravy in the roaster.

Christopher came in looking very comfortable in his jeans and purple polo shirt. He got the silverware and plates out and set the table, then began to prepare a Caesar salad. They worked together easily laughing, joking, and snitching food from each other.

When everything was ready, they stood back and looked at the dining room table critically. "Just right," Christopher said with satisfaction.

"Yep," Mickey said. "This table could be featured in *Gourmet* magazine."

"Absolutely. The perfect elegant dinner."

Then Mickey laughed. "Except for us. We look like the original couch potatoes. But hey, this is who we are, right?" She put on an exaggerated southern drawl. "After all, honey bunch, I'm just not in the habit of 'dressin' for dinner'."

"Me either, little darlin'" Christopher said, responding in kind. "I say eat in comfort."

"My thoughts exactly. I'm allergic to being dressed up too long." She grinned. "Seriously. I get a rash and everything."

Christopher pulled out her chair with a flourish. They enjoyed the meal thoroughly and cleaned up together afterwards. Mickey finished wiping the counter, then lifted her hand to cover a jaw splitting yawn.

Christopher laughed. "What is it about Sunday afternoons?" he asked. "I always get so sleepy."

"Me, too," Mickey said, yawning again. "I'm off to take a nap."

"Same here." Christopher put the last container of leftovers in the refrigerator. "See you later. Sleep well." She was already out of the room, so she failed to detect the note of wistfulness in his tone.

He shook his head while his mind conjured up the image of Mickey and himself, snuggling down together for a Sunday afternoon nap on a cold snowy winter day.

None of that now, he told himself firmly. *That's no way to encourage patience, torturing yourself with how things could be.* He took one last look around the kitchen, then headed for his bedroom.

~ *Eleven* ~

That evening Mickey decided to explore the attic. Christopher helped her pull down the trap door, which she was too short to reach, then headed for the living room saying he wanted to read some photographic journals. She climbed the ladder in anticipation.

I love attics, she thought happily. *This is going to be too fun.*

After groping around a bit, Mickey found a light switch. The space looked like a typical attic, with a sloping roof and tufts of pink insulation poking out here and there. A musty odor filled the air and dust covered everything in a thick layer.

An old, tattered recliner sat in one corner and beside the chair sat a large worn brown trunk. Mickey looked around the otherwise empty attic and seeing nothing else of interest, decided to investigate the trunk.

She brushed the dust off the chair and gingerly sat down. The old piece of furniture squeaked in protest and Mickey groaned when the springs poked her backside though the threadbare blue fabric. She spotted a faded gold colored pillow nearby and put the cushion under her.

"That's better," she said with a happy smile. She grasped the trunk's lid.

The trunk opened stiffly, and Mickey gasped with delight while she waved away the cloud of dust. One corner was stacked high with old books, while the rest was filled with an odd assortment of boxes. Carefully she began to lift the books out. The first ones were different ranching books ranging from care of cattle to planting crops. When she neared the middle of the pile, she grinned with delight.

A first edition McGuffy Reader, Mickey noted in amazement. *I can't believe it! This thing must be worth a lot.* She looked through the yellowed pages carefully, smiling when she thought of the generations of children who had probably learned from this very book.

After inspecting the reader thoroughly, she gently laid the book off to the side and went back to the stack. She found a volume of Robert Frost poems and an old leather-bound edition of *Pilgrim's Progress©*. At the bottom of the trunk, she found a large family Bible.

Eagerly checking the inside cover, she discovered the volume to be from the MacGregor family.

"I'll bet they forgot about this," Mickey said aloud. "They said we could have anything we found in the house and barn but surely, they want their family Bible. Oh, my word, the entries date back to 1703!" She carefully laid the Bible beside her in the chair.

As she looked through the rest of the trunk, she found one box of vintage Christmas ornaments, a larger box packed full of carefully wrapped objects, and a wooden box which contained a stack of old letters tied with a faded red ribbon.

I'll bet these are love letters, she thought with glee while she fingered the yellowed paper.

Curious about the large box, Mickey lifted the bulky package out of the trunk and began to unwrap the contents. The first item she discovered was a small toy truck. The faded red sign on the side proclaimed HOOK and LADDER, Fire Dept.® Mickey noticed the cut-out figure of a fireman sitting in the driver's seat and another cut out figure sitting at the back of the truck. The body featured an open design, with a ladder attached to the upper part of the truck by two hooks and a small rust-colored bucket set inside. Both the ladder and the bucket were removable.

Mickey smiled with delight. She placed the worn truck on the floor and grasped the pull string at the front. Gently she tugged and the black steel wheels moved easily. *That is so cute*, she thought. *I wonder how old it is.*

She reached a hand to push back a strand of hair from her face, then reached into the box again. She lifted out a heavy package which she placed on her lap. When she pulled away the yellowed tissue paper, she found a cast iron bank in the shape of a prancing horse. The shiny black finish bore a few nicks here and there but seemed to be in good shape.

Mickey placed the bank next to the fire truck and excitedly grabbed the next bulky package. *I love it! This is just like Christmas*, she thought, giggling with excitement while she pulled the paper away.

She discovered another automobile. She gently fingered the cast iron racer style roadster. The body of the car featured red paint with gold wheels. A silver painted driver hunched over the steering wheel. *Chris will love this. I'll bet he'll want it for his bedroom or maybe the office.* She smiled happily, thinking of his reaction. *He always did love old cars.*

A cast iron dual horse fire engine pumper wagon came out of the box next. Mickey smiled with delight. The whole toy was solid black, except for a bright red coat on the driver and some red on the horse's harness. She held the toy up, eyeing the condition critically. Like the first fire truck, this one also had many nicks and scratches.

This must have been one of the favorites, she thought, imagining the many hours of pleasure some small child must have had playing fireman.

At the bottom of the box, she found a puzzle and several books. The puzzle featured an old timey fire engine pulled by brown horses. The city could be seen in the background and one of the buildings pictured flames shooting out of the windows.

Mickey laughed out loud. "Boy," she said. "Somebody seriously liked firemen! I wonder if whoever played with these toys ever grew up to *be* a fireman." She smiled and placed the puzzle next to the other toys.

Mickey eagerly reached for the books. The first, a well-worn edition of *Little Red Riding Hood©* published by Hurst & Company, featured a picture of Little Red Riding Hood® in the woods on the front cover. She was an adorable little girl with a round face and rosy cheeks. Blonde hair peeked out from under a red cap. She wore a blue dress and a white apron that was covered with red polka dots. Over her shoulders was a red cape and over her arm a covered basket. She was looking at the wolf, who was emerging from the woods.

Mickey read through the entire story, turning each yellowed page carefully lest the old paper fall apart. She sighed happily when she finished.

What a find! She thought with excitement. *I just love old books. Especially kids' books.*

She pulled the last item from the box. This book featured the story of *Jack and the Beanstalk©*. Mickey laughed with delight. *Yes! I've always loved this one. I can't believe it's here!*

She brushed a bit of dust from the sides of the linenette book and began to look over her treasure. The cover showed a rosy-cheeked Jack at the top of the beanstalk just beginning to step onto the road. The giant's castle could be seen in the background. Jack wore red tights, a yellow shirt, and a gray tunic. Blonde curly hair poked out from under his red hat which had a yellow feather stuck jauntily in the side.

Mickey read through the story in its entirety smiling widely while she thoroughly examined each page. When she finished, she pushed her hair back and sat for a moment picturing in her mind the children who had lived in this house. She wondered how old the antiques before her really were.

Doesn't really matter though, she thought, shaking her head with a sigh. *I wouldn't part with these for anything unless the MacGregor's want them back.*

~ Twelve ~

Mickey rose, gathered her treasures, and put them all into the large box. Carefully she descended the ladder holding the side with one hand and balancing the box on her hip with the other. She put the box on the kitchen table and went to find Christopher.

He loved the small roadster and immediately decided to put the car on his dresser. They both looked over the old Bible excitedly and agreed the book should be returned to the MacGregors at once.

"I'll give them a call," Christopher said, pulling his phone from its holster.

Thirty minutes later Mr. and Mrs. MacGregor were standing on the doorstep. Mickey and Christopher welcomed them in and they all went to the living room. Mr. MacGregor picked up the old worn book from the couch. He ran his hands over the cracked brown leather reverently.

"You don't know what this means to us," he said, brushing away a tear. "This came over with my ancestors from Scotland. I thought it had been lost forever. We looked and looked before we moved." He glanced at his wife sheepishly. "I guess I just forgot about packing this away."

She hugged his arm. "Oh, Malcolm, you and your packing," she said tenderly. They sat down on the couch.

She looked over at Christopher and Mickey. "He loves to keep things neat and orderly. I'm just so glad you folks found our Bible. We really wanted to pass it on to our eldest son."

Mickey smiled and pulled out something she kept hidden behind her back. "These might be something you'd be interested in, too," she said with a twinkle in her eye.

Mrs. MacGregor's eyes widened. "My letters," she exclaimed, taking the small box carefully. "Oh, my." She gently opened the lid and fingered the papers inside. For a moment she sat still, overcome with emotion. Her husband put his arm around her and hugged her close.

"We met only days before I was called up to go overseas. She agreed to let me write to her and we got to know each other on paper," he said huskily. "She's always been sad she lost her letters. I can't imagine how they ended up in that trunk. I thought the thing only had old toys inside."

"Let me show you what else I found." Mickey hurried to the dining room table to get the box she brought down from the attic.

She and Christopher each took a chair while the MacGregors looked the things over. They smiled happily, reminiscing about their children who once played with the toys and the past Christmas holidays when the old ornaments graced their tree.

"You can certainly have these things back," Mickey said, rising to her feet.

"Oh, no dear," said Mrs. MacGregor. "You keep them. We don't need the toys anymore and we've got enough Christmas things."

"We can't find room for what we have," put in Mr. MacGregor with an impish grin. "Mildred loves to decorate for Christmas. Gets so we hardly have room to move around."

"Oh now, Malcolm," she said, swatting his leg. "It's not that bad."

Mickey folded her arms across her chest. "I'm pretty sure I saw a rule once that said a person can never have too many Christmas decorations," she said firmly, then giggled.

"You folks be sure to come to us when you're ready for a tree this year," said Mr. MacGregor. "We've got all shapes, sizes, and varieties."

"Absolutely," Mickey affirmed.

She returned to the kitchen and a few moments later came in with coffee and a plate of cookies. She and Christopher thoroughly enjoyed talking with the MacGregors, finding out all about the ranch's history.

They bade the couple farewell an hour later. When the MacGregors reached the car, they carefully wrapped the treasured Bible in a beautiful woolen blanket made of their Scottish tartan plaid.

"What wonderful people," Mickey said while they closed the door. "I'm glad they decided to stay nearby." She looked at the clock and sighed, running her fingers through her hair. "Time for my workout."

"What?" Christopher looked at her in surprise. "This is Sunday. Don't you ever take a day off? You should." "Chris! *Hello!* I just ate *two* cookies. Fat piles on just as easily on Sunday. I can't let it get the best of me. I cannot get fat." Her voice sounded firm but held a twinge of desperation. She turned and started for her bedroom. Christopher quickly reached out and stopped her, placing his hand gently on her shoulder. "Mickey, I want to ask you something. Do you think I'd not like you if you were a different weight? Do you do all this just for me?"

Mickey whirled around and pushed his hand away, her blue eyes flashing. "Christopher Gordon, you have no right to say that. You think of yourself way too highly. I exercise because it's the right and healthy thing to do. Being overweight leads to numerous health risks. I do it for *me*. I could care less what you think. Now lay off and leave me alone." She stomped angrily up the stairs to change clothes.

Whew, what just happened there? Christopher was unable to understand her reaction. He thought back over his words and groaned inwardly.

Oh man! I sounded like a pompous self-important egotistical pig, he thought with disgust. He decided giving Mickey some space would be the best move, so he grabbed a jacket and went out to take a walk. He left the house and continued to ponder her behavior.

It's so strange, he thought, meandering into the front yard. *I mean, I know I acted like a jerk to say that but usually she'd just tease me about it. Most of the time she's so easy going but then all of a sudden, she acts like someone's going to hurt her or condemn her. I wish I knew what to do.* He sighed. *Maybe it's just a woman thing, hormones, or something.*

Upstairs Mickey angrily changed into her shorts and tee shirt, put on her tennis shoes, and pulled her hair into a ponytail. She put on a sweatband and headed for the basement. While she leaned against the wall and put her left leg behind her to stretch her calf muscles, angry thoughts tumbled around like froth at the bottom of a waterfall.

Of all the nerve. What a complete and total jerk. I do this for me. I want to look nice for me. I like being in shape. I hate feeling overweight and I want to be healthy.

Her frustrated anger abruptly evaporated and gave way to sobs. She clearly remembered how Lee had constantly been at her about her weight. She was on a four day a week workout program at the time but decided she better start exercising every day. Even then, she could see the look of dissatisfaction in his eyes every time he looked at her.

Once while in the lunch line together, he looked at her with an air of extreme disappointment when she took a small piece of chocolate cake for dessert.

"I just don't know how long I can keep putting up with someone who can't even take care of her body," he said loudly. "You don't even *try* to eat right." He sighed deeply and shook his head. "You're never going to slim down at this rate." She felt her face burn while people stared.

The memory caused Mickey's tears to continue while she began to stretch her right leg. But in a few moments, she stopped and took a deep breath.

I've got to apologize to Chris, she thought miserably. *Even if he was being a jerk, I had no right to be so hateful.* She slowly but resolutely headed for the stairs.

She found Christopher sitting cross-legged in the front yard, staring at the distant shadowy mountains bathed in the light of a full moon. He looked up at her with sorrow and confusion in his eyes.

"Chris, I'm sorry." Mickey knelt in the grass beside him. "Ever since Lee, I've been afraid to get fat, even just a little. He was ..." she paused. "He was never happy with me."

"Lee was a freakin' moron," Christopher said angrily as understanding began to dawn. He eyed her slender frame with tender compassion. "You are the fittest woman I've ever seen. I know you work hard to keep it that way but I want that work to truly be for you, not because of anyone else."

He reached out and took her hand. "Mickey, take a day off if you want to. You're my dearest friend in the world and I hate to see you so driven. Don't let that guy keep renting space in your head."

He paused again, not wanting to upset her but really wanting to know. "Mick, I've always wondered, what happened to cause you and Lee to break up?"

Her silence lasted so long he thought his question must have offended her but finally she gave a deep sigh.

"I can't believe I was so blind to what he really was. He was the consummate manipulator. Brain washer, really. And he wove scripture and spiritual 'principles' all through his nonsense. He mixed me up so badly I didn't know which end was up. I wanted so much to please him, but it seemed like the more I tried, the more things he found that needed work."

Mickey stared off at the mountains. "And it was so weird. If I was having a good day, he would immediately start asking what was wrong. Then the lectures and preaching at me. Seemed like he couldn't stand for me to be happy. Anytime anything was going well for me, he had to pull the rug out emotionally and psychologically from under me. I read some literature later that called it 'Crazy Making.' I can vouch for the fact that he indeed nearly drove me crazy."

She crossed her arms to ward of the chill of the June evening and continued. "He came to stay with Mom and me for two weeks during the Christmas break of our senior year. I was so messed up by then that I was sick half the time and constantly felt like I was walking on eggshells. But thank the Lord, it finally came to a head."

Mickey paused and Christopher asked softly, "What happened?"

"I walked into the kitchen one afternoon," Mickey went on, "just in time to see him viciously kick our little toy poodle. Poor little Panda was crying in pain and scared to death. He started toward her again saying 'shut up, you stupid mutt' and, Chris, I really think he was going to kill her.

"I screamed for him to stop. He turned and came at me and grabbed me around the neck and said if I didn't shut my fat mouth, he would do worse to me.

"Mom came in and he shook his fist at her and yelled for her to stay out of it, then grabbed me around the neck again. Thankfully, his threats didn't faze her. She called 911 and before the police got there, he ran."

Christopher stared at her in horror. He had no idea things were so bad because Mickey always put on such a serene face in public during those years. He gently took her fingers in his and stroked her hand softly with his thumb.

Mickey squeezed his hand in return. "He called the next day and said he was so terribly sorry. That he'd been a monster and would never ever hurt me. That he loved me. Said it would never happen again, blah, blah, blah. I told him that I never wanted to see him again.

He was crying and kept saying 'please don't tell me I can't see you'. He kept pushing for us to go somewhere and talk. But Mom warned me not to go anywhere with him, so I said no. He kept begging and crying.

"But I had seen enough. That whole episode scared the soup out of me, and I finally woke up. I told him firmly I did not want to see him or talk to him again."

"Did he keep trying to see you?" Christopher asked quietly.

"Oh yes, he did. After a week of him calling and coming to the door, I finally told him if he didn't stop, I'd get a restraining order and since I lived in a small town and the local deputies were friends of mine, they would be more than happy to offer me protection. After that, he stopped. He wouldn't have taken a chance of any public humiliation. He wanted everyone to think he was kind sweet wise *Brother Lee*.

"I don't know why I was so blind but I'm glad I got away from him when I did. I really think my life would have been in danger. The way he grabbed me around the neck..." she shuddered at the memory. "He was going to strangle me, Chris. There was murder in his eyes."

Christopher moved to put an arm around her and hugged her close. "That's all over now. You're safe and I will never let anyone hurt you."

He paused and drew away so he could look into her eyes. "And Mick, I'm sorry the way I sounded earlier. Like everything revolves around me." He shook his head. "What complete bonehead I am!"

Mickey smiled at him. "I know, right? But hey, we all have those moments. The thing is, I have it on good authority that the world revolves around *me*."

They both got a laugh out of that, and the humor lightened the otherwise sad trip down memory lane. Mickey squeezed his hand once more and stood.

"I'm going to take your advice and skip the workout tonight. I'm dying to give those books I found another look through."

"Atta girl." Christopher smiled and rose to follow her. "I think I'll come, too. I'd like to see them."

He reached out and gave her ponytail a tweak. She squealed and began to race for the house. While she ran, she felt a warmth around her heart. Christopher's kindness while she remembered the breakup made her feel cared for and validated her pain. They spent the remainder of the evening laughing and enjoying each other's company.

~ Thirteen ~

Christopher looked around with pleasure while he loaded his camera gear in the green Jeep Cherokee®. The perfect early July weather afforded him the opportunity to do some shooting a couple miles away at a small waterfall they discovered one day when out riding. He smiled with satisfaction, and he drove off, knowing the location was just right for the subjects of his current project.

A few minutes after Christopher left, Mickey stepped outside. *What a gorgeous day*, she thought. *I think I'll go get a couple loads of shavings*.

Though the shavings were free of charge at a nearby sawmill, they offered no loading services. Christopher and Mickey depleted the one load they brought back a few weeks earlier and the stalls needed new bedding.

Mickey returned to her bedroom and donned purple shorts, an old tee shirt, and tennis shoes. Knowing the work would have her perspiring profusely, she decided against makeup and pulled her thick hair back into a ponytail. She did not feel very hungry, so she quickly ate only a piece of toast spread with blueberry jam before heading outside.

Mickey revved the engine of the Silverado®, thankful again for the handsome blue and silver vehicle. She got the first load into the truck and back to the barn without too much trouble. By the time she shoveled the second and was ready to head back, she suddenly felt exhausted.

Just get them unloaded, then you can rest, she told herself while she wiped her sweaty forehead and stretched her aching back before climbing wearily into the truck.

The drive back to the C&M gave Mickey a chance to rest a bit. She backed the truck into the barn, hopped out of the cab, and grabbed the shovel. *I can do this*, she thought. *I can do this.*

After she worked for a few minutes, her arms and legs began to tremble, and she knew she was in trouble.

I'm going to have to go slowly, she thought ruefully, *or I'm going to collapse right here.*

She knew she should go inside and rest but doggedly continued to toss shovelfuls of shavings onto the growing pile. *If I can just finish, then I'll go get something to eat,* she thought, trying to ignore her shaky legs and the bright lights that clouded her vision. *I can't leave the job half finished.*

~ * ~

With a click, Christopher got the last shot he needed of the yellow warbler family, whose nest was close to the waterfall. Pleased with his work, he packed up his equipment and headed home with a smile on his face.

When he pulled into the drive, he noticed the absence of the truck. After putting his camera and tripod in the house, he fixed himself a late lunch, then went down to the barn to begin installing some bridle hooks in the tack room. He heard the truck enter the passageway and stop.

She must be planning to pitch the manure directly into the pickup, he thought off-handedly, remembering they promised a load to the Greg and Lorrie for their garden.

After about fifteen minutes he realized he had not heard the expected sounds of stall doors opening or manure thumping in the back of the truck. His curiosity got the better of him and he poked his head out the door. The sight that met his eyes made his heart sink.

Mickey stood in the truck bed and her limbs were visibly shaking. About half the shavings were unloaded. She paused for a moment to catch her breath, then heaved out another shovelful. She grabbed the edge of the truck and dropped the shovel when her trembling legs nearly gave out.

Christopher stalked over and jumped up with her. "Go sit down, Mickey," he said firmly, picking up the shovel. She looked uncertain, so he took her hand and helped her down. "Go." His tone boded no argument, so she went and sat in a nearby chair, watching him effortlessly toss out the rest of the shavings.

When he finished, Christopher came over and stood in front of her, not saying anything while he rolled up the sleeves of his plaid shirt. Uncomfortably, she looked up and her heart sank. He was obviously upset. Memories of Lee's impatience with her shortcomings washed over her.

"Chris, I'm sorry I was going so slowly but this is my second load. We needed more shavings." Mickey threw up her hands in a helpless gesture, trying to make him understand. "We were almost out, and Fili and Kili needed new bedding."

The pleading in her voice almost undid him. "Why didn't you tell me you wanted to go today?" he asked, wiping his forehead. "I would have helped you."

"Christopher, I've been doing this kind of thing by myself for years!" She stood abruptly and turned from him with a frustrated sigh. "I was responsible to do the work. That's always been the price I paid for the privilege of having the horses I love. I just have to take things slow sometimes but eventually I do get finished. Besides, those bright lights have started, and I can hardly see straight."

Tears threatened and she bit her lip hard to keep them from falling, ashamed of her weakness. "I'm sorry. I know watching me take so long to do such a simple task must have driven you crazy. I get so frustrated with myself. I mean, good night, I should be able to do a little manual work without going all to pieces. For crying out loud, I exercise almost every day! I should be strong."

"Mickey, like it or not, that kind of physical labor is hard even if you are in fantastic shape," Christopher said firmly. "Of course, you have to go slow. I don't know why you'd think that would bother me. What does bother me is that you don't *have* to do stuff like this by yourself anymore."

He paused for a moment and the vulnerable look on her face made his heart clench. He continued in a softer tone.

"I don't want you doing work that's too hard for you. I know you can eventually finish if you go slow but that's not the point. I'm here to help now. You don't have to do that."

He eyed Mickey's small frame thinking with pain of all the times she had probably worked herself into a state of exhaustion.

Unless I miss my guess, something Lee said has a lot to do with this, too. It's no wonder she has headaches, he thought angrily. *She's probably pulled her back and neck way out of whack doing this kind of work all these years. Crazy dude is still messing with her mind, even after all these years.*

Mickey stood for a moment, her feelings of fear turning to frustration. *He can't tell me what to do. Just because I'm a woman doesn't mean I can't do the same things he can. I'm not some high maintenance little princess who needs to be pampered by a man. I can take care of myself.*

But when she looked down at her trembling hands and felt the weakness in her arms and legs, Mickey felt smitten within her spirit at her pride. Slowly she turned and looked at him.

"You're right, Chris." She shrugged helplessly. "I just don't want to be a burden to you."

Christopher noticed her shaking hands. "I'll bet you're also suffering from a drop in blood sugar, too. Here, Mick, eat these." He drew a pack of almonds from his shirt pocket. "And here's a Hershey's bar."

"I think you're right. Thank you." Mickey gratefully took the snacks and tore open the candy. The sudden drops in blood sugar plagued her for years but she never knew when they would hit.

When she finished eating, she pushed back a damp strand of hair that had escaped the ponytail holder.

"I'm sorry I didn't tell you about this morning, but I hadn't even decided to go until after you left." She sighed. "But honestly, even if I had planned ahead, I probably wouldn't have said anything."

Mickey smiled sheepishly. "You'll have to be patient with me. This is going to take me a bit. I mean getting used to having someone around who I can feel free to ask for help. I've spent so many years feeling that being 'one hundred percent one hundred percent of the time' meant I should be doing it all myself."

"Where did that phrase come from?" Christopher asked. "I mean, I'm all about doing one's best but that's ridiculous."

"Oh, just something Lee used to drill into me constantly," Mickey replied. "He heard it at a camp somewhere and decided to make it his mantra."

She thought for a moment, wanting to be completely transparent, then said, "But even before that I always felt like I was a bother if I had to ask someone for help. I felt I should be able to care for my own needs.

"Lee's little phrase reinforced that. Then self-reliance became a matter of pride. God has been showing me that, but change might take a while. That's been a part of who I am for a long time."

Christopher sighed with relief. He feared she would be furious even though he knew he was in the right.

"I'm glad you're not angry," he said. "And don't worry. We'll get used to working together. May take a while to figure things out but we'll get there. And please, don't ever hesitate to ask me for anything."

Mickey smiled again. "Okay. Can I have a million dollars and a room-sized reef aquarium in the living room?"

"No, ma'am you may not." Christopher reached out and tweaked her ponytail.

The rest and food were making her feel better. "Actually," she said thoughtfully. "I really am glad to have someone to help me."

Her voice took on a teasing note while she got up and strolled toward the truck. "I never did get my jollies out of loading and unloading shavings. Shouldn't be too hard to let you take care of that. Besides, they look so much better on you." Playfully she grabbed a handful and threw them at him.

Christopher lunged for her, and she took off running. He grabbed some shavings and proceeded to chase her out the door, through the gate, and into the yard, where she collapsed laughing on the thick green grass. He tossed the shavings over her head, then stood with his arms crossed, daring her to retaliate.

Mickey shook her head, unsuccessfully trying to get the mess out of her curly ponytail and bangs. The strands of auburn shone in the sun and her blue eyes sparkled with mischief. She smiled up at him while she brushed the shavings off her shirt.

Christopher caught his breath. She looked so very beautiful. For a moment, his feelings, and his promise not to mention them warred within him. He drew a ragged breath and prayed for control.

How on this earth am I going to live with her and not tell her I love her? He thought helplessly. *Maybe this wasn't such a good idea. This whole thing is going to be a lot tougher than I realized. I'm going to need Your help, Lord. I can't do this in my own strength.*

"I'll bring the truck up to the garage," he said, looking away while attempting to keep his voice calm. "You'd better get some more food and then rest awhile. You might be able to ward off the migraine." He turned and walked rapidly back toward the barn.

Mickey stared after him. She knew from the look on his face that something happened. Her womanly instincts told her exactly what was going on, but she refused to give the idea any thought. She slowly rose, finished brushing herself off, and headed for the house to shower and fix something to eat.

The look in Christopher's eyes continued to cause her concern and she worried for the rest of the day that things were not right. Her uneasiness remained that night when he returned to the house, but they ate supper in comfortable silence and spent a pleasant evening watching the movie *Silverado©.*

In the days that followed, Christopher seemed to be his usual friendly self. Mickey was greatly relieved and also grateful he accepted her completely, even when she was most vulnerable.

Over the next few weeks, they spent time examining each section of the barn, which was badly in need of updating. The one lone bulb that hung in the center of the passageway left most of the stalls in shadows. There was no water supply and much of the woodwork was quite worn.

The MacGregors planned renovations but since they mainly used the barn for storage, decided the house needed work first. Christopher and Mickey agreed they needed to consider some improvements if they intended to raise and train horses.

~ Fourteen ~

Christopher left for the day and Mickey just finished wiping down the kitchen counter when her phone rang. She said and was pleased to hear Lorrie Norris on the other end.

"Mickey, would you be free to come over for lunch today?" she asked. "I know this is kind of short notice but..."

"Oh, that's all right. I'd love to come."

"Great. About eleven-thirty then?"

"Okay. That'll be good. What can I bring?" Mickey asked.

"Just bring yourself. I've got a bunch of stuff here. People keep bringing food for when the baby comes, so we're overflowing. We've got more here than we could ever possibly eat."

Lorrie laughed good-naturedly. "We're very grateful, though. Having things we can just pop into the oven is so helpful. I'm just glad we have an extra freezer."

"I'll bet," Mickey said. "Does Greg cook at all?"

"Not a bit," Lorrie replied with a short laugh. "He even has trouble making toast. Although sometimes, I wonder. I think he just likes me to take care of him."

"Just like a man," Mickey said. "I'm blessed, though. Chris loves to cook and so do I, so we take turns making meals."

"I don't really mind. I'm just concerned when I have to be away. It's nice to have something simple for him to fix." She paused. "Mickey, I'll see you in a while, okay?"

"All right, Lorrie. Thanks for calling. I'll be there around eleven-thirty."

Mickey hung up with a smile, already looking forward to the visit. After cleaning the barn and spending the morning working on the manuscript the publisher emailed her, she got ready for her lunch date. She decided to dress casually, in her purple T-shirt, jeans, and Birkis sandals. She caught her curly hair back into a ponytail, then pulled a few bangs down over her forehead. Satisfied she looked okay, she grabbed her purse and went out to the truck.

She arrived at the Norris home at eleven-thirty on the dot with a bouquet of flowers she picked by the road and some cookies she baked the night before. Lorrie greeted her at the door, looking adorable in her maternity dress. Her hair, pulled back with a green ribbon, shone like a polished new copper penny. Lorrie smiled happily, her face alight with friendship, and Mickey immediately felt at home.

They proceeded into the kitchen of the small house and Mickey helped Lorrie get lunch on the table. While they sat down to eat, Lorrie groaned. "Any day now," she said, patting her rounded belly. "I'll tell you, Mickey, I feel like I've been pregnant for a million years. I can't wait to finally meet this little one."

"It must be so exciting," Mickey said, trying to keep the wistful tone from her voice. "I can't imagine what pregnancy would be like, carrying a little person around inside you."

Lorrie looked at her quizzically, puzzled at Mickey's tone. Gently she said, "I'm sure your turn will come someday if the Lord wills."

Mickey nodded, anxious to change the subject. She was sure Lorrie, being so in love and expecting her first child, would never understand about her nontraditional marriage.

Lorrie prayed over the meal, and they began to eat. The egg salad on croissants were superb and Mickey had never tasted a salad with that mixture of fruit before. She took a bite of a strawberry muffin, and something suddenly occurred to her.

"Now Lorrie." Mickey looked at her teasingly. "This spread doesn't look like something you'd keep in the freezer. Did you go and cook when you didn't have to?"

Lorrie blushed and grinned. "You got me. I felt guilty to be cooking when we had so much food on hand. But I've been craving egg salad for weeks. You were the perfect excuse to make what I really wanted. But the croissants and muffins really were in the freezer."

"Ah ha," Mickey said triumphantly. "And do we get ice cream and pickles for dessert?"

"Oh no, that was over after the first month. Now chocolate cake sprinkled with barbecue potato chips is the dessert of choice," Lorrie stated matter-of-factly.

"That doesn't sound too bad. I'm always up for anything chocolate. In fact, the cookies I brought are chocolate chip with Heath chips."

"Mmm..." Lorrie murmured dreamily. "Sounds perfect."

The two women laughed and continued to talk while they finished their lunch. After cleaning up, Lorrie took Mickey upstairs to show her the nursery. Mickey's eyes caressed the room and her throat constricted at the thought of the dear little person who would soon take up residence there. She walked through the doorway and stood in the center of the room looking around.

The top two-thirds of the walls were painted a soft shade of mauve and the bottom third featured a light cherry wainscoting. The crib in the corner was dark cherry matching the changing table and dresser combo on the opposite wall. A small closet was set in further down that wall and a dark cherry rocking chair with a mauve colored cushion sat in the corner.

"Oh, Lorrie, this is beautiful," Mickey said, looking at the tastefully decorated room. "I love that vase in the corner with the pussy willow branches. The whole room is so peaceful and calming. I'll bet you'll have the quietest baby there has ever been. I take it you know you're having a girl?"

"Oh yes." Lorrie smiled happily. "I had an ultrasound several months ago." Her eyes took on a faraway look. "That was really something, Mickey. We could even see her fingers and toes. She was sucking her thumb."

Mickey's lips curved gently, thinking how marvelous and miraculous the development and birth of a child were. She cleared her throat. "I figured this wasn't a boy's room," she said, with a grin. "You know, it looks like a professional decorator did this. Such a gorgeous nursery."

Lorrie looked a little embarrassed. "I did the decorating myself. I still need to get some wall art in here, though. I just haven't settled on what I want. Oh, by the way, I worked for an interior design firm back home in Boston before I met Greg. The lady who mentored me taught me everything I know about design." Her tone was a bit wistful.

"Do you miss your home?" Mickey asked.

"Even though this is my home now, I really miss the city." She moved to look out the window. "I know that's probably hard for you to understand," she said while she gazed down at the tiny, fenced back yard. "I know you love this part of the country but living here was hard for me, especially at first. I just like knowing things are close by if I need them. Aspen Ridge isn't exactly a metropolis!"

Mickey nodded in agreement. "Yeah, I know. But you're right, I really do love the West." She sighed. "I'm pretty much living my dream life right now. I can understand how it must be for you, though. I'm sure I'd feel the same way if I lived in a city."

"I miss my family, too," Lorrie said. Tears welled up in her eyes. "I have two sisters and three brothers, and they and their families all stayed in the East. And of course, my parents are there, too.

"I felt like a pioneer when we came out here and left my family behind. We were hoping to get back there this year for Christmas, but I don't think that's going to work out."

She sighed and wiped the tear from her face. "Oh now, I don't want to get all sad on you." She said with a watery smile. "This pregnancy has made me so emotional. C'mon. Let's go down to the living room and talk."

They spent several hours chatting about various things. Mickey was surprised at how she could feel such friendship with a person who didn't share her love of the country, but she discovered that she and Lorrie had many other things in common. When she headed home later that afternoon, she smiled with satisfaction, glad for the opportunity to get to know the pastor's wife better.

One of the ladies in the church called Mickey that Friday. Lorrie was in the hospital in Great Falls. After five hours of intense labor, little Zoe Rose finally made her appearance, a beautiful baby girl healthy and whole. Mickey was extremely happy for Greg and Lorrie and thankful that their little one arrived safely.

After Lorrie rested at home for a few weeks, Mickey and Christopher drove over to meet Zoe. They took turns holding her and admiring her beauty. Christopher insisted the tiny infant smiled at him.

Zoe was indeed a lovely child and already boasted a respectable amount of red hair. Lorrie said that currently, her red hair didn't indicate a bad temper. The baby appeared to be relatively quiet and content.

Mickey and Christopher congratulated the couple, then presented them with a painting featuring a cluster of mauve colored roses nestled in a field with the mountains in the background. The painting was set in a cherry wood frame and Mickey signed "To Zoe from M. Sterling" at the bottom. The Norrises were touched by the wonderful gift and Lorrie immediately decided the picture must be hung over the crib.

~ *Fifteen* ~

Christopher awakened with a start. His return home around 11:30 pm the previous night after doing some moonlight shooting caused him to oversleep. Glancing at the clock, he saw it was almost 10:00 a.m. He yawned widely and got up, wondering momentarily why the house was so quiet. When he ambled into the kitchen, he got his answer.

A box of cereal, a bowl, and utensils were neatly laid out on the table. Under a plastic wrapped plate holding two apple cinnamon muffins was a note which read: "Chris, I went to town to stock up on feed. Be back this afternoon, Mickey. P.S. Yes, the coffee is ready, too! Check in the cup over by the stove". She drew a face with a grimace beside the word 'coffee'. He laughed when he remembered how often she said she loved the smell of coffee but loathed the taste.

~ * ~

Mickey spent the morning in Aspen Ridge. She stopped at the grocery store to buy a few items, then drove farther down the street to Sam's Feed, Seed, and Hardware. Sam greeted her warmly.

"Hey there, Mickey," said the tall, gangly man. "Come to clean me out?"

"But Sam, its twenty-eight miles to town," she said with a pained whiney tone. "I like to get enough supplies to last a while. I'm not into running to the store every day."

"Yep, I can understand that," he said with a nod of his head and a grin. "With that purdy ranch of yours, I can imagine you stay mighty busy. Go on and bring the truck 'round back and we'll get you fixed up."

Mickey drove around and backed up to the loading dock. After filling the truck bed with bags of oats, Sam wiped his sweaty forehead with the back of his hand and looked at her teasingly.

"What's this I hear 'bout this feed going to grain Friesians? What on earth kinda ranch horse is that? Ain't they draft horses?"

"Now, Sam," Mickey said with a glint in her eye. "I know this is Quarter Horse country but they're my babies!"

Sam grinned. Their running discussion on the subject continued every time Mickey came in for feed. "I've yet to see one help rope a steer, Miz Mickey but I guess for *pleasure* ridin' they're all right."

Mickey put on a very superior air. "I don't *need* to rope a steer, Sam. We're going to be a horse ranch, not a cattle ranch."

"Oh, of course. I see." Sam nodded wisely and winked at her. They both laughed together, then Sam gave Mickey a more serious look. "Mighty glad to see you folks in church every week. Wonderful thing to see young folks who really love the Lord. It's such a blessin' to have new neighbors here who are believers."

"Oh, Sam," exclaimed Mickey. "That church was just what we were looking for! We love the Bible based preaching and soul stirring praise and worship. We feel so at home there."

"Good. I thought you'd like the people and Pastor Norris. He's a good fella. Was a real help to me when my Maud passed a couple years back."

"I've enjoyed getting to know Lorrie and the baby," Mickey added with a grin. "Zoe is quite a little bundle." "She is at that." Sam ambled over and opened the truck door for her. "Never seen a youngster with hair that red. Hope she don't have the temper to match."

Mickey climbed into the cab laughing. "I don't think she does so far. But just wait 'til she's a teenager!" She revved the engine. "Bye, Sam. See you Sunday."

"Bye now," he said with a grin and a wave. "You and Chris take care. And give them horses a pat for me."

Mickey started the drive home in good spirits. *The people in this area are so kind and friendly*, she thought happily. *I already feel like I've lived here all my life.* She drove along singing with the praise songs on her playlist.

About fifteen minutes from home, she neared a grove of trees off to the left and noticed a small gray Toyota parked on the side of the road. Slowing automatically, she looked around trying to see if someone was in trouble.

She peered into the trees and spotted a young woman wearing a red shirt and jeans, who appeared to be kneeling on the ground. After a moment, the girl stood abruptly and strode back toward her car with an angry expression on her face. She walked so hard her blonde ponytail bounded in rhythm with her steps.

Mickey recognized Jennifer Austin from church, so she came to a stop and rolled down the window. "Need any help, Jen?" she called.

The tall girl carefully climbed over the barbed wire fence that bordered the road and came over to the truck. "Mickey," she exclaimed. "I'm glad to see you. I don't really know what to do." She sounded frightened and angry. "There's a horse over there. I've never seen one so thin. I don't think he's been fed in weeks. And there are scars all over him."

She sighed, wiping a trickle of perspiration from her forehead. "I saw that strange looking corral when I drove by." She shaded her eyes with one hand and pointed to the haphazard enclosure with the other. Boards were nailed to the trees in a sloppy manner to form a rough circle.

120

"I wondered what in the world they had in there," continued Jennifer. "I slowed down to look and could make out the form of a horse. Then he just collapsed. He's still alive but I don't know what to do."

"Let me get out of the road and I'll come look," Mickey said. "Maybe between the two of us, we can figure something out."

She pulled the truck to the shoulder of the road, and they climbed over the fence. The two women walked the short distance and stood looking through the board fence at the miserable animal. He lay on his side, his head flat on the ground. Every rib showed from his painfully thin sides and the hip bones protruded sharply. His dirty matted coat and the dull expression in his eyes spoke of his misery. Every few minutes he gave a soft groan.

"Oh, my word," gasped Mickey in disgust and horror. "I used to see this kind of thing on that show Animal Cops. I never thought I'd see it with my own eyes."

"Abuse of the worst kind," agreed Jennifer, her voice cold with anger. "How could anyone do this? He can't even get out to fend for himself."

"I don't know. I've never understood how people can be so cruel." Mickey looked grim. "Let's see if we can get him up." They climbed over the board fence and Mickey knelt beside the horse, giving his frayed halter a light tug. He gave a low grunt and tried to raise his head but fell back.

Mickey patted him gently and murmured a few soft words of comfort before she rose. "I'm going to call Chris. He should be able to help." They went back to the truck and Mickey made the call.

She quickly related the situation and Christopher shared her concern. "I'll call Dr. Kent," he said. "He's a veterinarian I met the other day who just moved to this area. I was really impressed with him. I'll see if I can round up some other guys to help and meet you there shortly."

Mickey and Jennifer stood by the truck to wait. After about twenty minutes, Jennifer pointed in the opposite direction. "Look, here comes somebody."

A red Chevy Blazer® pulled in behind the Silverado and stopped. A handsome brown-haired man emerged carrying a small black bag. He wore jeans and a black tee shirt.

"I'm Dr. Andrew Kent," he said introducing himself with a friendly smile.

Mickey reached out and shook his hand. "I'm Mickey Sterling and this is Jennifer Austin. Jen, why don't you show him the horse? I'll wait here for Chris and the others."

Jennifer nodded. "He's over there in the trees." They walked to the enclosure where the horse lay. Tears began to form in Jennifer's green eyes while she looked at the wretched animal. "It's so horrible." She sniffed. "I'm glad I saw him in here."

Dr. Kent gave her shoulder a gentle squeeze and handed her a handkerchief.

"Thanks, doctor." She tried to smile. "I get so emotional about this kind of thing."

"I understand," he said in a kind voice. "And hey, please call me Andrew. I still look around for some old guy when I hear people say 'doctor'".

Jennifer chuckled through her tears and nodded. They climbed over the board fence and Andrew looked around the small muddy enclosure. "He's been in here for a while."

He glanced around at the piles of manure and noted the absence of grass. The surrounding trees showed marks where the horse had tried to eat the bark. An old bathtub held only about a half inch of scummy water.

He knelt and carefully ran his hands over the horse's sides. After a cursory examination, he sighed deeply and rose. Mickey, along with Christopher and five other men who just arrived, came walking toward them. They looked to Andrew for direction.

"Hi, folks," he said. "Thanks for bringing some help, Chris." He looked grim. "This animal will die soon if we don't get him some help. He's going to need a lot of care." He looked around. "We need to get him out of here. He needs a clean safe environment where we can work with him."

Jonathan Wilkins, the C&M's neighbor to the right, spoke up. "I've got a good, strong tarp in my pickup. We can roll him onto that and lift him up. I'll go cut that outer fence and bring the truck and trailer through."

As he walked toward the road, Christopher and the other men began to pull sections of the board fence away. After several minutes, Jonathan's trailer was neatly positioned in the opening. They spread out the tarp right beside the animal, then rolled him over gently. The men grasped the corners and sides and with much effort, hoisted the suffering animal up into the horse trailer.

Christopher spoke to Jonathan. "Let's take him back to the C&M. We've got plenty of room."

"I'll ride with him." Jennifer stepped up carefully into the trailer. Tears formed in her eyes again when the horse moaned softly.

"Be careful, Jennifer," cautioned Andrew. "He could start thrashing."

Jennifer nodded.

"I'm going to drop by my office and pick up a few things," Andrew said. "And I'll stop by the police department and apprise them of the situation. I'll meet you all back at the ranch."

He paused a moment. "Oh, Chris, be thinking of a way we can hoist him up in a sling. We've got to get him upright immediately or his systems will start to shut down."
"Will do," said Chris. "We'll find a way."

~ *Sixteen* ~

When they arrived at the *C&M*, Mickey and Jennifer ran into the barn and quickly prepared a stall. Chris and the men rigged up ropes over a large beam to attach to the tarp's metal rings.

The neighbor men carefully lifted the horse out of the trailer and carried him inside the barn. Using all their strength, they held him upright while Chris swiftly tied the ropes to the tarp. They situated the horse so his hooves touched the floor, allowing him to support his own weight when he regained strength.

Andrew stayed with them for the remainder of the day. He gave the horse several shots and set up a fluid drip. Jennifer gingerly tried to squeeze water into the corners of his mouth with a washcloth. She also offered him a small handful of oats which he took eagerly but most of the grain fell out of his mouth. He seemed too weak to chew.

Jennifer's efficient assistance of the veterinarian fascinated Mickey. She seemed to know just how to help, and they worked together smoothly like parts on a well-oiled machine. She wondered briefly why Jennifer was not planning to be a vet herself or at least a technician.

Andrew followed Mickey and Jennifer back into the house late that evening, where they all collapsed around the kitchen table. Christopher, who returned to the house earlier, had hot coffee and sandwiches ready. He grinned when he placed a tall glass of orange juice in front of Mickey. She looked at him with gratefulness in her eyes, pleased he remembered her aversion to coffee.

He sat down with them and asked, "Andrew, what do you think? Will he pull through?"

"Too hard to tell at this point." The veterinarian sipped his coffee, then continued. "He wanted to eat. That's a good sign that he hasn't given up. The fluid therapy helped a lot. He was very dehydrated."

He shook his head. "He's awfully weak but I gave him a round of antibiotics to ward off infections. You all need to be prepared, though. When a horse gets this bad, things can go downhill in a hurry.

"If he pulls through these first couple days, he's going to need a good worming. And his teeth need to be floated, too. We'll have to wait until he's a lot stronger for that, though."

Jennifer chuckled. "Yeah, trying to file down those sharp ends right now would probably knock him right off his feet, if he could stand, that is."

Andrew laughed. Usually a bit shy around women, he was surprised to find himself completely at home with Jennifer. "You're right," he said. "He's going to need a lot of good food and care before he's back to normal."

Jennifer's face clouded. Her soft spot for hard luck animal cases made situations like this difficult. "I wish I could keep him," she said, resting her chin in her hand. "But I'm lucky to be able to keep the horse I have. Since I'm away at school most of the time, my mom takes care of Gimli."

She smiled ruefully. "She doesn't mind feeding him and mucking his stall because she knows how much I love him but I would never ask her to take on another horse's care."

Christopher spoke reassuringly. "We'll keep him here until he's recovered. And we won't let him get into the wrong hands again."

Andrew finished his coffee and rose to go. "I'll stop by again tomorrow to check on him and give him some more fluids. But I'd better get a little shut eye before then."

Mickey and Jennifer bid him farewell, and Christopher went out to walk him to the Blazer®. "I'm really glad I met you the other day," Christopher said while they walked down the pebble path. "How much do I owe you?"

"Glad I met you, too, Chris," replied the veterinarian. "And no charge for today. I'm happy to donate my services in cases like this."

"We're happy to pay you, Andrew," Christopher protested. "You have to eat!"

"Oh, no worries." Andrew shook his head. "You may not know this, but the barter system is alive and well in Aspen Ridge."

"Are you serious?" Christopher asked.

Andrew laughed at his expression. "I'm serious, man. But you know, so far everything is working out. I get enough monetary compensation to pay my bills and enough bartered goods keep the fridge stocked. I have enough casseroles, homemade jam, and pies to start a small café."

Christopher laughed again, then looked at Andrew quizzically. "Apparently you have plenty in your larder, but would you be interested in joining us for church on Sunday and lunch afterward? I promise, we won't serve a casserole."

Andrew grinned and nodded. "Oh wow, that would be awesome. I was hoping to find a good church around here." They reached the Blazer and Andrew carefully placed his bag on the passenger seat.

"So, are you a Christian?" Christopher asked with a smile.

Andrew leaned against the vehicle and crossed his arms. "I guess I'm what you'd call a baby Christian. Not very long ago I was running down the wrong path at top speed.

"I guess you could say I was your typical wild and crazy college student involved in a lot of things I shouldn't have been. I tried drugs and alcohol looking for something to fill the void in my heart. Thankfully the Lord brought someone across my path who told me about the love of God, shared the gospel, and explained all I had to do was accept His gift of salvation."

Andrew looked up thoughtfully at the star-studded sky, his eyes moist at the memory. "I don't know what made me believe. I was so hard and cynical back then. But I know God sent that friend when He did because He loved me. I truly never thought about God loving me before. The thought was so amazing. And so personal."

Andrew sighed. "I guess I'd begun to realize just how futile and empty all the diversions of this world can be. Nothing was ever enough. I was ready for answers, and I found them all in Christ." He looked at Christopher. "The day I accepted Jesus, He changed my life and brought a ful-fillment to my heart that is unexplainable and totally amaz-ing."

Christopher reached out and shook his hand. "What a wonderful story. I had a feeling when I first met you that we shared the same faith. Just something about your de-meanor. You have a real peace about you. Thanks for shar-ing." The men talked a few moments more and Christopher shared his own childhood salvation experience. They prayed briefly together before Andrew started for home.

~ * ~

After the men left the house, Mickey turned to Jen-nifer. "Jen, why don't you spend the night here? I mean, look at the clock - nearly 11:30! I hate for you to have to drive all the way home. I'm sure I have an extra tooth-brush."

Jennifer thought for a moment. "If you're sure it's no trouble, I would love to stay over. Right now, the thought of a drive back to Aspen Ridge feels impossible. I'm almost asleep on my feet." She looked at Mickey with a smile. "Thanks."

They began to gather the cups from the table. Jennifer opened the dishwasher and Mickey deposited the glassware inside.

"I'd better call my mom, though," said Jennifer, pulling out her phone. "She's probably wondering where I am. I don't want her to worry." She went to make the call while Mickey started the dishwasher.

Christopher came back inside. "Hey, Mick, why don't you ask Jennifer to stay here tonight?" he said.

Mickey laughed. "Great minds do indeed think alike. I already asked her. She's in the living room calling her mom to let her know she's staying."

Christopher chuckled. "That's great! I was worried about her driving home."

He lounged against the counter while Mickey wiped the table with a dishrag. "I just had a great chat with Andrew. He's a Godly man and a great guy."

"He's a nice man," Mickey said. "We need to invite him to church. Since he just moved here, he might not know there's a church here."

"Been there, done that," Christopher said with a grin. "He's coming with us to church Sunday. Oh, and I invited him for lunch, too."

"Oh, are you talking about Andrew?" asked Jennifer when she returned to the kitchen. "We were talking about our faith out in the barn. Isn't it wonderful to meet other people who have a personal relationship with Jesus Christ?"

"Absolutely. We are certainly blessed." Christopher raised a hand to cover a jaw splitting yawn. "Why don't we have a quick prayer together before we call it a night?" Christopher asked.

"Sounds good," the women said in unison.

The three joined hands and Christopher prayed. "Father, thank You for Your leading today. Thank You for causing Jennifer to see that poor horse in need. Thank You that we were available to help. Thank You for using this situation to bring us together with Andrew and thank You for keeping us all safe while we worked. Strengthen Andrew's faith, Lord, and ours also. Please keep us in Your care and cause us to become more like You every day. Guide and direct our steps and continually point us to those in need. Thank You for Your grace and love. In Jesus name, amen."

"Amen," chimed in Mickey and Jennifer in unison. Mickey showed Jennifer to the guest room, then rounded up an extra toothbrush, toothpaste, and a bottle of Bamboo Green Tea Wen. She put the items in the bathroom, then took Jennifer a clean tee shirt and sweats to sleep in.

"Thanks, Mickey, this is great," she said gratefully. "Do you happen to have an extra contact lens case? These contacts are about to walk out of my eyes on their own."

Mickey laughed. "Mine, too. Let me get one from my bathroom. I've got extra solution, too."

While Mickey was gone, Christopher walked by on his way to his bedroom. "Night, Jen," he called through the open door.

"Night, Chris," she said.

Mickey returned with the contact case and solution, then bade Jennifer a good night. Once finished in the bathroom, Jennifer snuggled into the comfortable bed. Before she drifted off, she wondered why her friends had separate bedrooms. They seemed happy and content.

Maybe he snores, she thought and began to drift off.

~ *Seventeen* ~

Christopher, Mickey, and Jennifer sat eating breakfast when Christopher's phone buzzed. After a short conversation, he tapped the off button.

"That was a deputy from the police department," he
said. "He wants us to meet him out where we found the
horse yesterday so we can answer any questions he may
have."

He looked concerned while he finished his biscuit
and said, "I'm pretty sure he'll verify we did the right thing
in removing the horse. I'm just a little worried about the
fact that we did so without a seizure warrant being served
on the owner. But we were attended by a veterinarian."

"And I've got pictures on my phone," Mickey said. "I
had a feeling we might need proof of what we found."

"Great thinking, Mick," Christopher said. "Here I'm
the photographer by trade and I didn't even think of that!"

"I didn't watch all those Animal Cops shows for nothing, you know," she said firmly.

The threesome met Deputy Steve Morgan at the site
an hour later. "That's where we found the horse, Deputy,"
said Jennifer, nodding toward the dilapidated enclosure.
Deputy Morgan looked the area over thoroughly, then
snapped several pictures.

"That must lead to the house," he said, pointing to
the narrow dirt driveway just beyond the grove of trees.
"Follow me, folks. But please stay in your vehicle until I
give the all clear."

After passing a rusty bashed in mailbox with *J.C.Dale*
pasted to the side in faded letters, they followed the meandering drive for about a half-mile before pulling up in
front of a small shack.

"Oh, my word." Mickey's eyes widened. "Hard to believe people live like this. There's so much trash everywhere."

"Looks like that Ford has seen better days, too." Christopher noted the rusted truck parked next to the house.

Deputy Morgan approached them, and Christopher rolled down the window. "Folks, I don't know what I might find in there," he said. "Once again, please stay put until I give the word."

"Will do, Deputy," Christopher said.

They watched while Deputy Morgan gingerly knocked on the torn screen door. Only the sound of the birds twittering in the trees said him. The inner door opened when he turned the knob.

Slowly he disappeared inside. After a few minutes, he exited the house and returned to the Silverado®.

"I'm sorry to say, Mr. Dale is deceased," he told them. "I'll need to get some pictures and then taped off the door. Nothing leads me to believe foul play was involved but we'll have to start a death investigation."

"Do you have any idea what might have happened?" Mickey asked. "Do you think that's why the horse we found had no food or water?"

"I'm afraid not, ma'am," Deputy Morgan said. "Horses don't deteriorate like that overnight. Unfortunately, this was a true case of animal abuse and neglect. I couldn't tell you the exact time of Mr. Dale's death but judging from the condition of the body, I'd say he passed away within the last twenty-four hours."

He rested his elbow on the truck's passenger side mirror. "As to what happened, from the number of bottles and cans around the body, my first guess would be alcohol poisoning but of course I can't be sure. Guess we won't need to leave that seizure warrant after all."

"How horrible," Jennifer said, her face revealing her shock and revulsion.

Deputy Morgan nodded and retrieved his camera from the patrol car. "You all can get out but please don't enter the house. If you'd be so kind, would you have a look in that shed over there and check around out back? There may be more animals."

"Of course," Christopher said. "We're happy to help."

The three got out of the truck and when they approached the small outbuilding, they heard a faint moan and a scratching noise. Feeling sick Christopher pulled the door open. A scruffy looking sable colored Collie crawled out and cowered on the ground. Patches of hair were gone, and the rest was matted to the skin stretched tightly over her thin frame. Her backside was covered with sores. Clearly the shed had been her prison for days.

Tears slowly ran down Mickey's and Jennifer's cheeks while they knelt to caress the dog. "How could someone be so cruel?" A sob escaped Mickey's throat when she looked at the pathetic creature before her and thought of the horrors she must have endured. The dog put her head on Mickey's knee, her dark eyes calm and trusting but infinitely sad.

At that moment, Christopher though he heard a noise. "Oh, please tell me there's not more." He opened the shed door once again and shined his pocket flashlight around but saw nothing. Curious, he made his way to the back of the house and his heart sank. "Oh no!"

Chained to a post on the other side of the house was a small Chihuahua. He shivered uncontrollably when Chris approached and held out his hand. The tiny dog was obviously torn between fear of a stranger and joy at being rescued. Slowly he crept to Chris's outstretched hand. Christopher gently removed the too tight collar and heavy chain. The dog was painfully thin and had a raw spot on his neck where the collar had started to dig into the flesh. His body was covered with welts and scars.

Christopher lifted the small animal to his arms, stroking him gently and talking to him softly. The Chihuahua looked up at him with adoration in his brown eyes and shyly tried to lick his rescuer's chin. He walked back to where the women stood with the Collie. "Look what I found." The women gasped and Christopher shook his head, his face a mixture of compassion and heartbreak.

"I can't believe the little guy wasn't killed by a predator. He's obviously been out there for a while. You should have seen the size of the chain hooked to his collar. Must have weighed more than he does."

Mickey began to sob, and Christopher put one arm around his wife. "I know, honey, I know. I don't understand what drives people like Mister Dale in there to treat animals this way." He shook his head sadly. "He obviously had a drinking problem. I always wonder why on earth people like that even want animals anyway.

"I know sometimes, people who are otherwise decent individuals, turn into monsters when they drink. But there are others who just want something to boss around and control. Makes them feel bigger and stronger. I guess we'll never know what the situation was here."

"Whatever it was, treating these sweet animals this way was despicable," said Jennifer, her heart breaking. "He clearly didn't just fall on hard times and neglect them. He abused them horribly."

Deputy Morgan returned, and they showed him the animals they found.

"Deputy, we'll be very happy to take these dogs home with us," Christopher said. "In fact, I think you might have a hard time convincing these ladies to do otherwise."

"Yes, sir, I believe you're right." Deputy Morgan smiled slightly.

Christopher handed the Chihuahua off to Mickey. She and Jennifer returned to the truck and climbed into the cab. Christopher easily lifted the Collie up into Jennifer's lap.

"Thanks for taking care of these poor critters," Deputy Morgan said while they prepared to head for home. "I'll let you know what the coroner's investigation determines. Normally something like this would also have to go through probate but since there is obvious animal cruelty involved, I think the judge will allow you to take possession of the animals while we work out the legal issues."

"But Deputy, what if there are relatives who want to claim them who are unfit like Mister Dale?" Mickey asked, her face a mask of concern and fear.

"Oh, don't you worry, ma'am," he replied. "We'll do a thorough background check and require references. These animals aren't going to anyone who'll abuse them. I guarantee you that."

"Thanks, Deputy," Mickey said with relief.   Before starting out, Christopher called Andrew and explained the situation.

"He's going to bring some meds for the dogs when he comes to check on the horse today," he said after he hung up. "And he'll take a look at the sore on the little guy's neck." He looked down at the Chihuahua in Mickey's lap. The dog still gazed at him. He seemed to draw strength from Christopher's nearness.

"Chris, I do believe *you* have a dog," Mickey said with a grin. "I can already see you're his favorite."

Christopher reached over to gently stroke the tiny dog's head before putting the key in the ignition. "Let's get these kids home," he said with a smile.

When they arrived, Mickey and Jennifer took some old blankets and a couple feather pillows and made a bed for the dogs in the kitchen. Kip trotted into the room, his nails tapping out a brisk rhythm on the tile floor. He went over and proceeded to inspect the Collie. She never moved while he sniffed her over thoroughly.

Then he turned to the Chihuahua. He sniffed him over thoroughly in the way of all dogs, then wagged his tail gently. He looked up at Mickey with an expression that said, "Cool! You got me a sister and a dog!" He sat beside the two for a moment, then crawled into the makeshift bed with them and began to gently lick the Collie's wounds.

Mickey eyes welled up with tears and she smiled with love while she looked at them. "He's such a compassionate dog," she told Jennifer while reaching for a tissue. "I think he's really an angel in a dog's body."

Jennifer smiled. "He is sweet. So empathetic."

"Whenever I'm feeling down, he'll stick close by me," Mickey said. "He just keeps looking at me until I finally break down and tell him my troubles. The way he looks at me, I know he's trying to communicate. Hey, wanna know my theory?"

"Absolutely." Jennifer looked puzzled. "What theory?"

"Okay, animals can't speak, right? So, I think that's part of the curse from Genesis." Mickey continued. "I mean, the serpent spoke to Eve in the Garden of Eden, and she didn't think that was at all odd. Which leads me to believe that all animals talked before sin entered the world. Sin brought the curse on everything, but I think part of that curse is that animals can no longer speak to us using words."

"Very interesting," Jennifer said thoughtfully. "I know the Bible doesn't say for sure but that does make sense to me."

"We are certainly allowed our theories, if they don't contradict scripture, right?"

"Absolutely," Jennifer said firmly. "I believe that our pets will be in Heaven. People say they don't have souls and I say if that's true, then they don't have a choice to make to accept Jesus or not. Even more reason of course He would take them to Heaven when they die. He so clearly sends them to minister to us. I wish I could have a dog or cat but right now I just don't want to burden Mom with anymore animal care while I'm in school."

"You can share mine," Mickey said firmly.

She looked the dogs over thoroughly, taking in their filthy coats and overall foul odor. She turned to Jennifer.

"Let's give these dogs a good grooming." Determination was written all over her face. "I'll bet that would make them feel a lot better. Then we'll fix them a good meal."

Christopher walked in just in time to hear her words. "I'll bring up that big plastic tub from the barn. Then you can work on them in the mud room where you'll have warm water" he said. "I'll grab the clippers while I'm there."

"Oh, perfect. Thanks, Chris. I'll need to shave the Collie down completely. There's no way to comb out all those mats." Mickey turned and jogged out of the kitchen, her brunette curls bouncing. "I'll go get some of Kip's Wen Pet®. That'll make them feel better in no time!"

Jennifer looked after with a bemused expression. "When she gets an idea, she doesn't mess around, does she?"

"No, she does not," Christopher said with a grin. "She's quite a gal." His eyes softened when he thought of her caring gentle spirit.

"Of course, you might be just a wee bit prejudiced."

"No, ma'am. Not at all." His voice changed to a dry monotone with a British accent. "After years of careful painstaking research, the facts have led to the inevitable conclusion that the subject is, without question, the most amazing woman on planet earth." He looked at her with an innocent expression.

Jennifer laughed but was puzzled at the look of intense pain that suddenly crossed his face before he left the house. She looked after him for a moment, then shrugged and opened the cabinet door under the sink.

After rummaging around for a moment, she found a sponge and a clean rag. When Mickey returned with the container of cleansing conditioner, they took the Collie outside. After carefully shaving away all the matted filthy hair, the girls took her back into the mud room for her bath.

As Mickey lifted the Collie, whom they decided to name Kelsey, into the tub, she laughed. "You know, when her hair grows back, she and Kip will look like twins, except she's bigger."

"You're right." Jennifer laughed. "They'll make a great pair."

Patient throughout the bath, Kelsey sat quietly letting out only a small whimper when they carefully washed the sores on her backside. They dried her off gently with a large towel, then led her to the living room where Mickey had spread blankets and towels out on the floor. Kelsey immediately began to root and roll around in them. Poncho, the Chihuahua, was next into the tub. After cleansing his coat thoroughly, they rinsed him and wrapped him in a towel they warmed in the drier. They took him to the living room where he immediately took advantage of the chance to roll and dry off.

Mickey fixed two bowls with a small portion of dry dog food mixed with canned while Jennifer filled a bowl with clean fresh water. They watched while Kelsey began to lick at the food. She ate daintily, a little at a time. Halfway through, she looked up at Mickey and Jennifer and whined, wagging her tail gently. The girls smiled, each feeling the prick of tears at her obvious "thank you".

Poncho gulped down the first few bites without appearing to chew. He then looked around furtively, seemingly afraid someone would take the morsels from him. Turning back to the bowl, he gobbled the remainder of his dinner in huge gulps.

"Poor little guy," Mickey said. "I hate to think what he's been through."

After eating, they took the dogs outside to relieve themselves. During the whole affair, Kip hovered close, ever responsible for the well-being of all.

~ * ~

Andrew arrived while they were feeding the horses early that evening. After checking the rescue horse over, he turned his attention to the dogs. Mickey held Poncho while he administered a dewormer and took blood and stool samples to test back at his office. Kelsey stood bravely throughout the treatment and never whimpered.

"I'll check to be sure they don't have Coccidia or anything else going on in their guts and that blood test will tell us the story about heart worms. If the tests are negative, you'll need to get them on preventative medication monthly." He looked at Mickey. "Do you have something to put on them for fleas and ticks?"

"I've got Advantix® for Kip but his won't be the right size for them," she said, stooping to pat Kelsey's head with her free hand. "I did notice a lot of flea dirt and fleas when we cleaned them up earlier."

"No worries, I've got some in the car." Andrew retrieved two tubes of medication which he applied to their necks. "Getting rid of the parasites will help that skin heal faster but I've got some spray here for those sores that I want you to use. Just squirt this on them twice a day."

He knelt and caressed the dog's head gently. "They're great dogs. I think they'll be just fine with time and good care."

~ * ~

Later that evening, Wildlife Unlimited® called and Christopher asked do a photo series on red squirrels. "I'm sorry I'll have to be out every day with all of this going on," he remarked to Mickey later while they were making a final check on the rescue horse before going to bed.

"Don't worry. I can take care of things. I really love nursing animals back to health. In fact, sometimes I think I'd enjoy this more than raising horses. I'm not into show-ing and competition much and you really need to be up on all that to be going into the breeding business."
"You certainly have a way with animals. Let's just see how things go," Christopher said with a smile, pleased that Mickey found fulfillment in helping God's creatures. He reached to scratch the horse gently behind the ears. "I'll help however I can when I get back in the evenings."

Christopher left the stall and closed the door behind him. Then he stopped and looked back. "Mickey, we need to give this poor guy a name."

"You're right. Hmm..." Mickey looked at the horse critically. "You know, looks like his coat is kind of a tan col-or under the dirt. Buckskin maybe. Hard to tell right now when he's in such poor condition." She thought a moment, then said, "How about Tanner?"

"Tanner. Yes, that suits him perfectly." Christopher gave her a high five. "Tanner it is."

~ Eighteen ~

Christopher's phone buzzed early Sunday morning while they were feeding the horses. "Hello, Chris? Andrew Kent, here," said the veterinarian.

"Hey, Andrew, what's up?" Christopher asked.

"I hate to have to bow out of church and lunch today, but I just got a call. Fella's got a cow in trouble calving. Looks like it may be a tough one. I'll probably be out there all day."

"I'm sorry about that, man. We'll miss you."   "I certainly hope I can take a rain check," Andrew said with a chuckle. "I definitely want to visit the church and spend some time with you guys."

"Absolutely," Christopher said immediately. "Consider it a standing invitation."

"Thanks. I appreciate that. I'm off to birth a calf."

"Hope everything works out all right. Bye, Andrew."

"Is everything okay?" Mickey asked, coming up behind him with a bucket of oats for Fili.

"Oh, yeah. That was Andrew. He can't make it today. He's got to go help a cow in trouble birthing her calf."

"Oh, that's too bad. I hope he'll come again another time."

"He will. He said he wanted to take a rain check." Christopher smiled while he headed toward the feed room to procure oats for Kili.

~ * ~

Eager to see how Tanner, Kelsey, and Poncho were faring, Jennifer followed Christopher and Mickey home from church on Sunday. When they arrived at the ranch, Mickey suggested a picnic lunch instead of the sit-down dinner they planned previously.

"You two go ahead," Christopher said. "I need to start my research for the squirrel shoot and get my gear together." He headed for the office. "You two have fun," he called back.

The women packed a sumptuous lunch into their saddle bags and left generous portions on the table for Christopher. After saddling Fili and Kili, they checked on Tanner. Satisfied he was doing well, they mounted the horses and headed for Mickey's favorite mountain meadow.

As they rode, Jennifer took a deep breath of the fresh clean air happily. "I love these August summer days. Nothing like living in Montana. I could spend my whole life here," she said dreamily.

"Why don't you?" questioned Mickey while the horses walked through the north pasture.

"It's complicated," said Jennifer.

"You know, I noticed how good you are with animals. Are you planning a career with them?"

Jennifer looked a bit gloomy. "No, I'm a business admin major," she said flatly.

"Oh, that's right. I think you mentioned that at church before. But …" Mickey looked at her in confusion. Now that she knew Jennifer a little better, she absolutely could not picture her new friend working in an office environment. "Jen, I know I'm probably prying but why? You'd be such a fantastic veterinarian. Or vet tech."

Jennifer sighed deeply. "Robert said that's what I should do. He's my fiancée," she remarked absently. "We've known each other since grade school, and we've been a couple since high school. I brought up veterinary medicine once and he was not pleased. 'All dirt, sweat, and people who don't pay' were his exact words. He said wasting education on becoming a vet would be a foolish unprofitable decision and that business administration was the smart choice for us."

She patted Fili's neck absently. "Robert is majoring in pre-law and intends to get into Harvard for his Juris Doctor. He wants me to get a paralegal degree, too.

"He hasn't decided where we want to live, but I know he won't want to be in a small country town. Wherever we end up, he plans to work for the local prosecutor's office for a few years and then the public defender for a few years just to get experience in both sides of criminal law. He hasn't decided for sure what type of law will be his specialty, but he wants his own practice. I'll run the office and be his paralegal."

She sighed, looking resigned to her future. "He pretty much has our lives mapped out. He's a good planner."

As they went through the gate at the far end of the pasture, Mickey felt sad, remembering how her life had been so controlled by Lee for a time. They entered the woods and began to climb the mountain. Mickey spoke carefully while they negotiated their way between the Ponderosa Pines. "Jen, do you love Robert?"

"I suppose so. I've been with him for a long time. I mean, the fireworks are long over but they never last anyway, right? Yeah, I love him."

But Mickey was not convinced. *Sure doesn't sound like it*, she thought. She waved a fly away from Kili's ear. As they approached the small stream, she pulled the horse to a stop and looked at Jennifer. "I know this is probably none of my business, but you should be madly in love with him if you're going to spend the rest of your lives together."

Jennifer looked at her for a moment, then began to guide Fili carefully through the shallow water. "I owe him, Mickey," she said slowly when they were both on the other side. "I owe him a lot. His family is paying for my schooling. I could never have afforded higher education, and neither could Mom. Besides, we've been together forever. I'm sure his mom and dad covered my expenses because they expect me to be their future daughter-in-law."

Mickey protested. "No, Jen, what you owe him is honesty. If you don't love him, you certainly shouldn't commit to him."

As the words left her mouth, she felt smitten. She raised one hand and pushed a strand of hair behind her ear. Tears threatened and she bit her lip to hold them back.

That is how it should be. My situation is just an exception. But Jen's life doesn't have to be that way. They rode on in silence, but tears threatened.

When they reached the meadow, Mickey and Jennifer dismounted and let the horses begin to graze. Jennifer spotted the perfect place for their picnic a few yards away. They spread out a large blanket on the grass in the shade of a cluster of Quaking Aspens. After they were seated, Mickey could hold back her tears no longer. She began to sob quietly.

"Mickey, what is it? What on earth is wrong?" Jennifer looked at her, concerned.

"Oh, Jen," Mickey said, sighing and wiping at her wet face with her sleeve. "I have no business telling you about love. Here I am trying to play psychologist and tell you what to do when I am such a total hypocrite."

Mickey proceeded to share the story of her marriage. Jennifer listened quietly. When finished, Mickey found she felt much better having shared her secret with a trustworthy kindred spirit.

"Would you like to pray, Mick," asked Jennifer.

Mickey nodded and they bowed their heads, each petitioning the Lord for grace and wisdom. They both laughed when Mickey said 'amen' and both their stomach rumbled loudly. They eagerly began poking through the saddle bags.

"Been a long time since breakfast," mumbled

Mickey. She began devouring a chicken salad sandwich.
"You are so right, girlfriend." Jennifer eagerly grabbed the
other sandwich and scooped up a handful of ranch flavored
tortilla chips.

They ate heartily and topped off the meal with lus-
cious chocolate turtle brownies. When they could not eat
another bite, they packed the trash in the saddle bags and
stretched out on the blanket, full and happy.

Suddenly, Mickey sat up and began to snicker.
"What?" asked Jennifer with a bemused expression. She sat
up also. "What's so funny?"

"This is kinda mean but Jen, what if Robert can't
pass the bar?"

Jennifer thought for a moment and then began
snickering herself. "Oh, man, wouldn't that be crazy? All
those well laid plans." She began to laugh and the more she
laughed the more Mickey laughed.

Soon they were gasping for breath with tears running
down their faces. "I truly don't mean to be unkind, Jen but
it just struck me so funny. Here's this guy with the perfectly planned out life. I mean, isn't that just asking for something to go wrong?"

"I know what you mean," said Jennifer, still giggling.
"God has a way of not going along with our plans sometimes." She smiled but her tone took on a more serious
note. "I try to listen to His leading because I surely don't
want to do anything that is not God's will."
"Amen to that, sista!" Mickey said fervently. Inwardly she
was relieved. *Lord*, she prayed, *If Jennifer's relationship
with Robert is not of You, please show her. And show Robert.*

The girls laid back on the blanket and stared up at
the sky. "Look, Jen," Mickey said, shading her eyes while

she looked up at the sky. "That cloud looks just like a horse going around a barrel."

"You're right. It really does." Jennifer stared at the sky. "That one looks like a cowboy," she said, pointing. "See, he has his hat in his hand." She sighed and put her arm behind her head. "I really wanted to start showing Gimli this summer. He needs the experience." She glanced over at Mickey. "My secret dream has always been to make it to the barrel racing nationals."

"Oh, Jen, that's a wonderful goal," Mickey said, enthusiastically. "Why don't you just go for it?"

"I don't have time to train him being away at school and all." She sighed. "At least with taking these summer school courses, I'll be graduating at the end of the year instead of next spring. But that still won't give me enough time to make him show ready for next summer. I can work with him during the winter, but we'll have to spend the summer in the smaller shows. Oh, well." She hopped up, stretched luxuriously, and smiled.

"Enough of that. I want to explore up here." Jen's green eyes were eager, filled with anticipation.

"All right." Mickey rose and folded the blanket. "Enough sitting around. Let's go." She grinned in anticipation. "You're going to love this area."

They retrieved the horses and mounted, agreeing to head further up the trail. The two women spent the rest of the afternoon leaving the deep troubles of life behind and exploring the mountain. Discovering many common likes and dislikes, they also found they shared the same opinions on many issues and a similar sense of humor. Mickey felt like she had discovered a wonderful treasure.

Around 4:00 pm, they headed back to the main trail and began to make their way down the mountain. "You know, Jen," Mickey said, reaching to push a branch out of her way, "I have an idea. You want your horse to be worked

146

regularly, right? Why not bring him out to the C&M? I could give him some schooling every day so he'll be ready when you can take over.

"I do have to devote time to my job, but I think between the two of us we can get him ready for next summer's shows. Maybe that way you can even get to some of the bigger events. Most of my experience is with pleasure horses but I did do a little barrel racing for a while when I was a teenager. I just didn't have enough competitiveness in me to continue for long. And I never owned my own horses until I was older."

"Oh, Mickey, are you serious?" Jennifer sat straight up in the saddle, causing Fili to jerk his head up in alarm. She laughed and patted his neck, reassuring him that all was well. She smiled at Mickey.

"Wow. That would be fantastic. I wanted so badly to get him started while I still have him. I don't know what will happen once Robert and I get married."

"I would love working with him." Mickey grinned, her blue eyes sparkling.

"I plan to be home again next weekend," said Jennifer, her brow furrowing while she mentally reviewed her schedule. "I'll only be able to stay Friday night and Saturday morning, but I should have time to get him moved out to your place."

They reached the barn, excitedly making plans for Gimli's training.

~ * ~

The next few days passed quickly. Jennifer returned to school and Mickey continued to lavish tender care upon Tanner, Kelsey, and Poncho. The dogs improved rapidly, and the good food began to fill out their gaunt frames. Tanner, now out of the sling and strong enough to stand on his own,

147

progressed well and was allowed a half-hour at pasture each day.

In fact, by mid-week, Mickey decided that Tanner was strong enough to be bathed. "I'm going to wash Tanner this afternoon," she announced while she and Christopher were eating breakfast. "I cringe every time I pat him. His coat is filthy, and he smells like a pig pen."

Christopher smiled and began to spread cherry preserves on a biscuit. "I'm sure he'll feel a lot better once he's clean."

"Absolutely," Mickey said firmly. "He probably needs coat conditioner, too."

"Now, Mick, you know he's not going to look all glossy and beautiful right away. It'll take months of good feed and care before that hair begins to look healthy again."

"I know that." Feeling defensive, she put her spoon down in her bowl causing milk to splash on the table. "But I'm going to do the best I can right now. Can't hurt."

"Hey, hey, I wasn't trying to rain on your parade. I just don't want you to feel disappointed if he doesn't look up to snuff when you're finished today."

Mickey reached over and grabbed a napkin to dab at the spilled milk. She smiled sheepishly, feeling she should apologize. "Thanks, Chris. I'm sorry. You're sweet to think of that. Don't worry. I know he won't be perfect but at least he won't be covered with dirt." She frowned slightly. "Unless he decides to have a good roll afterword."

Christopher chucked. "Isn't that maddening the way they always do that after a bath?"

"Yes, it is." Mickey sighed and finished her cereal. "Oh well. The best I can hope for is to have him clean for a few minutes. I'll have to walk him to get him dry so maybe we can avoid the roll."

"I'll keep my fingers crossed," Christopher said. As Mickey cleared away the breakfast dishes, she found herself amazed at how unaffected Chris seemed whenever her defensiveness rose to the surface.

He never seems to get rattled, she thought. *He is such a patient man.*

~ * ~

Mickey hauled two buckets of warm soapy water out to the back yard along with a large sponge. She went down to the barn and led Tanner slowly up the path.

He pricked his ears sharply forward and looked around eagerly, curious about his new surroundings. He was most eager to graze on the lush green grass of the lawn, but Mickey let him have only a few mouthfuls.

"Sorry, boy," she said softly while she wrapped the lead rope around the trunk of a tree and fashioned the ends into a quick release knot. She adjusted the length so Tanner could move his head around but could not reach the grass.

"We can't have you eating too much and getting sick on top of everything else. A round of colic would probably kill you." Tanner nickered softly and lowered his head to be scratched.

Mickey obliged him for a few moments, then dipped the sponge into one of the buckets and began to gently work the cleansing conditioner into his coat. She washed him over thoroughly and then rinsed with the hose.

She cleansed his coat for a second time and then allowed the conditioner to sit for about five minutes. After a final rinse with the hose, she was satisfied she had done her best.

"You were so good, Tanner," she murmured, caressing his face. "I'll bet you feel better now, don't you?" She pulled a carrot out of her pocket and fed it to the dripping horse.

He nickered softly and reached eagerly for the treat. He munched away happily while Mickey used a rubber squeegee to get the excess water from his coat. She led him back to the barn praising him for his good behavior. All at once he stopped and shook mightily.

"Ooh, Tanner," she exclaimed, wiping drops of water from her hair. "I thought I'd gotten most of the water off you. Now we're both soaked." He blew through his nose softly and rested his head on her shoulder.

Tears pricked in Mickey's eyes. *Wow. It's like he's thanking me for cleaning him up. What a wonderful horse.* She smiled happily and stood with him for a few moments before giving his new blue halter a gentle tug.

She walked him slowly around the barnyard, giving him a chance to enjoy the sunshine. When his coat dried, she took him into the barn and gave his coat a good brushing. The cleansing conditioner helped smooth out many of the tangles in his mane and tail and she combed them out with a minimum of breakage.

When finished, she stepped back and looked at him critically. Then with a huge smile, she led him back outside and took a quick photo with her phone.

"Tanner, oh my word. Your coat is so soft, and you look amazing! The before and after pictures are going to be striking. I'm posting these on Facebook for sure!"

Mickey hugged his neck, and he nuzzled her gently. Tanner's clean coat turned out to be the color of creamed coffee which blended into a dark brown from his knees down. His mane and tail were a light blonde. Though still thin, his potential was clear. She gave him another treat, then led him to his stall to rest.

"Bye, Tanner. You are going to be one handsome boy when we get through with you." With a pat to his nose,

Mickey closed the stall door with a great feeling of accomplishment.

~ * ~

Mickey had her hands full after Gimli came to the ranch the next weekend. She enjoyed working with the young horse and his quick progress pleased her greatly. She prayed that Jennifer's fiancée would be understanding and would not make her give up the horse after they married.

Tanner continued to improve while the summer waned. The ample supply of oats, hay, and green grass helped him to slowly fill out again. Mickey kept up the daily grooming and his coat grew shinier each day.

His personality proved to be loving and calm and Mickey even rode him around the barnyard a few times. His manners were impeccable, and he said to every cue with ease, suggesting at one time he must have enjoyed good training.

Andrew came out periodically to check on him and finally pronounced him fit. The coroner's report on the death of Tanner's owner confirmed alcohol poisoning. Since no relatives were located, the judge ordered that Mickey and Christopher be permitted to take ownership of the abused animals or adopt them out.

As soon the veterinarian heard these developments, he asked if he could adopt Tanner himself. Though sad to see the horse go, Mickey knew him to be in the best of hands.

"Andrew has the kindest face I've ever seen," Jennifer said during a call to Mickey to see how Gimli was adjusting. "He makes you feel safe, somehow. I'm glad Tanner has such a good home."

~ *Nineteen* ~

Thunder boomed overhead when Mickey flopped into the easy chair Thursday evening with her iPad while Christopher went upstairs to change. This had become routine for her each night after supper, and she looked forward to the chance to sit and relax.

She aimlessly flipped channels trying to find something suitable to watch but nothing caught her interest. She finally settled on the Weather Channel, then tapped the Facebook app on her iPad.

Christopher came in wearing his comfortable old gray sweats and a royal blue long sleeved tee shirt. He patted Kip and Kelsey who were lying beside Mickey's chair, then stretched out on the couch with his hands behind his head.

Poncho, who had been nestled in Mickey's lap, immediately jumped down and joined Christopher on the couch, looking at his face with love. Mickey caught her breath for a moment when she looked at them.

Chris is so handsome, even in his old duds, she thought. *And the way Poncho loves him is so special.* She felt her face getting warm and decided she should take her train of thought down a different track.

She chuckled and said, "You know, Chris, Poncho likes me but you do realize he totally adores you, right?"

He stroked the tiny dog and laughed. "Seems that way, huh? I guess it's because I found him and took him away from that horrid place. Dogs are so intelligent. I don't think humankind can even tap the surface of what goes on in their brains." Poncho enthusiastically licked his hand, then curled up beside him in a tight ball.

"I think you're right," Mickey said thoughtfully. "Dogs are a lot more intelligent than most people give them credit for."

She held up her iPad and tapped the camera icon. "Smile for Facebook, Chris," she said, tapping to take the photo and then posting it online.

"I'm supposed to be the photographer you know," he said with a friendly sigh and a shake of his head.

"Speaking of that, what's up for tomorrow?" she asked placing the iPad back in her lap.

"I really want to complete the red squirrel project," he said, trying to read the next day's forecast at the same time. "Wildlife Unlimited wants me to finish up. They're already planning next fall's issue." He sighed with relief when he read the screen. "Oh, good. No rain tomorrow, just tonight."

"How much do you have left with the squirrels?" Mickey asked.

"I only need a few more shots. Catching the little guys at the right time is the trick. I think I can get what I need tomorrow, though, if they'll cooperate. I'll probably be up on the mountain all day."

He yawned and put a couch pillow under his head. "Those squirrels are like a bunch of nervous terriers. When I first started shooting their nest, they would make a racket every time I moved. And I was using the telephoto lens, so I wasn't even that close."

He laughed. "I've never heard such screeching and squawking. And they'd flip those little tails like nothing I've ever seen. They were completely unhappy with my invasion of their space. They must be used to me now because they don't have much to say to me anymore. They just chatter back and forth to each other."

Mickey grinned. "I've had some of the gray squirrels back home screech at me when all I do is walk by under their tree. They think they own the world."

Christopher glance over at her. "What's on your plate for tomorrow?"

"I'm going to work on a new manuscript in the morning and then work Gimli after lunch. Jen wants to try him out in the Aspen Ridge show next weekend. He's coming along well but he'll need some more work to be ready, I think, even though that show is small."

"Jen picked herself a fine horse," Christopher remarked, thinking of the beautiful bay Quarter Horse. "Sure is smart for a three year old. I don't think I've ever seen a horse learn so fast."

"You got that right. He's been a joy to train. I'm going to be sorry when she graduates and has time to work him at her own place. I'll bet they'll be big names in barrel racing before long if she gets to stay with it."

"Yep." Christopher yawned again. After a few moments of silence, he ran his hand through his hair. "Boy, I just can't keep my eyes open. I think I'll hit the hay since I have to get up early."

He rose and started for his bedroom, then poked his head back through the door. "Oh, hey, why don't I feed the horses for you in the morning since I'll be up anyway? That way you can sleep in a bit."

"Oh daahling, that would be heavenly," Mickey said in her best British accent, while thinking how considerate and kind he always was with her.

"Consider it done, madam," he said with his own imitation. "I shall also feed the dogs and take them out so you can be a lady of leisure. Good night, Mick."

"Night," she called to his disappearing back. "Sleep well."

154

As he climbed the stairs and headed for his bedroom, Christopher sighed heavily. *I wish I didn't have to say good night at the living room door*, he thought sadly.

As he crawled beneath the covers, his love for his wife once again plagued his thoughts.

I wish there were no 'his and hers' bedrooms. He rolled over onto his side and prayed once again for patience and self-control.

"Father, I need Your strength. I believe You led us into this marriage, strange though it is. Help me to die daily to my own selfishness and personal desires. Help me to always put Mickey's needs before my own.

"And dear Father, please," he choked back tears while his feelings overtook him. "Please dear Lord, work out Your will for us both. Please heal whatever hurts and wounds from the past that still cause my Mickey pain. I feel with every fiber of my being that You caused me to fall in love with her all those years ago. And that love has done nothing but grow since then. I know our marriage is of You. Please, Father. Bring us together as true husband and wife in Your time and in Your way. And help us to learn what You have for us to learn in the meantime."

~ Twenty ~

Mickey awoke the next morning and stretched. She yawned and glanced lazily out the window at the trees swaying lightly in the breeze. Suddenly she sat straight up, causing Snippit to leap down and scramble under the desk looking insulted. Kip, Kelsey, and Poncho jumped up, immediately on alert. Poncho let out a sharp bark.

"What time is it?" she said in a panic. "The horses! Oh, no!" The clock said 9:28 am. "Oh, the poor babies." She ran to the closet, frantically grabbing her jeans. "I'm two hours late. How could I have slept through the alarm?"

As she reached for a tee shirt, she suddenly remembered Christopher's early shoot and his offer of the night before to care for the animals. Mickey flopped back down on the bed. Her heart was pounding but she was grateful for his thoughtfulness. *Wonder how he got the dogs out of here without waking me up? I must have been dead to the world.*

"Wow, kids, at least I'm awake now," she said, with a giggle. Snippit slowly emerged from under the desk. She jumped onto the desk chair and sat stiffly, giving Mickey and the dogs a look of disdain.

Mickey laughed again. "Ah, c'mon," she said, patting the bed. "You can come back over here and sleep some more."

After a few minutes of coaxing Snippit allowed herself to be soothed and leapt lightly over onto the bed. She curled up on the pillow and began to purr loudly. Mickey gave her and the dogs a final pat, then headed for the shower.

The hot water pounding on her back felt exceptionally good and the luxurious scent of the cleansing conditioner in her hair made her inhale through her nose with delight. *This is going to be a great day*, she thought happily.

Mickey stepped from the shower ten minutes later, feeling much refreshed. While she pulled on a hunter green turtleneck, she planned her day.

I'll try to get at least three chapters edited before lunch. She pulled her hair out from under the collar, then reached for her work jeans. *Then I'll clean the barn and give Gimli a workout.*

Remembering the temperatures were forecast to be cool, she added a green sweatshirt that said 'Salty Dog Café' on the front.

Mickey stopped in the kitchen to grab a quick bite before settling into work. She sat down at the table and took a bite of a large pumpkin muffin. Suddenly she spotted a note under the saltshaker. She put the muffin on her plate and reached for the small slip of paper.

Mick, left Gimli in for you – let everyone else out. Be home late tonight – will call if later than eight though. Chris.

Mickey put the note down and absently picked up her muffin again. She took another bite and chewed slowly, staring out the window. She was unable to understand her feeling of letdown. She really did not expect him to leave a note at all, much less write an epic. After all, they had just talked the night before.

She finished her muffin and put her dishes in the dishwasher. She read the note again, crumpled it with a sigh, and tossed the paper into the trash can while she headed for the office.

~ * ~

Gimli heard her footsteps on the path and greeted her with a loud whinny. He then looked pointedly out the open door at the other horses grazing in the pasture. Mickey smiled when she walked up to him and began to scratch behind his ears.

"I know, I know. You can go play after we work a little." Gimli lowered his head and stood very still, enjoying the gentle scratching.

Mickey continued for a moment, then headed for the tack room. Gimli sighed loudly and she laughed again. "You guys are so hilarious," she said, thinking of the varied personalities of the animals.

Her smile widened when she glanced out the window and saw the splendor of the mountains in the morning sun. Bits of bright color in the trees hinted at the glory to come. The air turned cooler every day while autumn edged out the last vestiges of summer.

"Oh, Lord," she said aloud. "You've been so good to me. This is what I always dreamed of: lots of land, horses, and the mountains. Thank You, Lord, for allowing my dream to come true. And thank You for Chris, Lord. Without him, this wouldn't have been possible."

Mickey felt vaguely uncomfortable when she said this. *I am thankful for him. I don't have to be in love with him to be thankful for him.*

She thought of the few times in recent memory when she found herself attracted to Christopher.

That's just a physical thing, she thought firmly. *I felt that way before about Lee and then when I got what I wanted it was awful. Besides, a mere physical attraction or chemistry is not love.*

The verse echoed in her mind again. *Ask and ye shall receive, seek and ye shall find, knock and it shall be opened unto you.*

Right, she thought sarcastically. *Like I'm really going to ask to love someone after what happened with Lee. At least I finally had the good sense to get away from him.*

I'm sure that scripture does not refer to asking for love.
Love for all humankind perhaps but not romantic love.

Mickey stared out the window remembering the day when thoughts began to flit through her mind that her relationship with Lee might not be healthy. The end of the first semester of her senior year fast approached and she felt imprisoned. She often wondered why. One's senior year was always said to be the most enjoyable.

She left her last class of the day feeling exhausted. She missed two questions on the pop quiz and dreaded the thought of telling Lee. He always complimented her when she received a perfect score, but anything less earned her one of his stern lectures about being one hundred percent, one hundred percent of the time. She decided to skip supper and just go back to her dorm to lie down.

As she entered the room, Mickey caught sight of her face in the mirror. *That doesn't even look like me anymore.* Dark circles spread out under her eyes and her features looked haggard. Her once bright blue eyes were dull, listless, and tired.

I used to be so happy, she thought while she put her books on the desk. *Seems like these days everything I do makes Lee unhappy. I try so hard to please him, but he always gets so irritated. I just don't understand. He used to be so sweet. But the other day he said, If I feel like you love me, there's nothing I won't do for you. But when you do stupid things like this, I know you don't really love m'.*

She climbed up and stretched out on the bed. She lay there thinking and tears welled up in her eyes. *What things? I don't how to make him feel loved. Nothing I ever do suits him.*

Deborah Godfrey, Mickey's roommate, came in and stopped short. "Oh, Mickey, what's wrong?" she asked, dropping her books on her bed, and coming to stand beside her friend. "Can I help you somehow?"

Mickey sniffed and reached for a tissue. "I just don't know what to do. Why can't I make Lee happy anymore? What's wrong with me, Debbie?" Mickey began to sob. "What's wrong? I feel like the real me is lost and I don't even know who I am anymore."

Debbie looked stern. "Mickey Sterling, there is nothing wrong with you." Her tone softened and she reached for Mickey's hand. "I don't want to tell you what to do but I don't think you should keep dating Lee. I mean, it's just not a right kind of relationship, you know?

"He completely dominates your life. He wants you to spend all your time with him, he won't let you have other friends, and face the music, Mickey, he's just plain mean to you. He is a classic abuser and if you stay with him and end up marrying him, the abuse will only get worse. I'm sorry to be so blunt but I've been wanting to talk to you about this for a long time."

She sighed deeply before she continued. "My sister got into a marriage with an abusive man. Mickey, trust me when I tell you things *will* get worse. If Lee is this abusive now, just imagine how bad he'll be in the privacy of your own home. He won't stop at verbal and emotional abuse." Debbie paused for a moment and then continued. "My sister's husband was like Lee but one day she saw a change in his eyes and in the tone of his voice that scared her to the core. She knew the physical abuse was coming.

"He even made veiled threats. Nothing you could take to the police, of course. The man was very careful to keep his nose squeaky clean. Lizzy called our mom that morning on her way to work to ask her to pray. Mamma and Daddy prayed together and then called her back and told her they felt strongly she needed to get out of there.

"That night Lizzy got home a few minutes late from work. Carl tied her to a tree and drove his truck at her for two hours. She thought he was going to kill her. One time the front bumper grazed her forehead. He left here there tied up all night."

Mickey's tears continued to fall, and Debbie handed her another tissue. "Believe me, Mickey, she did not take the idea of leaving her husband lightly. She really had to wrestle with that even after that horrible night because she believes marriage should be for life.

"But after hearing the Godly advice from our folks and praying her heart out, she packed all she could two days later and fled while he was at work. I know he would have eventually killed her."

Debbie shook her head. "He never did change. Always acted like she was the one who made him act that way. He would never admit he had a problem, even after she left. Mickey, you don't deserve that. No one deserves to be treated like that."

Mickey nodded slowly and inhaled deeply. "I guess I have some thinking to do."

Debbie squeezed her hand, then gave her a hug. "I'll be praying for you. I know breaking the relationship off won't be easy, but this is no way to live. Just remember, his behavior is not the proper, God honoring way for a man to treat a woman. Don't enable him by allowing him to continue abusing you."

During Christmas break, Mickey ended the relationship after Lee kicked her dog and then tried to strangle her. When classes resumed, Lee sent her a long email saying that the breakup was probably for the best anyway. He just couldn't overlook her faults anymore, especially since she didn't even try to correct them.

He said that her rebellious independent attitude would earn her God's wrath and judgment before long. For weeks afterward, Mickey remained sad and afraid. Every time something went wrong, she inwardly flinched in anticipation of the hateful words of reproof she had come to expect.

~ * ~

Brokenhearted that she wasted a season of her life in that relationship, Mickey did not see that she needed to surrender her past to the Lord. She pushed the troublesome thoughts from her mind.

I will not ask for love, Lord. I don't know why I keep thinking of that verse but I'm sure that passage should not be interpreted as a green light to ask for love.

She concentrated on gathering the tack for her ride. After a few moments she calmed down and felt so badly that she prayed again.

"I'm sorry, Lord," she said contritely while a tear rolled down her cheek. "Forgive me. I need to be content with all the wonderful things I have and with this situation.

"Thankfully, Chris is not abusive now. But if we were husband and wife in the true sense, the jealousy might take over and he might harass me about everything I do or say just like Lee. There's nothing I want more than to truly be in love, but I absolutely cannot risk asking."

With a small shudder, Mickey pulled a tissue from her pocket and dabbed at the tears before leading Gimli outside. She tied his lead rope to a fence rail, then looked around her and sighed. Large white fluffy clouds floated along in the bright blue sky. A light breeze blew Mickey's hair away from her face while she tightened the cinch. The horse stood quietly, his glossy bay coat shining in the sun.

"Thank You, Lord," she whispered. The beauty around her soothed her rumpled emotions. "Thank You for this gorgeous day. Thank You for this balm for my spirit."

Mickey slowly mounted and murmured, "Good boy, Gimli," while she patted his neck gently. He stood perfectly still until she gave the command to move. She rode around for about fifteen minutes in the ring which they built inside the barnyard area. The young horse walked, jogged, and loped flawlessly, responding quickly to her every command. He changed leads well and even gave her several excellent runs at the barrels.

"This day is too pretty to stay in this ring," Mickey told Gimli in a matter-of-fact tone. "Besides, you deserve a reward for doing so well. Let's go for a fun ride."

She turned Gimli to exit the ring, intent on heading for the nearest trail. Then she remembered her promise to Chris.

"Oh, crumbs!" she exclaimed, pulling Gimli to a halt. "I hate not being able to trail ride unless someone can go with me. I really enjoy the solitude."

But Mickey knew Christopher's concern was well founded. Trail riding alone was just too dangerous, and she had given her word.

"Okay, boy," she said with a frustrated sigh, "Let's just ride around in the north pasture since your friends are over on the south side right now. At least we can look at some different scenery." Gimli turned obediently and they headed out.

He performed beautifully when they entered the field, allowing Mickey to open, close, and latch the gate without dismounting. "You're doing great, Gimli." She patted his neck affectionately. "You're going to make Jen a great horse. I'll bet you'll take all the blue ribbons at that show." He tossed his head proudly, hearing the praise in her voice.

They began to follow the perimeter of the pasture, Mickey quietly enjoying the environment she loved. She inhaled deeply, breathing in the scents leather, horse, and a hint of fall. Her eyes soaked in the majestic beauty of the mountains.

This view is just plain good for the soul, she thought with pleasure.

She grinned when she remembered a quote from Winston Churchill which had also been used by her favorite President, Ronald Reagan. "The outside of a horse is good for the inside of a man."

With all due respect, Mr. Prime Minister and Mr. President, she thought, *that applies to the women also.*

When they reached the far end of the pasture, Mickey turned Gimli, then pulled him to a halt near a large Ponderosa Pine. From this vantage point she could look back at the house.

Off to her right, a quick flash caught her eye. She turned her head and smiled when she spotted a pair of chickadees feeding on flowers gone to seed.

They're so adorable, she thought while she watched the small black capped birds.

She was intently watching the pair go from flower to flower and didn't notice when Gimli suddenly pricked his ears sharply forward. He stepped back nervously. A moment later he suddenly jumped sideways, half reared, and bolt- ed.

Mickey hit the ground before she knew what had happened. She saw the horse tearing madly away as if his tail was on fire. She felt a sharp pain in her leg and in her head, then the world went black.

~ Twenty-One ~

When Mickey came to, she lay for a moment trying to figure out where she was and remember what happened. Everything came back in a rush. She hurt all over but rolled her head to one side trying to see what spooked the young horse. There was no apparent cause for his alarm. Mickey sighed inwardly.

It's my own fault. I should have been more alert. They spook at everything at this age.

When she gingerly tried to sit up, excruciating pain stabbed through her right leg. Mickey gasped and tears involuntarily welled up in her eyes. She looked in despair at the gash on her leg.

How on earth am I going to catch Gimli and get back to the house? I can hardly breathe my leg hurts so badly. I wonder if there's a broken bone.

She looked around and saw a fallen branch nearby that looked strong enough to use as a crutch. She crawled toward the piece of wood, trying to keep her injured leg from moving. Despite her best efforts, the intense pain nearly caused her to pass out again. By the time she finally got to the branch, her entire body was shaking uncontrollably. She sat resting for several moments.

When Mickey caught her breath, she grabbed the branch and pulled herself up, resting all her weight on her good leg. Careful though she was, every movement made her gasp and bite her lip in pain.

When she finally straightened up, her head swam, and she was afraid she would lose consciousness again. She closed her eyes and held tightly to the branch, breathing deeply until the dizziness passed.

165

Christy R. Diachenko

She reached into her jeans pocket for her phone and then remembered. Before she started working Gimli on the barrels, she put the phone into a small, zippered compartment at the back of the saddle seat so the phone would not be jarred from her pocket. She groaned in agony, not knowing what to do.

She looked out across the pasture and spotted Gimli grazing peacefully in the center. She managed to push a whistle through her trembling lips, then she called to him weakly. The horse looked up and started toward her, then snorted, turned, and galloped back toward the barn, bucking and kicking all the way.

Mickey's heart sank. Her only hope of getting back quickly or calling for help just ran off.

At least he's okay, she thought thankfully. *But what am I going to do? Chris won't get back until late. I can't just stay here. I need help. This leg is bad.*

Tears of fear and pain filled her eyes while she hopelessly looked at the insurmountable distance to the house.

"Oh, Lord, please help me," she sobbed in despair. "I can't do this, alone. I just can't."

The breeze gently caressed her cheek and the birds twittered in the tree branches. All else was still. While she stood there frightened and hurting, she remembered one of her favorite promises from Hebrews 13:5, *"I will never fail you. I will never abandon you."*

Gradually she got a grip on her fear and pain and common sense took over.

I'm going to have to make it on my own, she said to herself, wiping her eyes with her sleeve. *There's no other way.* She repeated to herself, *'I will never fail you. I will never abandon you.'*

She pushed the hair back from her face, wishing she had a scrunchie. She prayed again for strength and carefully set out, using her good leg and the branch to slowly

166

make her way across the pasture. Time and time again she nearly fell, passed out, or tripped. The tall grass seemed to deliberately twist around her leg to pull her down.

Strains of one of her favorite songs by Chris Tomlin played through her mind, reminding her that God was always by her side. With a power that was not her own, she forged ahead, repeating her favorite Bible promises and singing "Whom Shall I Fear" in her mind while she went.

Two hours later, Mickey arrived at the gate. Gimli, now docile, came to her immediately. She retrieved her phone, let Gimli into the barnyard, and then painfully made her way to the house.

She stumbled through the door and dragged herself to the living room. She sank onto the couch, drenched with sweat and trembling all over. She sat for a moment, feeling as though she could not move another muscle. She looked unseeingly at the phone in her hand and, for a moment, could not remember how to use the device.

How many minutes passed she could not have said but the pain in her leg began to throb, and her body began to shake uncontrollably again. She knew she could not wait until Christopher came home. She tapped the phone and managed to dial 911. Just when she finished giving them the information they needed, everything went dark once more, and her body went limp.

~ * ~

When Mickey awoke, Christopher's pale face and his worried brown eyes looking into hers was the first thing she saw. She lay still racking her brain, trying to figure out where she was and why on earth Christopher looked like he had just seen a ghost. Then she remembered the accident. She was lying in a hospital bed and could see that her leg was now in a cast.

Oh, boy, she thought, wincing when pain shot thorough her head when she sat up. *He's going to be so angry. That squirrel shoot was so important and now he's gotten pulled away right in the middle.*

Tingles of panic washed over her, and she started apologizing. "Oh, Chris, I'm so sorry. I should have told them not to bother you. I didn't mean for you to have to come. I'll be all right. Please, you don't have to stay. I know you want to finish up that project today. I'm sorry I messed you up." She felt frantic and fear gripped her heart like a vise.

Christopher put a gentle hand on her arm and looked at her with sorrow. "Mickey, when are you going to realize that *you* are more important than anything else to me? I'm not going to be angry with you because accidents happen. Life doesn't always happen on our terms. I know that." He put his hands up in a gesture of helplessness. "And why would I blame you? Do you really think I could keep working, knowing that you were hurt?"

Christopher sighed deeply and looked at the floor. "They said my wife had an accident and was on her way to the emergency room in Great Falls. They said the clinic in Aspen Ridge couldn't handle the injuries. That's all they would tell me. I had no idea what happened or how badly you were hurt. I was scared to death, Mick!"

His voice caught. "You just don't know," he whispered. "I prayed my heart out the whole way here. Like it or not, you're my best friend and I couldn't bear to lose you."

Mickey felt ashamed when she saw tears glisten in his eyes. Here he was, so concerned, and all she could do was be afraid for herself.

"I'm sorry to have frightened you so badly," she said softly. "I'm glad you're here." She explained how Gimli spooked and she was thrown from the horse.

"I can't believe you came all the way across that pasture with a broken leg," he said, shaking his head at the thought of her being in such pain. He felt helpless and neglectful. "You should have waited for help."

I should have been there to protect her, he thought with chagrin.

"But Chris, I would have been there all afternoon and who knows how late into the night," Mickey said, feeling defensive. "You said you were going to be late and even then, you would have had quite a search before you found me. I couldn't just lie there. You remember. There are cougars and grizzlies in those mountains."

Her tone took on a sarcastic note. "As I recall that was one of the reasons you didn't want me trail riding up there alone. Predators could very easily come down into the pastures at night. So even though I wasn't actually on the mountain –"

"You're right," he conceded, realizing she had a point and also knowing he would have done the same thing had he been in her position. "I guess you did what you had to do. But from now on, you've got to carry your phone in your pocket or in the saddle bag whenever you ride, okay?"

"Okay," Mickey replied, feeling too weary to point out that the phone *was* in the saddle bag but hadn't done her much good since the horse and saddle bag headed for home without her. Her eyelids felt like lead weights and her body ached all over. Her head throbbed, and she felt like someone was boring into her right temple with a screwdriver. Christopher could see she needed to rest.

"Go ahead and sleep," he said tenderly, helping her scoot back down into the bed. He pulled the blanket up around her and laid his hand on her forehead. "I'll be right here when you wake up. I called Jennifer. She was coming home tonight for the weekend anyway, so she's going over to the house to care for the horses and the dogs. That way I can stay here."

Mickey nodded slightly and yawned. Then her eyes opened wide. "But Chris, what about Gimli? He's still all tacked up wandering around the barnyard. What if he gets hurt or something?"

"He'll be all right until she gets there, don't worry. Jen will take care of him. He *is* her horse you know. She knows what to do."

He smiled and kissed her forehead gently. Once again Mickey's eyes closed while sleep overtook her.

~ Twenty-Two ~

Around three that morning, Christopher awoke. For a moment, he looked around in confusion. Then his stiff body reminded him he fell asleep in the chair at Mickey's bedside. He stood and stretching gingerly. Mickey appeared to be sleeping peacefully, so he decided to run down to the lobby to get a cup of coffee from the machine. He tip toed out the door, closing it gently, and walked down the quiet hallway.

The nurse at the desk smiled at him when he walked by. "How's your wife, Mr. Gordon?" she asked.

"Sleeping well," he replied. "I'm going for some coffee."

The nurse told him where to find the vending area and went back to her charting. A few minutes later a buzzer on her panel sounded. She listened briefly, then rose. One of the patients needed more pain medication. She gathered her supplies and headed down to the room at the end of the hall.

~ * ~

After Christopher left the room, Mickey began to stir, then toss restlessly while she dreamed of college. She was walking along the sidewalk, enjoying the bright yellow daffodils, and smiling with delight at the beautiful spring day.

Suddenly, she tripped. Looking down in horror, she saw the bone sticking out of her leg. Blood spattered everywhere and she was in terrible pain. Tears streamed down her cheeks, while the excruciating agony increased. She fell to the ground. People began to gather around her, but no one offered assistance.

A harsh voice came from behind her. "Stop crying, you freakin' moron. Why do you have to be so emotional

171

about everything? You just fall apart. You can't handle any-thing."

With effort, Mickey looked around and there stood her boyfriend, Lee Davidson. He stalked toward her, his face dark with anger and his icy eyes flashing blue fire. "You are the clumsiest person I've ever met," he said with a sneer. "You can't even walk down a simple sidewalk with-out doing yourself bodily harm."

Mickey cowered on the ground. "Please, Lee, it was an accident. My leg is broken." Mickey heard a low nicker. Gimli trotted up and began to graze in the lush, green grass in front of the science building.

"Oh, there's a brilliant deduction. Of course, your leg is broken but not by accident. It was by your own stu-pidity," Lee said angrily. "If you were the right kind of Christian woman, you'd be more graceful. You're even more idiotic than that dumb animal."

He looked toward the grazing horse with hate filled eyes. From nowhere he pulled out a rifle and shot Gimli in the head. The horse looked at Mickey and gave an agonizing whinny, then slowly collapsed.

"No!" Mickey screamed in anguish, reaching help-lessly toward the dead animal. "Lee, how could you? He was just standing there. He didn't do anything to you." Tears of grief streamed down her cheeks and her shoulders heaved with sobs.

"Oh, Mickey, dear," said Lee haughtily. "*I* didn't do anything. *You* killed that horse. He had to die because you refuse to change your ways. If you were right with God, I wouldn't have to continually encourage you to shape up. This was your fault. Everything is *your fault*."

Then he reached down and grabbed Mickey's arm, pulling her up roughly. He began to jerk her along behind him. She tried to stumble after him on her good leg but fell when she put weight on the broken one.

"Get up," Lee said angrily. *"Get up.* You are such an embarrassment. Good grief, you're not worth the space you occupy, which is a good bit with all the weight you've gained. No wonder you wear body hugging clothes. You can't find anything big enough. And no wonder your leg broke. The poor limb could no longer support your weight." The crowd roared with laughter.

Lee looked down at her in disgust. "You're just lucky I'll even go out with you. Not many guys would put up with an ugly, fat hag like you, Mickey."

He laughed cruelly. "I've thought of a pet name for you, my dear. 'Icky Mickey'. A moniker which suits you perfectly." The crowd began to chant the name over and over.

Thunder suddenly boomed and the sky rapidly darkened. Rain and hail began to fall from the sky like pellets and lightning zigzagged everywhere. Lee, along with the rest of the crowd, ran for cover leaving Mickey alone where she had fallen. She sobbed in pain, fear, and humiliation.

As the rain soaked her to the skin, Mickey felt strong hands around her neck. "No," she choked out.

The sinister voice of Lee whispered in her ear. "I'm going to kill you, Mickey. You're just no good. The world must be rid of you." His hands tightened while she clawed at them. She choked for breath, and all began to go dark.

~ * ~

Christopher stepped off the elevator back on the second floor just in time to hear Mickey's agonizing scream echo through the halls. He dropped his half empty cup and ran for her room. The coffee splashed across the floor.

Mickey writhed in the bed, still not fully awake. "Oh, dear Lord," she said, choking back tears. "I know it says 'Ask and ye shall receive' but I'll never ask to love a man again. I won't, I promise. I didn't know. I thought he

173

was nice. I just wanted someone to love and someone to love me. I won't ask again. I won't. I promise." Her voice broke completely, and she sobbed hysterically.

Christopher gathered her gently into his arms and tried to awaken her. "Mickey, honey, wake up," he said soothingly. "Wake up. You're safe now. Everything will be okay. No one is ever going to hurt you again, not while I'm around."

The nurse came in looking alarmed but saw what was happening and stepped back. Slowly Mickey's mind surfaced back to consciousness. The horror of the nightmare still lingered, and she clung to Christopher in desperation while sobs shuddered through her. Christopher held her close until she calmed, then asked her about the dream.

Clumsily she tried to make sense of what just happened. The medication made her thoughts foggy but gradually she pieced things together.

"I guess it was a combination of what happened today and memories of my time with Lee," Mickey said brokenly, her eyes full of anguish. "He wasn't mean at first. He seemed to be a good man. The abusiveness just kind of gradually surfaced, then got worse and worse."

She sat back and looked off into space, still breathing heavily, remembering. "I always used to try to figure out what in the world I did to make him so angry."

"You didn't do anything," Christopher said, his jaw clenched with anger. "Lee was the one with the problem. He just wanted someone he could control."

Christopher remembered well that day in college when he came very close to physical violence against the man. He, Mickey, and some friends were enjoying a snack in the campus café. Mickey and Lee's break up was months behind them.

Lee sauntered by and stopped, looking at Mickey. "Geez, Mick, what happened? Did your treadmill break down? You look like you've put on fifty pounds. Are you all right?" His tone was scornful and sarcastic.

Though her friends' faces showed their disapproval of Lee, Christopher could see Mickey's deep humiliation. He rose menacingly, his hands curled into fists, but Lee hurried off. Christopher slumped back into his chair, not understanding how someone hateful and hurtful as Lee Davidson could claim to be a Christian.

Christopher's thoughts returned to the present. He never realized until now just how deep and lasting the scars were on Mickey's sensitive soul.

Mickey continued softly. "I realized later, thanks to you and my roommate Debbie, that I wasn't to blame," she said, easing her body down and laying her aching head back on the pillow.

"I probably would have been soured on men for life if it hadn't been for your friendship. I know Lee had no right to be abusive. Of course, he wasn't quite as bad in real life as he was in that dream just now but I think in time, he would have been."

She sighed painfully. "Still, I got what I asked for. I told the Lord I wanted love no matter what. That *was* my fault. I'll never make that mistake again."

Christopher's heart sank. He wanted to refute her statement but could not think of what to say. He knew something was still not right about her thinking on the subject but sat in silence, feeling helpless. He remembered again the story of Hosea.

No matter how long, Lord, he prayed inwardly. *No matter what she says or does. I will love her until the day I die. Please Father, give me wisdom and the right words to say at the right time. And please heal her wounded heart.*

Mickey put a hand to her temple and closed her eyes with a soft moan. "I feel like my head is about to explode," she whispered in agony. Christopher stood and reached to squeeze her hand.

"I'll go get you something, dear," said the nurse who had been watching attentively.

After about half an hour, Mickey slept peacefully. Christopher sat in the chair beside her bed thinking hard. A few things were beginning to come together in his mind.

All this time I figured she really just felt like I was a brother figure. He rested his head on the back of the chair and stared at the tiles of the ceiling. *But maybe she's afraid to let herself love me. I think that business with Lee affected her more than I realized.*

He remembered the makeup episode when they first moved. When he looked back over the three months of their marriage, he could plainly see the times when she feared he would be angry with her if she were in any way imperfect, made a mistake, or angered him.

Christopher thought a bit longer, then prayed. *Lord, I'm not sure I understand all that's going on here but help Mickey to realize that You are a loving Father. Help her to see that, though You allowed the situation with Lee, it wasn't to vindictively punish her. Help her to see that asking You for things is not a risky business if she asks in Your will.*

Help her to see Your faithfulness and help her to seek Your healing from the hurt that man inflicted on her. Thank You that You have sent me to love and protect her here on this earth. But I know You love her more than I do, Lord. Heal her, I pray. Use me. And if it is Your will, bring us together in love someday.

~ Twenty-Three ~

The hospital released Mickey after two days. Fearing a possible head injury, they performed a CT scan and kept her for observation. By Friday the doctor was satisfied she was out of danger and released her to return home.

Mickey inhaled deeply when they left the hospital, breathing in the crisp autumn air. She was amazed at how much the weather changed in such a short time. Christopher helped her into the back of the Jeep so she could stretch her leg out on the seat. After pushing and pulling, she sat in relative comfort.

"I can see already this cast is going to be a major pain," she said in exasperation, looking at the unwieldy mass.

Christopher climbed into the front seat and started the engine. "I know but we'll manage. You'll see. The time will fly by and before you know it, the cast will be history. I'm just thankful you didn't have a more complicated break. The doctor said it was a slight fracture and should heal quickly."

"I'm thankful for that," Mickey said with gratefulness. She said nothing more while he drove out of the city, basking in the fact that Christopher was so positive and kind.

She rested her head against the glass and stared out the opposite window. The beauty of the passing scenery filled her soul with peace.

"You know, I've been wondering," remarked Christopher. "What spooked Gimli the day of the accident? Do you remember?"

Christy R. Diachenko

Mickey sighed. "I think it was just a flighty young horse thing. Although," she said knowingly, "it very well might have been an orc."

Christopher burst out laughing. "I'm glad your sense of humor wasn't damaged," he said grinning at her in the rear-view mirror.

He plugged in his phone and tapped the 'instrumental' playlist. Soft mellow piano music poured from the speakers. Mickey's eyes were soon drooping. Her ordeal and the hard hospital bed did not contribute to good rest. The rhythm of the tires on the road and the pleasant soothing music began to lull her to sleep.

Christopher noticed her head nodding when he glanced at her through the rear-view mirror. "Here, put this behind your head." He handed her pillow back to her. "Try to get a little rest. We won't be home for a good forty-five minutes."

Mickey yawned. "Yeah, I think I will." She put the pillow behind her and settled back. "I'm really tired. Thank you, Chris. Thank you for everything."

She fell fast asleep as soon as her head hit the pillow. Christopher drove on, thinking and praying. He tried to think of ways he could help her during this time. Thankfully he was not currently on an assignment with a deadline, so he could be home most of the time. He intended to completely pamper Mickey while her leg healed.

~ * ~

Mickey still slept soundly when Christopher turned into the ranch's long driveway. When he reached the house, he quietly cut the Jeep's engine and turned in his seat. Mickey looked so vulnerable, her eyes closed and her face peaceful. While he gazed at her, his heart constricted. He could not believe how intensely he loved her.

Gently he touched her arm. "Mickey, honey, we're home."

178

After several seconds her eyelids fluttered and she gazed back at him, a bewildered look in her sleepy blue eyes.

"We're home, Mick," he said again.

She yawned widely and after a moment or two began to perk up a bit. Christopher helped her out of the Jeep and handed her the crutches. After putting them under her arms, she looked around and slowly smiled.

"It's all the same," she said happily. "I'm so glad to be home."

"I'm glad to have you back." Christopher smiled. "The place was awfully quiet and empty without you here."

Mickey took in the house, then turned to look at the yard, then the barn. When Christopher looked down at the beautiful woman before him, he was overcome with tenderness. When Mickey's gaze met his own, he looked into her eyes for what seemed like years before he stepped closer and slowly lowered his head.

For a moment Mickey could not move. The abruptly she put a hand on his chest. "Please don't, Chris."

He stepped back instantly. With a deep sigh of regret he said, "I'm sorry, Mick. I'm sorry. I just ..."

"It's all right," she said softly after an awkward moment of silence. "No worries." She shivered when a slight breeze wafted over her.

"We'd better get you inside before you get chilled," Christopher said. He grabbed her suitcase and went ahead of her to open the door, glad for something to ease the awkward moment.

Kip ran eagerly to her when she entered the kitchen. Mickey put the crutches aside, balanced on her good leg and reached down to pat his head. "Oh baby, Mama's so glad to see you," she murmured. He licked her hand ecstatically, his tail waving madly.

Mickey stopped then and looked around. "Chris, where are Kelsey and Poncho?"

"They're with Andrew until tomorrow," he replied, then quickly hastened to explain when he saw Mickey's look of concern. "He'll drop them by first thing in the morning. They're fine. I just took them to his clinic so they could be spayed and neutered. I know we'd discussed that, but we never decided on a time. Kelsey was starting to show signs of coming into heat, so I figured I'd better get a jump on things before we ended up with Chi-Collie puppies. And before all the male dogs from miles around show up in our yard."

Mickey grinned ruefully. "They still might, you know. Sometimes if a dog is in heat when she's spayed those lustful guys still want to come around. I'm glad you went ahead. She surely doesn't need any litters after what she's been thorough. Thank goodness Kip is fixed."

Suddenly Mickey felt a wave of extreme weariness wash over her. Christopher handed the crutched to her.

"You need to get to bed," he said firmly. "Do you want to eat first?"

"No, I don't think so. I'm so tired. I wanted to go see the horses but ..." She reached one hand to cover a jaw splitting yawn. "I guess right now what I want most is just to sleep in my own bed. I'll eat later when I wake up."

Christopher helped her to her room and put her suitcase on the floor beside the bed. He started to go but then stood by the door for a moment, uncertain how to proceed. He wanted to help but did not want to invade her privacy.

Noticing his dilemma, Mickey spoke. "I can take things from here, Chris. I'm just going to wash my face, brush my teeth, and fall into that wonderful soft comfortable bed. I probably won't move again 'til morning."

"Okay but if you need any help or want me to get you something just yell, all right?" A concerned look filled his brown eyes.

"I will."

"I mean it now, Mickey. None of this, I don't want to bother him, I'll do it myself business. If you need help or even think you might need help, you call me.

"In fact, why don't you just call me before you do anything at all. Here's your phone. I'll put it right here on the bedside table. Oh, and it's all charged. You can text me or call me. I'll always keep my phone with me."

Mickey stopped him with a laugh. "Chris, I'm fine!" He looked doubtful. "Okay, okay," she said with an exasperated but good-humored sigh. "I will ask for help if I need help. I promise. Now get out of here and let me sleep."

Christopher smiled and closed the door. He puttered around the house for the rest of the afternoon. He did the barn chores in record time that evening, afraid Mickey would awaken and need something right away. He slept lightly all night, waking at every noise. He opened her bedroom door and checked on her several times, but she never stirred.

~ * ~

Saturday morning Mickey awoke raring to go. Her night of good rest left her feeling refreshed and rejuvenated. She sat up and stretched, then reached down to give Snippit a hug.

"I missed you, baby girl," she said, scratching the cat under her chin. Snippit purred heartily in response.

Kip reached a paw to her and whined softly. "I know, you sweet boy. I missed you, too."

She pulled the dog toward her and hugged him gently. Kelsey moved in for her share and Mickey hugged her also.

"I'm glad you're back, sweetheart," she said softly.

At that moment Mickey's stomach growled loudly. "I'm starved, kids," she said, giving the animals a final pat. "I'm going hurry up and eat so I can go down to the barn. I hope everybody still remembers me. I feel like I've been gone for months."

Just when she was ready to get out of bed, Mickey heard a knock at her door. Christopher peeked in and, seeing she was awake, said, "Stay put." Then he disappeared.

Mickey looked puzzled but followed his instructions. He returned a few minutes later with a tray containing an enormous breakfast. Poncho trotted in at his side, looking none the worse from his recent surgery. Mickey caught her breath for a moment, then giggled.

"Boy, if I eat like this every day, I'm going to weigh a million pounds. And I can't even exercise until this cast comes off." She reached for the tray. "But hey, right now, I don't care. I'm totally starving."

Christopher looked sheepish. "You looked peaked after that hospital food. I figured you'd be hungry for some home cooking."

Mickey looked at the meal before her. A large dinner plate with pancakes, sausage, and eggs sat on the tray. A dessert plate contained two blueberry muffins with a couple pats of butter. A large glass of orange juice completed the meal.

"Aren't you having any?" she asked, noticing there was only one tray.

Christopher ran a hand through his hair, looking ashamed. "I'm sorry, Mick but everything smelled so good I just couldn't wait. I ate mine already. I mean, it *is* mid-morning you know."

"Oh, Chris! I really didn't mean to sleep right through. No wonder you went ahead." She picked up her fork. "And I can't wait anymore either. I'm going to say the blessing and then devour all this deliciousness!"

Mickey looked at him happily. She could smell the spicy pine scent of his aftershave. His brown eyes were alight with fun and amusement and the burgundy and green sweater he wore brought out their warmth.

His strong gentle hands balanced the tray on her lap, and he smiled again. "Madam, I'll leave you to feast in peace. I'm going to go clean up in the barn."

After finishing the sumptuous brunch, Mickey got up clumsily and washed herself as best she could. Putting on clothing proved an unexpectedly difficult chore. She began to wish she had Christopher asked for help but could not quite handle the thought of his being close enough to help her dress.

After struggling with pants, she finally decided the easier route would be to just wear a skirt. Even her sweats would not pull on easily over the bulky cast. She donned a navy turtleneck, a navy and plum colored wool cardigan, and her denim skirt.

She managed to get a sock on the foot of her good leg but after several tries, gave up entirely on the other. *Guess you toes will just have to be cold 'til I can get Chris to help,* she thought. *I absolutely cannot reach you.*

Mickey grabbed the crutches, put her phone in her sweater pocket, and headed downstairs. After putting on her jacket, she stuffed the sock into her pocket. Slowly she made her way out of the house and down the path to the barn. When she walked through the door, Christopher dropped the manure fork and rushed out of the stall.

"Mickey Sterling what's going on?" he demanded. "What are you doing out of bed and how did you get down here?"

"Oh, for Pete's sake, Chris, I'm not incapacitated," she retorted. "I got here on my own one foot. I've only got a slight fracture in this leg, and nothing could possibly happen while it's in this monstrosity." She tapped the case with her finger.

Her blue eyes darkened and her chin raised slightly. "I do *not* want to be treated like an invalid, Chris. I want to be outdoors. You know how much I love fall weather."

Christopher stood before her, his hands on his hips, wanting to give her a lecture. But when he thought about what she said, he realized she was right. *Besides, being outdoors is probably the best thing for her*, he thought.

"Okay, Mickey. Sorry, I just want to take care of you. I'm afraid you'll try to do things you shouldn't just because you're afraid to ask me for help.

Mickey's annoyed look evaporated. "I know. I promise, if I need help, I'll ask. In fact, I could use some assistance in one small area."

She extended her bare toes out and wiggled them. "These guys are going to get cold. In fact, they're already freezing. I can't reach down that far without bending my leg. The poor little guys really need a sock."

Christopher grinned and took the sock she held out to him. He knelt and drew the sock onto her foot, resisting the urge to tickle the digits. "There now," he said with satisfaction. "That'll keep 'em nice and warm."
The denim jacket he wore made his shoulders look even broader than usual. The sight of this gentle man kneeling on the barn floor to help her made Mickey's throat tighten. She swallowed hard and deliberately changed her train of thought.

"Thank you, my valet," she said with a haughty air. "Now back to your stall."

Christopher groaned. "I may live to regret this," he said while he went back to his work. But his look told her he would enjoy every chance to assist her.

Mickey's lips curved into a happy smile while she made her way to the pasture for a visit with Fili, Kili, and Gimli. The horses lifted their heads when she came through the gate. All at once they broke into a brisk trot, then began to gallop, tossing their heads and arching their tails. Her smile widened while she watched them approach, her heart full of their beauty and majestic power.

The horses crowded around her, eagerly nosing her pockets for treats. Thankfully she thought ahead and chopped up some carrot pieces before leaving the house. She doled them out with much love and affection. Mickey spent several minutes with each animal talking, scratching favorite places, and just letting them know she cared.

Fili, Kili, and Gimli remained by the gate when she slowly began to make her way back to the house. Finally, Fili let out a shrill piercing whinny. Mickey looked back and laughed. They were all looking at her, heads held high, ears pricked sharply forward.

"Don't worry, now. I'm not leaving for good," she said. "I just need to rest. I'll bring some more treats later."

The horses stood at the gate for a few moments more, then as if on cue they all turned and ambled back out into the tall grass. After wandering around for a few minutes taking bites here and there, they settled down for some serious grazing. Mickey shook her head and smiled. She went to stretch out in one of the Adirondack chairs in the back yard so she could rest and enjoy the outdoors at the same time.

~ * ~

The days of Mickey's recovery were spent in relative ease. She helped with some of the barn chores and even once thought of trying to ride. Christopher firmly told her he would not hear of her riding in her cast again. By the time the month was up, Mickey was exceedingly tired of being limited by her injury.

Mickey felt free at last on October first when they drove to the clinic in Aspen Ridge for removal of the cast. Though several days passed before her leg regained full range of movement, she was overjoyed to be back to normal.

Mickey enjoyed working with Christopher around the ranch again and they quickly settled comfortably into a nice routine. They took several long rides, exploring other parts of the ranch while enjoying their easy and friendly relationship.

We're doing all right, thought Christopher proudly one afternoon while he carefully attached his camera to the tripod positioned in front of the barn.

His new assignment came from Rancher's Life magazine and would feature a photography spread of the different structures of area barns. The project departed from his usual wildlife subjects, but he welcomed the challenge and the opportunity to expand his portfolio. The tight deadline proved to be the project's only drawback.

Self-control with Mickey isn't such a problem anymore, he thought while he peered through the view finder seeking the best angle for the shot. *I'm doing all right. I guess this arrangement won't be so bad after all.*
As Christopher's barn shoots continued, the project became increasingly exhausting. He rose very early most mornings to get to his shooting locations. Often, he stayed overnight in a neighboring town to be on location when the best light for his shot occurred.

By the time he time returned home, Christopher barely paused for a meal before going to the office to start processing pictures. After hours at the computer, he fell into bed and slept as soon as his head hit the pillow. Mickey missed their usual time of scripture reading and prayer after supper but did not feel she should say anything when he was working so hard.

Several times Christopher looked at his Bible on the bedside stand but felt he could not comprehend anything even if he did read. He tried to pray when he crawled into bed but was asleep before he got past, "Dear Father". After a few days, he gave up entirely, vowing to resume his personal time with God when the work was finished.

~ *Twenty-Four* ~

When Mickey entered the kitchen to prepare breakfast the morning of October fifteenth, she stopped short and then began to laugh. Balloons filled the room and a large colorful bouquet of roses and carnations, her favorite flowers, sat on the table. A large banner read *HAPPY BIRTHDAY, MICKEY STERLING.*

He must have gotten up in the middle of the night and done all this. Mickey shook her head. *What a sweetheart. I love a big deal on my birthday even if it does mean I'm a year older.* She got out the eggs and bacon with a happy smile.

When Christopher sauntered into the room fifteen minutes later, he stopped and stared at her intently. For a few moments she ignored him, then whirled around with her hands on her hips, her curls flying. "What?" she asked, in mock exasperation.

"Turn around, would you? I need a three-sixty." "Chris, you are nuts," she said, while obliging his request.

When she turned back to face him he looked very smug. "Nope, can't even tell," he said with satisfaction. "I would never guess you're thirty today."

He became playfully stern. "Maybe I need to have a look at your birth certificate. I'm having a really hard time believing that you're really thirty. Are you telling me the truth? I think you're just turning twenty-one and somebody's going to show up here any day now and beat me up for robbing the cradle."

Mickey laughed happily, enjoying his complimentary teasing. Turning the big three-o bothered her more than she cared to admit but his banter made her see how little one's age mattered.

"No, I'm telling the truth," she said with a laugh. "But," her voice lowered to a whisper. "I have a secret. The arsenal of skin care products in my bathroom is key. But don't tell anybody, okay?"

Christopher laughed and shook his head. He sat down at the table and said, "Don't plan anything for supper tonight because we're going out."

"Oh really?" Mickey chuckled knowingly and waved a wooden spoon at him. "Isn't that convenient? Tonight was finally your turn to cook again since you've been gone so much, remember?"

"Seriously?" he asked. A frown furrowed his brow. "Hmmm. What do you know about that? I must have forgotten." The mischievous look in his brown eyes and the crinkles at the corners gave him away.

"Right." Mickey put plates and silverware on the table and went back to the stove. "And I totally believe you. Um hm. Sure do."

She retrieved the skillet and returned to the table. "No matter. We haven't been out in a long time." She placed a steaming hot omelet on each plate.

Mickey went to the cupboard for a glass and a mug. "So where are we going?" she asked while she poured orange juice for herself and coffee for Christopher.

"That, my dear, is a secret," Christopher said, his eyes twinkling. Then he put on his best gangster voice. "But you do need to dress up. I'm takin' you to a classy joint, doll. We're celebratin' your birthday with style."

Mickey laughed at his foolishness and brought a basket of apple cinnamon muffins to the table.

"But seriously, this is for your birthday and to celebrate that I finally finished that barn project."

Mickey smiled in understanding. "I know you're glad those shoots are done. That was one of the most time-consuming projects you've had lately. Took a long time to finish, didn't it?"

"Oh yeah. I'm just ready to kick back and relax for a while. Tonight will be fun."

"I can't wait," she said in happy anticipation.

~ * ~

That evening while she got ready, Mickey felt as nervous as a girl going on her first date.

I don't believe this, she thought while she freshened her make up. *It's not like I have anything to prove. What do I care?*

She moved to put on her favorite little black dress, then looked at herself critically in the full-length mirror. She smiled while she looked at the dress. Worn only once to a formal Christmas party at her former employer's town-house, the dress still looked amazing.

After a few minutes of reminiscing, Mickey ran her fingers through her curls to fluff them a bit and turned to her jewelry box. Christopher's face kept coming to her mind and her heart began to pound. Her shaking fingers did not help when she tried to fasten the clasp of her chunky silver link chain.

She squeezed her trembling hands together. *I have to be sure everything is just right. I have to be perfect. I know it'll be important to him since we're going out. He'll be embarrassed to be with me if I look dowdy. And then he'll be mad.*

She carefully chose dangly faux diamond earrings set in silver and managed to get them in without punching more holes in her lobes. Honest emotions screamed to be heard in midst of the cacophony of twisted thinking.

But I do care. I really <u>want</u> him to find me attractive, her heart cried. *He will never be an abuser. You know that.*

190

She shook her head in frustration and bit her lip. *No, I won't think that way. Never again. That's what got me into trouble before. I didn't think Lee would be an abuser, either.*

Firmly, she grabbed her purse and headed to the coat closet downstairs.

No way will I do that again, she thought while she shrugged into her black faux mink coat and walked into the kitchen where Christopher waited. *I will not consider loving him. Friendship is safe. Love is just too dangerous.*

~ * ~

Despite her mixed emotions, Mickey enjoyed a wonderful evening. Christopher, every inch the perfect gentleman, treated her like a queen. They went to an elegant restaurant in Great Falls and dined by candlelight on succulent steaks.

Throughout their time together, Christopher was so overwhelmingly drawn to Mickey that he could barely stand the pressure. She looked stunning in her black knee length dress with the scalloped neckline. The style fit her slim form perfectly. The auburn strands in her hair caught the light and glistened brilliantly. Her eyes sparkled with fun and seemed even deeper blue than usual while they laughed and talked.

When they finished their entrees, the waitress returned to the table.

"Would you enjoy dessert?" she asked.

Christopher looked at Mickey, a question in his eyes. "Absolutely," she said, holding out her hand for the dessert menu. "It's cheesecake or die, baby."

Christopher and the waitress chuckled. "I think I'll have something, too. Would you give us a few minutes?" he asked.

"Certainly. Take all the time you need," the waitress said.

After they decided on decadent desserts and placed their orders, Christopher reached to the side and brought out a long box about two inches in depth. Wrapped in gold paper, the box had a single red rose gracing the top.

"This is for you, birthday girl," he said in a low voice.

Mickey took the box gently and looked into his brown eyes, so full of tenderness. Hours seemed to pass before she finally tore her gaze away and gave a nervous giggle.

"Now then, let's see," she said, shaking the box gently. "What could this be?"

"I think you'll be pleased." He smiled. "Go on, open it."

Mickey carefully put the rose to one side and tore open the wrapping. She took the lid off the box and pulled out several sheets of paper rolled together to form a tube. She unrolled them carefully.

"Blueprints," she said, not entirely sure what was going on. "Uh ..."

"They're for renovations of the barn," explained Christopher. "I know how much we both love the look of the outside of that old barn, so I didn't think you'd want to trash the whole thing and build a new one."

He went on and tears began to prick in Mickey's eyes. "With these plans, we can completely modernize the inside and leave the outside the same with just some touch ups here and there and a new roof.

"We'll have everything we talked about, running water, better lighting, an office, a tack and feed room, and those stalls with the iron bars around the top half and the sliding doors. We'll even put Dutch doors on each stall leading to the outside. That way if there's ever a fire, we can get the horses out without going into the structure."

Mickey sniffed and whispered. "I need a tissue." She dug into her purse.

"I take it you approve?"

"I love the plans." She dabbed at her eyes. "This is wonderful. You've thought of everything. You even put in a wash rack. But I thought it would be a long time before we could afford something like this."

"That barn project I just completed may have had a tight deadline, but I got a nice fat check in return. I figured the best way to invest money from a barn project was a barn renovation. I guess this really isn't a birthday present, since it's for both of us but I wanted to surprise you."

Mickey gave a short laugh and reached a hand to push a stray strand of hair from her face. "And you have succeeded! I am completely blown away. This will make caring for the animals so much easier.

Christopher smiled in satisfaction. "The construction guys will start work tomorrow." He moved back slightly so the waitress could place the large slice of peanut butter pie before him. "They wanted to start last week but I couldn't let them because then you'd have known something was up."

The waitress placed a slice of raspberry cheesecake in front of Mickey and told them to enjoy their dessert. Mickey took a small bite and savored the outstanding flavor.

After a bite of pie, Christopher said, "Now, for present number two."

"What?" Mickey said, her eyes opened wide. "You're kidding. There's more?"

"Yep." Christopher looked smug when he beckoned to the waitress who was watching from near the kitchen.

She brought over a large bulky package, which she handed to Mickey with a smile. Mickey eagerly tore off the paper and gasped with delight. Set off perfectly by the frame and matting was her favorite Thomas Kinkade print 'End of a Perfect Day'.

"Oh, Chris, I love this," she said softly, gazing at the beautiful representation of a mountain cabin made of stone sitting beside a small stream. The setting sun cast shades of pink and yellow across the sky and the colors were reflected in the water. Several trees beside the cabin boasted bright red autumn colors. The dimness of the restaurant brought out the trademark light which came from the cabin windows and spilled out onto the porch.

` "Thomas Kinkade was my favorite artist and I've always loved this painting. I can't believe you found one, especially a Renaissance Edition," Mickey said, looking across at Christopher. "I always wished I could just jump into the picture and live there. It's so peaceful. I'm going to hang this over the fireplace." She smiled. "Thank you, Chris. You've made this day worth turning thirty."

Christopher smiled and helped her prop the picture on one of the extra chairs at the table. "Maybe someday we can build a cabin up on our mountain," he said thoughtfully. "There are some boys at the church who I'll bet would love to go for camping and fishing trips."

"What a great idea! We should absolutely do that. I'll bet some boys of the grown-up variety would enjoy that also," Mickey said teasingly.

"You know, Mick," Christopher said, changing the subject. "I've been thinking of inviting Kirsten, John, and the kids for Thanksgiving. They really enjoy the country especially up this way. And I haven't seen them in ages. I probably won't even recognize Lisa and Jeff."

"I hope they can come. I would love to meet them."

"That's right. I forgot. You've never met them."

"I'd really like to get to know my new family, since I don't have any siblings of my own. Plus," a teasing look entered

Mickey's eyes. "I to thank your sister in person for raising such a gentleman."

"Aw, c'mon," Christopher said with a lopsided grin. He picked up his fork and lowered his gaze, unable to look into her mesmerizing blue eyes any longer.

Desperately trying to keep his thoughts under control he said, "I'll call Kirsten tomorrow."

Mickey continued to eat her cheesecake. *What a wonderful man,* she thought while she looked at his strong handsome face. She took another forkful and chewed thoughtfully. *And he's nothing like Lee. You know that.* Her true emotions and her heart again demanded to be heard. *He would never do anything to hurt you.*

No. I will not think that way, she told herself firmly. *I will not risk that kind of pain again. I learned my lesson and learned it good. I didn't think Lee would be abusive but boy was I wrong. Once the 'thrill of the chase' was over, the abuse began. If I return Christopher's love, it will just be history repeating itself. Remember the old saying 'those who don't learn from history are doomed to repeat it'.*

After they walked back to the Jeep and Christopher carefully put her gifts in the back, Mickey took his hand. He nearly jumped back. Her touch sent a shock clear through him.

"Thank you for the wonderful birthday, Chris," she said softly, knowing he put much thought and care into her day. "You've made everything so special, and I'll never forget it."

Christopher's emotions were running wild, and he felt he could barely contain them. "You're welcome," he choked out in low voice. Mickey noticed his odd tone and suddenly felt a chill come over her.

They climbed into the Jeep and after starting the engine, Christopher turned on the heat to ward off the chill of the October night.

I can't talk to her anymore, he thought with agony. *It's just too painful. I've got to focus on the last surprise. That will help get my thoughts off Mickey for a while.* He plugged in the iPod and tapped his favorite oldies playlist for the drive home.

~ * ~

When they pulled into the driveway at nearly 11:15 pm, Mickey was dozing. She slowly opened her eyes when they approached the house. "What on earth is that?" she said, coming fully awake with a start. "That looks like a semi in our driveway."

Christopher said nothing but smiled slightly.

"Looks like it says ATM on the side," Mickey said. "There's a picture of a fish so I guess it's not related to a bank ATM. I wonder if somebody's in trouble."

Concern filling her eyes. "I mean, why would they pull in here unless something was wrong?"

They exited the Jeep and Christopher steered her toward the front door. "But Chris, we need to see what's up with that truck."

"We will in just a minute, but we need to go inside first."

Mickey felt just a bit put out. *What if someone needs help? Why is he insisting that we go inside? And why aren't we going in the back?*

Christopher opened the door and before she entered, he said, "Please close your eyes."

Mickey still felt exasperated with him but honored his request. He led her inside, closed the door behind her, and positioned her facing the living room.

"Okay, Mick, you can open your eyes now."

196

Mickey's eyes flew open, and she stood stock still in amazement when Christopher and several men she didn't know shouted, "Surprise!"

Before her was a huge aquarium mounted on an elegant mahogany wood stand with a matching canopy. Live rock atop a two-inch sand bed was arranged in a beautiful design, leaving holes and crevices for fish to swim through.

"There's nothing in there but rock right now but I know you know all about tank cycling," Christopher said with a smile.

"Oh sure," Mickey said, tears beginning to run down her cheeks. "I can't believe this! Do you have any idea how long I've wanted a set up like this where I can have marine fish and corals? Oh, my word. I don't believe it! My own little slice of God's amazing underwater creation right here in my living room." She reached for a tissue from the end table.

One of the men stepped forward. "I'm Brent. Let me show you all the workings," he said with a smile.

He proceeded to open the stand which revealed a large sump set up with chambers containing a protein skimmer, a heater, more live rock for filtering, and a refugium. He showed them all the plumbing hook ups and gave them the paperwork for all the tanks components.

He shook hands with Chris. "All right, man, we're going to head out. We hope you enjoy your tank, ma'am." He shook hands with Mickey also.

Christopher walked the men to their truck and thanked them again for their quick work in setting up the tank while he and Mickey were away.

"Thanks again, guys. I seriously had doubts that we could pull off this surprise. But you did it and the tank is gorgeous. We're both going to enjoy that aquarium for years to come."

"Everything went off without a hitch on our end," said Brent and he shook Christopher's hand once more. "Call us if you have any questions or problems." He and his crew climbed into the cab and Christopher waved while they headed down the driveway.

Christopher returned to find a pair of high heels scattered on the living room floor, a coat tossed carelessly on the couch, and his wife on her knees in front of the tank peering through a magnifying glass. He laughed out loud.

"You didn't waste any time, did you? You didn't even change clothes. See anything?"

"Not yet. I'll have to look with a flashlight after the room has been dark for a while. I'll bet that rock is teeming with life that we won't see during the day."

She placed the magnifying glass on a shelf inside the stand and rose. "Chris, I am like ... I'm in total and complete shock over this. I..." her words trailed off and she looked at him helplessly. "I don't even know what to say other than thank you. This is so over the top! Way beyond anything I ever dreamed would actually be mine."

Christopher smiled. "You're worth it, Mick." Now that the excitement died down, his thoughts and feelings of earlier rushed back with a vengeance.

"I'm really beat, Mick. This has been a great day but I'm going to bed. Happy Birthday."

"Thank you," she called at his retreating back. Mickey stood in the middle of the living room feeling puzzled. The chill that came over her heart when they left the restaurant returned once more. He seemed to enjoy her company and clearly enjoyed his birthday surprises but now he could not get away fast enough.

Confused, unsure, and suddenly afraid, she took her coat from the couch and hung the garment in the closet. She grabbed her shoes and went to her bedroom, deciding to read a bit to wind down before bed.

Broken Promise

I guess it's all for the best, she thought. *I don't love him anyway and I never should have taken his hand earlier. This just proves my point. Besides, he may care enough about me to get me amazing birthday gifts but apparently, he's not attracted to me anymore. It's much better this way.* But the sadness persisted and would not be dissuaded.

~ * ~

Christopher sat in his recliner with his feet propped up on the bed. His thoughts whirled like a wild kaleidoscope though his mind.

After all, she is my wife. I have the legal right before God and man to love her. The Bible even says 'husbands love your wives'. I have tried to honor her and love her without demands. I've controlled my feelings but after all, I'm only human.

He grew more and more agitated, clenching and unclenching his fists. *I'm certainly within my rights to at least tell her I love her. She had no business making me promise not to. After all, I'm not a bad person. Why should I have to suffer like this?*

His jaw clenched. He leaped from the chair and strode purposefully across the room, his face flushed. *How much does she think a man can take? I'm not made of stone after all.*

His hand was on the knob, ready to jerk the door open, when a verse flooded through his thoughts. *Love is patient and kind.* He turned the knob. *Love is not jealous or boastful or proud or rude. It does not demand its own way.*

A cold sweat broke out on his forehead when he recalled the rest of the passage from First Corinthians thirteen. *(Love) is not irritable, and it keeps no record of being wronged. It does not rejoice about injustice but rejoices whenever the truth wins out. Love never gives up, never*

199

loses faith, is always hopeful, and endures through every circumstance.

Slowly, he went back to the chair and collapsed into the soft depths. He stared at the painting Mickey gave him and remembered again, the love Hosea had for his wayward bride. He put his hand to his forehead, in a state of shock at the road his thoughts were him driving down. Tears welled up in his eyes.

Marriage is supposed to be a picture of Christ and the Church, he thought miserably. *My Heavenly Father never forces me to love Him. How could I have even entertained the thought of breaking my promise? She would never trust me again. I could have lost her forever and frightened her to the core, just because I put my needs before hers.*

Christopher's eyes filled with tears, and he put his head in his hands. "Dear Lord, forgive me. Oh please, forgive me," he prayed. "Help me to have patience and give me victory over selfishness. Help me to be a servant." He gripped the arm of the chair. "Please help me, Lord," he continued. "Help me to come directly to You whenever I face these feelings."

He grimaced when he remembered his self-reliant thoughts of the weeks before. "I was so proud of how well I was handling things. I was forgetting to go to You for strength, Lord," he prayed. "I was trying to do it on my own. And I haven't been spending time in Your word and praying like I should. Please Lord, forgive my pride and arrogance."

Painfully he remembered his obsession with work during the barn project and how he ignored what should have been his most important priority, his personal relationship with his Lord.

He straightened and looked heavenward. "Help me to stay close to You, Father God. Help me to love Mickey the way I should, with kindness, patience, and gentleness. And I pray that someday, despite my weaknesses, she'll love me, too."

As Christopher sat quietly, peace filled him. "Thank you, Lord," he whispered. "Thank You for loving me even when I fail. Thank You for forgiving me." Feeling drained but with a quiet settled soul, he crawled into bed.

~ *Twenty-Five* ~

A week later, Mickey had just finished kneading the dough for a new bread recipe when she heard a knock on the front door. Kip and Poncho both let out a bark and trotted to the front door, sniffing intently. Kelsey joined them and they all sat in the entry way looking back at her questioningly.

Mickey laughed. "Thank you, kids. Yes, I heard the knock."

Quickly she rinsed off her flour covered hands. When she opened the door, she grinned. "Lorrie!" she exclaimed happily. "And Zoe!"

"Oh, Mickey, I'm so sorry," Lorrie said, struggling through the door with the baby and a bulky diaper bag. "I realized the other day I never came over to see you. With the baby and all, it's been just, well..." she faltered uncertainly.

"No worries, Lorrie," Mickey said with a smile while she put the bag on the counter. "I can only imagine the adjustments of having a new baby in the house."

Kip wined impatiently and Mickey laughed while she reached down to pat him. Poncho stood on his hind legs against Lorrie's leg, his tail wagging madly and his face filled with eagerness to make a new friend.

"This is Kip, that's Kelsey, and Poncho is the one trying to climb your leg." She fondly patted Kelsey's head. "We rescued Kelsey and Poncho from an abusive owner this summer. You'll probably meet my cat Snippit later. She has favorite nap spots in every room of the house."

Lorrie reached to pat the Chihuahua's head and he squirmed with delight. She moved to pat Kip, who accepted the affection graciously and then offered her a paw. "You've trained him well," she said. "What nice manners!"

Mickey smiled and looked down at the dog with love and pride. "I've had him since he was eight weeks old. He's a good friend. Chris really loves him, too."

Zoe's face puckered up and she began to fuss. "Mickey, I need to put her down for a nap," Lorrie said. "She's just tired. Is there somewhere she can sleep?"

"Sure, come on up to my bedroom. She can rest on my bed. We'll surround her with pillows, so she won't roll off."

Mickey failed to notice the puzzled look on Lorrie's face when she said, my bedroom. They made the baby comfortable and after a few cries and sobs at being left alone, Zoe fell asleep. Taking a baby monitor so they could hear if she woke up, they headed downstairs.

"I've been so anxious to see your horses," Lorrie said when they reentered the kitchen. "I haven't done much riding, but I really love horses."

"Don't get me started," Mickey said with a wry chuckle. "I'll talk your ear off when it comes to horses. Let's go out to the pasture and I'll introduce you. Oh, wait." She looked toward the mixing bowl. "Let me get this into loaf pans so it can be rising."

Mickey divided the dough, then covered the three pans with a damp towel. She rinsed her hands again and grabbed her barn coat.

As she and Lorrie walked down the path, Mickey whistled sharply. A few seconds later an answering whinny was heard along with the sound of hoof beats. By the time the women reached the gate to the North pasture, the horses were standing there looking alert and ready for action.

Mickey laughed when they approached. "They know I always have a treat for them. Here, Lorrie," she said, handing her several lumps of sugar. "This is the best way to introduce yourself."

Lorrie extended her hand to Fili who gently lipped up the sugar. Kili impatiently pushed Fili's nose away in search of his share. Lorrie laughed delightedly and quickly offered him a treat. He grabbed the sugar and chewed vigorously. Mickey took care of Gimli so there would be no jealously.

They stayed a few moments longer, petting the animals and scratching them behind the ears. While they turned to walk back to the house, Lorrie said, "Your horses are gorgeous, Mickey. Did you raise and train them?"

"Fili and Kili I did," she said, patting Fili fondly. "Gimli belongs to Jennifer Austin from church." She reached to scratch behind Kili's ears. "I've always loved Friesian horses but never thought I'd be able to own one because they're so expensive.

"But one day I heard about a Friesian rescue out of Arizona. They had just taken in two Friesian crosses who needed a home. I could handle the adoption fee and as you can imagine, I jumped on that immediately. The real miracle was that I was chosen to adopt them. I know there were a lot of people who submitted applications."

They turned to walk back to the house and Mickey continued. "I truly believe God meant for me to have these two horses. They've really met a need in my life."

She laughed. "I love Friesians so much. I've even thought about trying to raise and train them but there is a lot I don't know about showing and breeding. We'll see. I know that the Lord will direct. We have all this wonderful space. I'd love to see it filled with horses!"

Lorrie looked at her with a twinkle in her eye. "I can see it now. Mickey riding into the sunset aboard a powerful wild stallion who will allow her, and her alone, to ride him."

Mickey laughed. "Okay, okay, I admit it. Ever since I read The Black Stallion books when I was a kid, I was hooked on horses."

"Have you ever done a painting of them?" asked Lorrie while they strolled around the back yard. "I've done one of them in the pasture, but I just couldn't seem to get close ups right," Mickey said. "I mostly stick to scenery and landscapes."

"I'd love to watch you work sometime," Lorrie said with a smile. "I think watching a picture develop from a blank canvas is absolutely fascinating."

"Lorrie my dear, you're in luck," Mickey said with a laugh. "Believe it or not, I was planning to begin something new today. I want to paint the view from here to give Chris for Christmas. Just let me run in and get my supplies."

"Fantastic. I'll come with you and check on Zoe." Mickey went down to her studio to gather her painting supplies while Lorrie checked on the baby. Zoe slept peacefully, safely ensconced on her pillow surrounded bed. Easel, palette, paints, brushes, and rags in hand, Mickey and Lorrie returned to the back yard.

Mickey walked slowly around the yard seeking the best angle. Finally settling on the shady right corner, Mickey put the blank canvas on the easel. Lorrie grabbed two chairs from the back deck, and they made themselves comfortable.

"I may not last long today," Mickey said ruefully. "This air is pretty cold, and my hands get stiff. But I need to get started, so here goes."

Mickey was lost to the world when she began to paint the beautiful scenery. A slight breeze blew, rustling the remaining leaves on the trees. She paused every now and then to reach her free hand to push the dark curls back behind her ears, while looking critically at the view before her.

"This is so incredible," whispered Lorrie after a good fifteen minutes had passed, and the picture was beginning to take shape.

"I really love painting," Mickey said. Then her voice unexpectedly took on a sadder note. "It's therapeutic."

"And do you need therapy, Mickey?" asked Lorrie gently. The kindness and caring in her voice took away any sting the words might have had.

Mickey put her brush down for a moment. "I'm sorry, I didn't mean to be negative. There have been some things on my mind lately that I really didn't want to be there. Painting helps me to relax and forget for a while."

Lorrie looked out at the mountains towering tall against the deep blue sky. She sensed that her friend did not want to go into detail, though she had a feeling those things she had on her mind needed talking out. After a moment, she turned.

"Mickey, if you ever need someone to talk to, I'm available. I know we've only been acquainted for a short time, but I feel like I've known you all my life. Please feel free to share if you feel comfortable to do so."

Mickey looked at her for a moment, then sighed deeply. "I guess I should tell you one thing. My marriage is not a traditional one. I'm not in love with Chris, even though I do care for him. He is a very dear friend. I had nowhere else to turn and thankfully the Lord brought him along at just the right time. He proposed a business partnership type of marriage and I agreed." She held her breath, waiting for the horrified response.

"I had a feeling," Lorrie said calmly.

Mickey looked at her in surprise. There was no condemnation in her voice, no unkindness. She heard only gentle acceptance and understanding. Mickey suddenly felt free to share her heart.

"I absolutely felt peace about the marriage. What I don't understand is, sometimes I almost feel the way I imagine someone in love would fee. But it's only momentary. I guess that would just be physical attraction or something. Sometimes I've really wished I *could* be in love with him, but I won't ask for that again. I learned my lesson a long time ago and believe me, that's one mistake I'll never ever make again."

Close to tears, Mickey picked up her paintbrush once more. "Besides, I don't know if Christopher even feels the same way about me anymore. Sometimes I think he really does enjoy just being friends."

Mickey painted quietly for a few moments. "I'm really thankful Chris is such a good man." Mickey carefully blended one small area on the canvas that didn't look right. "I think he struggles with anger, though. I've seen his jaw really clench a couple of times. But I have to give him credit, he does control himself pretty well."

Her face clouded. "I knew someone once who just flew off the handle every time he got upset or things went wrong. He always blamed m..." She paused. "He always blamed others and didn't hesitate to tell them so. And he made sure everyone within a ten-mile radius heard, too. And of course, he was never wrong about anything."

Lorrie turned and looked at her searchingly. Mickey's blue eyes were welling up with tears. She reached for a clean paint rag and dabbed at them roughly with frustration. Changing brushes, Mickey paused for a moment to steady her shaking hand. She looked out at the landscape while she struggled to get her emotions under control.

With a sigh, her eyes dropped back to the canvas, and she began to paint in some small wispy trees with careful light strokes. Then she painted in the yellow leaves, most of which surrounded the tree's bases, looking like pools of gold.

Lorrie watched her friend paint but prayed inwardly.

Oh Lord, that poor girl is hurting. Someone has put a terrible wound in her heart that certainly hasn't healed. She'll never be able to feel safe to love Chris unless she allows You to help her. Open her eyes to Your love, Lord. Help her to come to You for healing.

Before Lorrie and Zoe left later that afternoon, Mickey invited Lorrie to come again when she could ride. Promising to come when she could get a sitter for Zoe, Lorrie drove home praying that her friend would know peace and complete healing.

~ *Twenty-Six* ~

Christopher drove up with a screech of tires and raced into the house.

"Mickey, guess what?" he shouted, throwing his keys on the counter. "Wildlife Unlimited's® top underwater photographer offered to let me go to the coast with him for a week. He's going to teach me all about underwater shooting. They're also doing a film documentary the magazine wants to run on Nat Geo Wild©."

He ran one hand through his hair. "I never thought I'd get the chance to shoot sea life. This is such an amazing opportunity!"

He took off his jacket and hung the garment in the small coat closet in the entry way, then walked over and sat down at the table. "I can't believe I'll get to learn from Wes Graham," he said, his face animated. "He's only one of the best underwater photographers in the U.S.!"

Mickey sat across from him. "Chris! Wow! Oh, my word I am so envious," she said, excited for him. "That is going to be incredible. I can't wait to see the pictures."

She smiled and shook her head. "I would love to scuba dive, but I get frantic underwater. Just can't handle that. I feel like I can't get enough air." She toyed with a napkin left on the table. "At least I'll have my own private mini reef up and running soon and that will not require scuba gear. Have I mentioned how much I love it?" she asked.

"Only every day and sometimes twice," he said with a grin. "How's the cycling going?"

"The ammonia levels are starting to come down. I'd say another month to six weeks, and I can start adding critters." She grinned. "What will be hard is not getting too many too fast. But I know better. I'll have to pace myself because I surely do not want to ruin things."

"I'm afraid I'm no help with aquariums," Christopher said with a sigh. "I'm glad you know what you're doing. I can't wait to see how it turns out."

Mickey's thoughts turned practical. "So, when do you leave for your trip?"

He eyed her cautiously. "I'll have to fly out tomorrow morning from Great Falls International."

Mickey leaped from the chair. "Tomorrow! Oh, my word. Lot of advanced notice, huh?" She paced the floor, biting her lower lip until she calmed a bit.

"You better get packed." She opened the refrigerator. "I'll get some food ready, so you'll have a snack on the way."

"Sounds good," Christopher said with a grin. He headed for the stairs. "I'll get my gear and some clothes."

"Christopher Gordon, now don't you forget your toothbrush, young man," Mickey said sternly, doing her best mother imitation.

"Awww, Mom," he groaned in a whining little boy voice.

Mickey grinned and waved him away while she began taking out sandwich materials. By the time she finished, she looked at the pile of turkey and cheese sandwiches, corn chips, bottled water, and double chocolate turtle brownies.

There's enough here for an army, she thought with a giggle. *Oh well, at least he won't starve. I just hope it will all fit in his carry on.*

~ * ~

They were up before dawn the next morning. To-gether they carefully loaded Christopher's duffel and car-ryon equipment bags into the back of the Jeep. Kip, Kelsey, and Poncho looked concerned and followed them outside to sit beside the Jeep.

After one more trip to the house to retrieve the fleece lined waterproof coat he forgot, Christopher stood, keys in hand, ready to leave.

"I guess that's everything," he said, mentally making one last check.

He looked at Mickey with a bit of concern. She looked so vulnerable hugging herself against the early morning chill. Her eyes blinked sleepily. She wore a bulky down filled jacket over a rumpled pink sleep shirt and sweats. Her small feet were encased in bright purple fuzzy slippers and her hair made a riot of waves about her shoul-ders. He longed to bury his hands in the beautiful brunette curls.

Christopher noted with pleasure that she seemed to be at ease with him, even before fixing herself up for the day. *Maybe we are making progress*, he thought.

"Are you sure you'll be okay here by yourself?" he asked. "What if it snows or something?"

"Oh, Chris, I'll be fine." She reached up to cover a wide yawn. "I'll probably ask Jen to come over for a while if she's not too busy. She's taking a few days off from school. Don't worry about me. Besides, I have three won-derful watch dogs here."

She patted Kip, Kelsey, and Poncho and their tails slowly began to wave back and forth. Poncho, who hated the cold, put his front legs on her leg and shivered all over.

"Baby boy, you win the blue ribbon for 'Most Pitiful in Show'," Mickey said with a laugh while she scooped him up and tucked him inside her jacket.

Christopher looked unconvinced. "Here are the numbers where you can reach me. There's one for the hotel and one for the marina."

He handed her a small slip of paper. "And you can always call my cell. I probably won't have a signal when we're out on the water but don't hesitate to call or text if you need me okay, Mickey?"

"Right," she said. "You'd better get going or you'll miss your flight."

Wishing he could kiss her good-bye, he gave the dogs a final pat, climbed into the Jeep, and started the engine.

"Bye, Chris." Mickey smiled and yawned. "Have a good time and be safe. Say 'hi' to Southern California for me!"

"Bye now," he called through the window. Under his breath he added, "I love you."

Mickey watched until she could no longer see him, then walked slowly back into the house. She flopped down on the living room couch and curled up. She felt bad all over, like she was coming down with the flu and she bit her lip to keep from bursting into tears. Kip and Kelsey sat looking at her in a puzzled manner and Poncho leaped up into her lap.

"Stop that, girl," she scolded herself aloud. "Get hold of yourself. You've got the whole place to yourself for a week. Good grief, after the way he hovered over you the whole time you were in that cast, you should be glad for a little alone time."

She decided firmly that she would stop moping and enjoy herself. *After all, I can finally get some things done without worrying about him being under foot*, she struggled to convince herself.

She called the dogs to follow her and headed back to her bedroom to catch a few more minutes of sleep. She laughed when she walked through the bedroom door. Snippit, curled up right in Mickey's spot, looked at her with an innocent expression. The cat blinked sleepily and chirped softly.

"You," Mickey said chidingly while she scooped up the cat. "You always move into my spot when I leave, don't you?"

Snippit purred loudly in response. Mickey sat cross legged on the bed holding the cat close for several minutes. Kip and Kelsey leaped onto the bed and curled up together on the other side.

Stifling a yawn, Mickey reset the alarm and crawled back under the covers. Poncho jumped up and curled in a tiny ball snuggled tight in the small of her back, while Snippit curled up on the other side next to her stomach. "I hope I don't have to make any sudden moves here. I'm trapped!" Mickey laughed. The cozy group soon slept peacefully.

~ *Twenty-Seven* ~

Christopher used the time during the drive to Great Falls to pour his heart out the Lord, seeking further direction about Mickey. After his episode of weakness on her birthday, he vowed never again to let his spiritual life slip. He listened to a mix of New Testament passages and his favorite praise songs while he enjoyed the beautiful Montana scenery.

The flight to California proved uneventful and after landing at the John Wayne Airport, he rented a car and made the short drive to his hotel. He checked in and unpacked his gear, then returned to the car, intent on finding the marina at Newport Beach.

He located the marina and the boat he was to sail on without difficulty. After stopping to grab a burger, he returned to his hotel to rest up for the next day.

Morning dawned overcast and misty. He hurriedly packed his duffel bag and headed out to the marina to meet Wes and the rest of the crew.

He pulled his raincoat tightly around him and when he approached the *Lone Star*, he saw a short man in a green rain slicker waving to him.

"Chris, over here," he shouted. His head was covered with what looked like a sea captain's hat and he wore knee high rubber boots. Over his shoulder he carried a large camera bag.

"Hey," Christopher said, reaching to shake Wes Graham's hand while he approached. "I can't tell you how excited I am! Thank you. This is such a great opportunity."

They walked across the dock and boarded the boat. "I've always wanted to try my hand at underwater photography," continued Christopher. "I even got my scuba train-

214

ing but then the Lord took my career in a different direction. I really appreciate your generosity."

"I figured you'd enjoy the chance to photograph some marine life," said Wes with a grin. "It'll be cold out there, but we won't actually be diving today. C'mon and meet the crew."

He introduced Christopher, who was greeted warmly by everyone. "Now, let me show you our gear," said Wes, heading toward the stairs that led to the hold of the boat. "Oh and there are bunks down here where you can leave your personal stuff."

As they reached the opening, a beautiful shapely woman emerged from below. Her wavy blonde hair cascaded around her shoulders, and she smiled wide, revealing white perfect teeth. She eyed Christopher up and down with obvious interest.

"You didn't tell me our guest was so handsome," she murmured seductively. She came to the top step and offered her perfectly manicured hand. "I'm Gillian Fitzgerald."

Christopher's upbringing demanded he always be a gentleman. Though his senses were on alert, he shook her hand firmly. "Nice to meet you, Gillian," he said, keeping his voice carefully neutral. He pulled his hand away quickly.

"Gillian is our marine biologist," Wes said with a knowing look at Gillian as though they were sharing an inside joke. "She's been a tremendous asset to our expeditions."

Gillian smiled smugly. "I just love working around all these hot guys," she said, doing her best breathy Marilyn Monroe impression. She gave Christopher a wink and stayed close to the stairs, forcing him to brush against her when he moved down.

"I can't wait to get to know you better, baby," she murmured, patting his arm.

Whoa, Christopher thought in alarm. *I'm going to have to really watch out for her. Protect me, Lord,* he prayed fervently.

Christopher spent the day refreshing his knowledge of scuba diving and learning about underwater camera gear. The next morning, they took the *Lone Star* out to sea. Temperatures were already in the 80's and climbing and the sun shone brightly.

Gillian clearly dressed for the warmer weather. The revealing hot pink bikini top and frayed short denim shorts showed off her curves and shapely legs to perfection. Christopher was uncomfortably aware of her, and she took every opportunity to sashay into his line of vision or brush up against him.

I wonder if she does any work or if she's just eye candy, he thought sarcastically.

By the time they finally stopped and dropped anchor, Christopher was most relieved to leave the boat. He and the film crew got into their wet suits and scuba gear and one by one splashed overboard into the cold sea water. The water temperature shocked his system at first but after a few moments he caught his breath.

Soon Christopher began to relax and enjoy the experience. The watery underworld made him feel he had traveled to another planet. He was fascinated by the variety of fish, sponges, and plant-like organisms surrounding him. Slowly he swam around, snapping shot after shot.

He looked above him and watched a school of Yellowfin Tuna. Below he spotted a striking Copperband Butterflyfish. Colorful Gobies darted here and there, and he also recognized several varieties of Brittle Stars and Cucumbers.

You are amazing, Lord, he prayed while he viewed yet another magnificent show of God's creation. *I can't even imagine the joy You took in forming all these incredible beings. Thank You, Lord. Thank You for the opportunity to see this with my own eyes.*

By the time they surfaced an hour later, Christopher was hooked.

"Wow!" he exclaimed, while he and the rest of the crew removed their black rubber wet suits and put tee shirts and shorts over their bathing trunks. "I can't wait to get back to my laptop to see these pictures. I've never shot anything like this. Now I can see why my wife wanted a reef tank so badly."

"Yeah, pretty great stuff, especially the first time you see it." Wes seated himself in a deck chair. "But you should really try to get to the Florida coast or down to the Caribbean Islands sometime. That's where the serious coral reefs are. They're amazing."

"If I go there, I'll have to take Mickey. She's not comfortable with the idea of scuba diving but I'll bet she'd be ok with snorkeling. She can't wait to fill her aquarium with corals."

Christopher looked out to sea thoughtfully. *That would make a great anniversary trip, if only ...* He stopped his thoughts in their tracks. *Nope, don't go there man. Don't go there.* He refocused his attention on his host.

Wes put his hands behind his head and leaned back. "We'll go down again in an hour or so. As you know, we're doing a photo and film documentary on Puffers. We got some shots and footage just now we've been trying to get for months. You must have brought us good luck."

He looked at Chris with a friendly smile. "Glad you could come with us. I've been following your work for a long time. You've gotten some amazing stuff. And I know how many hours it can take to get those shots."

Christopher laughed while the captain revved the engine and steered the boat toward another location. "You got that right," he said ruefully. "When I think of the hours I've spent stomach down in the brush, freezing and waiting."

They both laughed with understanding. Christopher stood on the deck and leaned against the rail, enjoying the feel of the wind and sea spray in his face.

Mickey would have loved this, he thought, gazing at the miles of blue gray Pacific as far as the eye could see. *I wonder what she's doing right now. I hope she's okay.*

Gillian chose that moment to saunter over and stand close beside him. "I just love nature," she murmured, taking his arm. "So strong. So wild. It's just so, stimulating." She hugged his arm against her chest and ran her fingertips up and down his biceps.

He instantly stiffened to give no sign of interest, even though fleshly desires surged through him. Like Joseph of old, he knew that flight was the only answer.

"I have to go," he said firmly, pulling his arm free. "Enjoy the ride." He strode swiftly away and went to talk to the captain.

Gillian watched him go with a calculating look. "You won't get away so easily, Mr. Gordon," she whispered softly, her full red lips curving into a smirk. "I always get what I want. And I want *you*."

~ * ~

Each day passed in similar fashion. The weather stayed warm and sunny, and Christopher enjoyed his underwater time immensely. New fish and life forms were spotted each day. His collection of photographs rapidly grew by the thousands.

On the last day, the highlight of the trip occurred. Just when they were about to splash into the ocean, Wes

218

stopped and pointed. "Guys, over there," he whispered excitedly. "Blue Whale!"

Everyone on the boat rushed to the side. The whale swam near and seemed to be checking them out. She slowly made a circle around them as if seeking to determine what strange new sea creature this might be.

"C'mon, we've got to get underwater," Wes said in a low voice. "Bill, get some topside shots, would you?" he asked the captain while he rummaged through his duffel bag for his extra Nikon.

"Will do," Bill replied, grabbing the camera immediately.

The diving crew and Christopher quickly splashed overboard and began shooting still shots and film footage of the magnificent gentle giant.

Gillian had rushed to the side of the boat along with all the others. But once the photographers were underwater, she casually edged toward the stairs to the hold. Once satisfied that everyone's attention was on the whale, she ducked through the door and swiftly made her way to the bunk where Christopher left his things.

"So, you've got a little woman, have you," she said with a sneer while she went through his wallet and found a snapshot of Mickey. "Oh, Christopher, you poor thing. What a little doormat. You need a real woman." She removed the picture, tore it to shreds, and put the pieces in her pocket.

She picked up his phone. "Yes! No unlock code!" she whispered with glee.

She quickly tapped his contacts list. She pulled her own phone from her pocket and tapped in several numbers. She then looked through his email and deleted several unread messages from Mickey that had come in earlier that day. With a wicked self-satisfied grin, she carefully placed each article back exactly as she found them.

Christy R. Diachenko

~ *Twenty-Eight* ~

Mickey carefully planned her time during Christopher's trip, making sure each day would be packed full of activity. The first two nights she went to bed exhausted but awoke unrested in the morning. By the third day, she was miserable.

Even having Jennifer there did not help improve her mood. She appreciated her friend wanting to spend her time off at the ranch, so she tried to be pleasant. Jennifer could tell something was amiss but wisely decided not to press the issue, sensing the time was not right.

Mickey got up early Saturday morning, tired of another night of tossing and turning. Since Jennifer was still asleep, she went down to the living room and sat in the recliner to read her scripture for the day.

She sleepily tapped into YouVersion© on her iPad®, selected her favorite New Living Translation, and went to First John chapter four. Several verses seemed to leap off the page while she read.

Dear friends, since God loved us that much, we surely ought to love each other. No one has ever seen God. But if we love each other, God lives in us, and his love is brought to full expression in us. We know how much God loves us, and we have to put our trust in his love. God is love, and all who live in love live in God, and God lives in them. And as we live in God our love grows more perfect. Then she noticed verse eighteen. *Such love has no fear, because perfect love expels all fear. If we are afraid, it is for fear of punishment, and this shows that we have not fully experienced his perfect love.*

She stared at the aquarium for a moment, then changed to the King James Version to read the same verse.

220

There is no fear in love; but perfect love casteth out fear: because fear hath torment. He that feareth is not made perfect in love.

Again Matthew 7:7 ran through her mind. *Ask and ye shall receive.* And then, *There is no fear in love. Fear hath torment.* Mickey tried to read on but the phrases tumbled over and over in her mind like churning whitewater.

With a frustrated sigh she got up, put the iPad on the end table, and headed for the kitchen. She put some sourdough bread in the toaster and poured herself a glass of juice. When the bread toasted, she spread cherry preserves on top and ate quickly, anxious to get out of the house.

Before going out the door, Mickey started jotting a note to Jennifer, telling her to make herself at home and enjoy whatever she wanted for breakfast. While she wrote, the tip of the pencil broke. She rummaged furiously through a drawer, her frustration at the boiling point. She yanked out a pen and completed her note. After slapping the missive on the table, she stalked out to the barn to feed the horses and begin cleaning stalls.

When the animals finished their morning grain, Mickey headed for Gimli's stall. "I can't believe this," she told the horse. "I miss Chris. I mean, of course he's my friend but I don't *want* to miss him this much."

She put on the horse's halter, latched the buckle, and then gave him a pat on the neck. "We're like brother and sister now, thank goodness. I just don't understand why I feel so badly about him being gone. I mean, he's been away before and it's not like he isn't coming back."

Gimli looked at her with knowing brown eyes and seemed most sympathetic until she moved away from the stall doorway. He tossed his head and shot out the opening.

221

He galloped through the open barn door and into the pasture, kicking his heels up and bucking with abandon.

"Some friend you are," Mickey said sourly. "You'd better be ready to get back here when Jennifer wants to ride."

She let Fili and Kili out, then placed her phone on the speaker dock and tapped 'shuffle' on her worship playlist.

While she walked toward the first stall, she heard the first few notes of one of her favorite songs by Matthew West. Mickey stopped and stood still, staring out the door at the pasture beyond. The first words of "Hello My Name Is" began to pour from the speakers.

The words Mickey heard hundreds of times now completely captured her attention. She leaned on the manure fork while the song played, the lyrics speaking of how regret can continue to harass one's mind and defeat can drag one to the depths of despair.

Mickey's tears began to fall and the cracks in the dam around her soul began to deepen. The chorus spoke of the lies of satan, and she began to sob. But when the next phrases played, revealing the grace, salvation, and freedom available through Christ, the blinders were removed from her eyes. The truth stood starkly before her and could no longer be ignored.

Mickey sank to her knees in the soft shavings on the passageway floor while the emotions came tumbling out, free at last. Tears began to stream down her face in earnest and heart wrenching sobs shook her body when she finally recognized her sin and her unbelief.

"Oh, Lord, I've been deceiving myself. I am not okay. For years I've been holding onto anger and bitterness over what Lee did to me. Regret and defeat have become who I am because I would not turn from those sins.

"Oh, Lord, forgive me. Forgive me for not coming to You for strength. Forgive me for never asking You to heal my heart and soul. But I am asking You now. Please, God, forgive me for not forgiving Lee and please heal my heart. Forgive me for trying to make it on my own. I don't want to continue living like a victim. I want to live a victorious life filled with your peace and joy. I *am* Your child, my dear Lord Jesus Christ, my God and my King!"

She wiped her eyes and fumbled for a tissue to dab at her runny nose.

"Oh, thank You, Lord, thank You," she breathed, and a peace she hadn't felt for many years slowly pervaded her heart and soul. "Oh, dear Father," she cried, smiling through her tears. "Thank You for setting me free from the past. Your word is so true. Fear most definitely has torment."

She hiccupped and sniffed while she tried in vain to find another tissue. Finally, she gave up when tears began anew. "And, Lord, I've been deceiving myself in another area, too. I don't love Chris as just a friend. I'm *in* love with him. I love that man with all my heart."

She put her face in her hands and the brunette curls fell forward while she sobbed. "I never thought this day would come. I never thought my feelings would change. I thought we'd just live out our days comfortably as good friends but now..." Her sobs continued until she felt drained.

She sat back against the wall. The last notes of the song died away and another began. She wiped her eyes and stared at the majestic mountains beyond the pasture. Again, she was smitten.

"Forgive me, Lord, for not surrendering this whole thing to You years ago. Forgive me for not truly trusting

You. I should not have let fear dominate my life. How many years I've wasted being afraid."

She paused thoughtfully. *Lee's abuse colored so many parts of my life.* She remembered the times she feared Christopher would be angry or disapprove of her. *I knew the two men were nothing alike, but I guess I was still trying to measure up to Lee's unreasonable expectations. I figured that, deep down, every man thought and acted like he did.*

Mickey prayed aloud again. "Lord, I thought I put all that behind me, but I was trying to do everything in my own strength. But even so, You were still using Chris to heal little bits of my heart even though I never asked You to make me whole again."

She continued. "I wouldn't ask to love Chris because I was so afraid that if I asked for love, he would turn out like Lee. I see now that when I truly desire to follow Your will, You won't let me go wrong. Help me to always put my trust in you."

Mickey remembered the verses she read earlier and smiled in wonder. She felt the Lord's amazing love and grace encircle her heart and soul like a warm blanket, healing the wounds and softening the scars. She felt completely safe and secure for the first time in her adult life.

Jennifer had entered the barn but remained quiet, seeing her friend needed this talk with her Lord. Now she approached and softly put her hand on Mickey's shoulder. "Is everything all right?" she asked gently.

"Oh, Jen, yes!" Mickey exclaimed, her blue eyes softening in amazement. "This is the first time in years I've really had complete peace."

She rose and brushed the shaving from her jeans. They went to sit in the barn's office and Mickey related her experience with Lee and how her life had been overshadowed by the abuse ever since.

"I didn't realize until today just how much that experience still affected me," Mickey said. "That was my fault." She looked at Jennifer pointedly. "Totally my fault. If I had confessed my bitterness and anger, been willing to forgive Lee, and asked for healing, Christopher and I might have been together a long time ago."

"So, you do love him then?" Jennifer asked, grinning widely, already knowing the answer.

Mickey giggled. "Oh yes, ma'am, I do! It's funny because now I feel like I've always loved him."

She leaned back in the desk chair, looking at her painting of the horses grazing in the north pasture. "I've always wondered why I didn't feel anything for him. I mean, we got on so well from the very first day we met in college.

"Of course, at that time, I guess I was still looking for the perfect man. You know, 'chemistry and fireworks'. I really didn't have romantic feelings toward Chris then. He was attracted to me, but I just couldn't return those feelings. He was like a pal. A brother."

Jennifer nodded. "I know how that feels."

"After the Lee thing, I was just plain afraid to ask the Lord for love again," continued Mickey. "I was sure if I did, I'd end up with another abuser."

Tears began to well up in her eyes once more. "How I must have grieved the Lord, a loving Heavenly Father, who wanted only the best for me. And I was so afraid He would give me someone hurtful. What caring dad would do that? I mean, I never knew my father, he died before I was born. But from what my mom told me about him, I know he loved me and would never have done anything to hurt me. Why would I think God would?"

Jennifer reached over and grasped her hand. "The Lord loves us unconditionally despite our fears and shortcomings. That truth is so wonderful. He is such an amazing God. He will never fail us like people do. He is always there to hold us up if we'll just depend on Him." Mickey smiled and nodded. She sat in silence for a moment, over- come with love for her Lord. She felt sad realizing how much precious time her fear and lack of trust cost her in fellowship with God and with Christopher.

The women rose and Mickey hugged Jennifer tightly. "Thanks for being here, Jen," she said with feeling. "I'm so thankful God allowed you to be here. I needed a friend to share all this with. I'm sorry I've been such a bear these last few days."

"I knew something was wrong, but I didn't want to pry." Jennifer smiled. "I'm glad I could be here. And I'm so glad the Lord brought you to live here. I haven't had a friend I could really talk to for a long time. Most of the folks at college don't have a personal relationship with Je- sus, so we don't have much in common regarding things that really matter. I just hope I don't have to leave right after I graduate."

Mickey reached a hand to push a curl back from her face. "Jen, why would you have to leave? I know you love this area. Couldn't you and Robert work here?"

Jennifer's face fell and she twisted her hands to- gether. "Robert really wants to get married before he goes to Harvard. And once he's gotten his degree, he won't want to waste his time in a small town like Aspen Ridge. He'll probably set up his practice somewhere on the East Coast in a large city."

Mickey felt alarmed for her friend. Jennifer's spirit would slowly die being cooped up in a city away from the animals and the outdoors she loved.

"I'll be praying for you, Jen," she said. "I know you want to do the right thing about Robert. Just be open to whatever the Lord brings."

"Speaking of doing things, what are you going to do about Chris?" asked Jennifer while she grabbed and extra manure fork.

They each entered a stall and began to toss waste into the wheelbarrow. "I'm not sure," Mickey said thoughtfully. "I can't wait for him to come home tomorrow but I'm not exactly sure what to do or say when he does."

"Just tell him," Jennifer said with a laugh. "You'll make his day. No, you'll make his year! That guy is going to be the happiest man on earth."

"But Jen, I'm not sure how he feels now. I mean, do you realize how many years I've been putting him off? And I made him promise never to speak of his love for me again. That must have hurt him terribly."

She frowned. "He went way over the top on my birthday gifts, but he hasn't acted the same since then. He used to look at me so tenderly at times and would put his hand on my shoulder or take my hand. But he hasn't done that for a while. What if he doesn't even love me anymore?"

"Mickey Sterling! Hello! That man loves you more than life itself," Jennifer said, forcefully throwing a forkful of manure onto the growing pile. She looked over at Mickey with a jerk of her head that made her blonde ponytail whirl around. "Anyone with eyes can see that."

Mickey's heart quickened at the thought. She smiled, enjoying the delicious, tingly feeling of embracing her love for her husband. "I think I'll just play it by ear. He'll probably call tonight. I sent him a couple emails early this morning and I know he'll reply when he gets them. We'll see."

Despite her euphoria, niggling doubts remained. *What if he's not attracted to me romantically anymore?* she wondered. *What if I waited too long?*

227

Suddenly she recognized those tired old voices. *I guess negative thought habits die hard*, she thought ruefully. *Lord, help me to trust You with my future*, she prayed, *whatever lies ahead*.

~ Twenty-Nine ~

Saturday night the film crew, photographers, and the *Lone Star* crew met in Christopher's hotel room to eat pizza and watch the game. Christopher would be leaving the next morning. They planned the party to celebrate the good work done and the completion of that phase of their project.

They all piled into his room around 8:00 pm. Wes' arms were filled with pizza boxes. To Christopher's dismay, Gillian accompanied the group. She swung into the room and removed her light raincoat revealing a bright blue low cut top and tight jeans.

She immediately went over to Christopher and gave him a hug. "Nice to see you again, baby," she said, her seductive green eyes gazing into his.

He quickly disengaged himself, shocked at her forward actions. One of the guys laughed at Christopher's obvious discomfort.

"What's the matter, Chris? Too much woman for you?"

Gillian smiled and squeezed his arm. "Yeah, hon, what's the matter? Don't you like me?" Then she put on a pouty expression and stepped back looking hurt. "I'm not good enough for you, is that it?"

The guys guffawed loudly, and Christopher felt his face grow warm. *Help me, Lord,* he prayed desperately. He cleared his voice and spoke.

"I'm a very happily married man," he said firmly, looking Gillian directly in the eyes. "And I love my wife more than anyone or anything on this earth. I've loved her ever since college and I will for the rest of my life."

Christy R. Diachenko

"Oh, good night, like you'd be doing something wrong just to be nice to me," Gillian said disdainfully.

She turned sharply, swishing her wavy blonde hair while she went. She crossed the room and sat on Jake's lap. "You like me, don't you Jake? You wouldn't be mean to me, would you?" she asked, putting her arms around his neck.

"Oh, baby." His tone was lecherous, and he hugged her close. "I'd never hurt a hair on your head. You can be my darlin' any time. I like every piece of you."

Christopher felt sad. He knew Jake was married also and had two young children, but he seemed to have forgotten that fact.

"Let's just watch the game and eat," he said lightly, trying to ease the tension."

When everyone became engrossed with the game, he stepped off to the side to call Mickey. Gillian watched him with a devious look in her eyes. When she was sure Christopher was talking with his wife, she motioned for everyone to be quiet. She took the remote and pushed the mute button.

"Chris, baby, are you going to talk all night, or can we get on with the party?" she asked in a loud voice. "I miss you, honey. Come on."

The guys snickered and Christopher stiffened. Mickey was in the middle of telling him how well Tanner was doing with Andrew. Her voice sounded different somehow, warmer and more open and she seemed very happy to hear he would be home by mid-day Sunday. When she heard the female voice in the background, she broke off abruptly.

"The film guys and the crew of the *Lone Star* came over to watch the game and eat pizza," he explained.

"Oh." Mickey's voice was a dull monotone, a sharp contrast to her lively tone of moments before. "I won't keep you."

Christopher knew she was upset and longed to tell her he loved her, but his promise forced him to keep the words to himself.

"They brought their marine biologist, too. She's helping them with their project," he said, knowing the whole thing sounded lame. Several of the guys doubled over with laughter and Gillian gave him a knowing grin.

"I see. No problem, Chris. I understand." Her tone became brisk and businesslike. "I'll let you get back. I'm going to go check the horses before I go to bed."

"Okay, Mickey. I'll see you tomorrow." He tapped 'end' feeling somewhat better and put the phone back in the holster on his belt.

I guess she's all right, he thought. *I thought she was really going to be upset. Why did Gillian do that?* The truth would not dawn on him until later that her timing was precisely planned.

After the game finished, the guys and Gillian prepared to leave. Christopher thanked Wes once more for giving him the opportunity to try underwater photography. He bade the group farewell while they filed out of the room.

Gillian was the last to go. She stood in the doorway, then looked back at him with a sad expression. She sniffed and pulled a tissue from her pocket. Dabbing her eyes, she said in a quavering voice, "Good-bye, Christopher Gordon. Nice knowing you."

He felt awful. *I didn't mean to hurt anybody but I'm sure she didn't want to just be friends. I'm so clumsy, though. I should have found a kinder way to put her off.*

Gillian fluttered her hand in a brief wave, then allowed her arm to collapse to her side, caught back a sob, and left the room. Once outside she put the dry tissue back in her pocket. Her mouth curved into a self-satisfied smirk.

She got into her red Porche and drove off, leaving a cloud of exhaust behind.

~ * ~

Mickey still sat at the kitchen table where she had collapsed after she hung up the phone earlier. She had been so sure of her feelings and could not wait for Christopher to come home.

How could I have been so stupid? He doesn't love me anymore. How could he? I haven't given him any reason to hope that I would ever change. I've been such a fool.
Her mind was in a fog of pain and disappointment and tears to begin streaming down her cheeks. *I'm going to lose him.* She felt so helpless. *He's already found someone else.*

Kip, Kelsey, and Poncho came and sat close to her. She patted them absently. When her tears were spent, she looked down.

"Oh, kids, I guess this is going to be a real test of putting my trust in the Lord. I'll just have to ignore my feelings. After all, I've spent most of my life *not* being in love. I do have practice."

Mickey stared out the window at the beautiful full moon. She grabbed for the box of tissues when tears began to flow again.

But I <u>am</u> in love. He's just not in love with me anymore. I don't know how I can go on living in the same house with him. I'll just have to avoid him if I can.
She shook her head and tossed another soggy tissue on the table.

Oh the irony, she thought. *All this time when he loved me, I didn't love him. Now that I do, he doesn't love me anymore. That explains why he didn't answer my emails today. He was busy with his new love.*

Mickey sighed deeply and reached for yet another tissue before going down to the barn to make a quick check on the horses. After returning to the house, she listlessly prepared for bed, knowing she would not sleep.

Christopher would return tomorrow. The event she looked forward to with such excitement only hours ago, now caused her dread. She lay staring into the darkness, praying for strength during the coming months.

I waited too long, she thought while tears moistened her eyes again. *Now I'll have to pay the price.*

~ *Thirty* ~

*W*hen Christopher returned around 1:00 Sunday afternoon, Mickey greeted him quietly. Saying she had a lot to do, she swiftly exited the room. He headed slowly upstairs to unpack, puzzled at her behavior.

I thought she'd at least want to hear about the trip and see the pictures, he thought while he tossed his duffle bag on the bed and set his carry-on equipment case to the side.

After pulling his clothing and other personal items out of the bag, he left them in a heap on the bed and went down to the living room where Mickey was vacuuming.

She usually doesn't do housework on Sunday, he thought. *That's odd.*

She glanced up and smiled at him. Her expression seemed perfectly normal. Feeling somewhat better, he went outside to visit the horses.

A few minutes after he left the house, Mickey could hear a faint ring over the noise. She turned off the vacuum and ran for her phone, which she left on the kitchen counter.

"Hello, may I speak with Christopher or Mickey," a polite voice asked.

"This is Mickey."

"Hi, Mickey, my name is Martina Hill. I'm with the Cascade County Abused Equine Rehabilitation Society. We read the story of your recent horse rescue in the Aspen Ridge Gazette and were quite impressed."

"We were so glad we could help him," Mickey said. She returned to the living room and sat on the edge of the couch while she talked.

"Tanner was in awful shape, and we really didn't know if he'd pull through. He had a lot of spirit, though, and a real will to live. Our local veterinarian adopted him."

"Your actions proved that you are the type of concerned loving people we're looking for. Our Society has a proposition for you," continued Martina. "We need a place with lots of room where we can foster some of the abused horses we find. We need folks like you and your husband who will give them the care they need to get well again and additional therapeutic training if necessary to address behavioral issues."

Mickey's eyes widened. "Wow," she said. "I'd love to do that! There's something so satisfying about giving animals the love and care they deserve after they've been treated badly. Watching them finally recover is tremendously rewarding."

"I hoped you'd feel that way," Martina said warmly. "That's how we all feel here at the Society."

"Do you need references or anything?" Mickey asked. "How does this work?" She slid down to sit on the couch.

"I hope you're not offended but we took the liberty of having background checks performed and we also spoke with your veterinarian in South Carolina. Everything checked out on both you and your husband, although we understand he did not have animals in his care until now."

"Oh, no offense taken," Mickey said. "I'm glad to know you're careful. Yeah, Chris traveled so much with his photo shoots, he knew keeping pets wouldn't be an option, even though he loves dogs. Our rescue Chihuahua, Poncho, adores him and vice versa."

Martina chuckled with understanding. "Here's how our program works. When we find an animal in distress and have taken the proper legal steps to remove them from the owner's property, we'll give you a call. If you have room, we'll bring the horse to your ranch.

"The Society pays for all medical bills; we just need you to house the animal, administer care, and provide feed. Once the horses are sound again and have had any behavioral therapy they need, we'll adopt them out to approved homes. Oh, and we will also cover farrier services and equine dentistry. Just save your receipts or have them send the bill to us."

"That's fantastic and very generous," Mickey said excitedly. "We've got lots of room. We only have three horses here right now, my two and one who belongs to a friend, so there are plenty of free stalls. And of course, we have pasture space in abundance."

"Sounds like just the ticket," said Martina.

"Of course, I'll have to talk your proposal over with Chris," Mickey said. "But I feel sure he'll want to go ahead with the plan. May I call you back in a day or two?"

"Sure. Take as long as you need to decide. And if things just don't work out or circumstances change, you're free to stop taking animals at any time, no hard feelings. We understand that sometimes this kind of arrangement doesn't work out over the long term."

"Okay, I should be getting back with you very soon." Mickey took Martina's number and tapped the phone off. *How wonderful!* She smiled, feeling a sense of relief and excitement while she walked back to the kitchen. *This is just what I need to get my mind off Chris. And I love caring for animals.*

She went to the mud room and grabbed her tennis shoes from beside the door. The afternoon was sunny but chilly. The forecast called for snow by the end of the week. Mickey shrugged her way into her coat and walked down the path to the barn.

She explained Martina's idea to Christopher, who immediately agreed the proposition sounded workable. They walked around the barn, inspecting stalls and discussing the care and training of abused animals.

Christopher stopped suddenly and looked at her. "You know, might be a good idea to check out that society online to make sure they're legit. These days, you never know and since they called you ..."

"Hmmm..." Mickey thought for a moment. "That's a good thought. I'm sure they're fine but a little research first is always a good idea. I'll do that this evening."

"And are you sure taking on extra animals who need special care won't be too much work, Mick? I mean, you're already working with Gimli, caring for Fili and Kili most of the time when I'm gone. Plus, you're working on manuscripts every day."

He looked at her with concern. "I may have to be out on assignments a lot of the time and that means you'll be left with the lion's share of the work."

Coping will be easier with him away, she thought, her heart clenching with pain.

She reached one hand to tuck a stray curl behind her ear. "Oh, Chris, I can handle things," she said assured him. "Most of the care of the rescue animals will involve getting good feed into them, grooming them, and giving them lots of love. Andrew will take care of any medical needs they have. Everything will be fine. I'd rather be busy than bored."

"You certainly have a way with horses. I'm sure you'll do well with them. They're going to need someone who is kind and gentle." Christopher smiled, his brown eyes warm and tender.

Mickey's heart pounded at his look but she could not let herself hope. *He just thinks of me as a sister,* she thought miserably. *That look didn't mean anything. He's got what's her name now.* She turned to go.

As Mickey walked down the passageway to return to the house, she called back over her shoulder, "We'd better stock up on shavings. We could get some new animals any time."

"Right." Christopher pulled out his phone. "I'll see if some of our neighbors would be willing to help. The more truckloads the better."

~ * ~

Mickey's research that evening revealed the Cascade County Abused Equine Rehabilitation Society's excellent reputation. The organization even won several awards for their rescue efforts. She made a couple phone calls the next day and all references checked out.

At the end of the week, the C&M had their first new arrival. The medium sized brown pony was very thin but not too weak to stand. Her filthy matted coat needed attention desperately and the corners of her eyes were filled with creamy discharge.

Long, cracked hooves made the small mare's every movement an excruciating chore. Her forced walking on the back on her heels caused the skin to be rubbed raw and dirt infected the wounds. The pony hopped along, swinging her head up into the air with each step trying to avoid the pain.

Mickey called the local farrier right away. He had an appointment at a neighboring ranch that day and agreed to stop by when he finished. Within half an hour of Melvin's arrival the pony's hooves were trimmed and shod with a light shoe to protect from further cracking and to provide support. Mickey led her out at a walk, then a trot. She seemed to float over the ground.

"Oh, my word, Melvin! She must feel so much better," Mickey exclaimed with delight.

The short muscular man grunted while he put his tools back in his truck. "Yep. A bit a' proper care makes all the difference."

He climbed into the cab and started the engine, then rolled down the window. "Might want to put 'er some kinda hoof conditioner on there. Help make 'em not to crack so easy. And be sure to keep 'em cleaned out good. She's got a bit a' thrush in her hind hooves. Spray a little bleach in 'em. That'll dry it up quick."

"Right, I'll do that. Thanks, Melvin." Mickey waved while he drove away, then reached over to give the pony a pat on the neck. Relief and thankfulness were reflected in the large brown eyes.

Andrew came out the next afternoon and examined the pony thoroughly. He gave her several vaccinations and a good worming. The gentle mare stood calmly through the procedures, flinching only a bit when the shots entered her rump.

"Nice little pony," he said, rubbing behind her ears. "She's got wonderful manners."

"I named her Chocolate," Mickey said with a grin. "A little grooming and a couple months of good feed and I'm sure we'll have no trouble adopting her out."

They walked outside to Andrew's vehicle. "You'd better get back to town soon," Mickey said, looking at the sky.

"Looks like that snow could start any time."

"Yep." Andrew opened the door, then turned back to Mickey. He started to speak, then fell silent.

"What is it, Andrew," she asked.

"Oh, I'd just really appreciate if you and Chris would pray for me right now. I've a bit of a difficult situation and I don't see how it will ever work out. I just wish I could see now what's going to happen."

Mickey touched his arm gently. "I know how hard believing this can be sometimes, but the Lord's timing is always best. That's something I'm trying to learn myself right now. I'll certainly be praying for you, Andrew. And I'll mention your request to Chris, too."

She smiled sadly to herself after he drove away. *Easy to say, not easy to practice, this waiting on the Lord. Especially when you can't see how the situation could ever turn out with a happy ending.*

Mickey led Chocolate back to her stall and gave her some hay. While she stood watching the pony devour the food, she thought, *There's nothing to do but wait and pray. Only the Lord can make Chris love me again.*

With a sigh, she closed the barn door and headed for the house.

~ Thirty-One ~

Mickey walked leisurely down the driveway after retrieving the day's mail, when snowflakes began to float lazily down around her. 'First Blizzard of November' was the word the forecaster used for the coming weather, so she hurried her steps.

I'm so glad Christopher strung that rope from the kitchen door to the barn door, she thought thankfully. *The last thing we need is to get lost in a snowstorm and have the animals in need.*

Her phone started buzzing about the time she reached the house. She fumbled with her bulky gloves, trying to get one off so she could use the touch pad. She finally freed her hand and tapped 'answer'.

"Mickey, it's me," came Christopher's faint faraway voice. "I'm on my way down the mountain. I should be there in about an hour unless the snow starts coming harder."

"Okay." Mickey held the phone to her ear with her shoulder and removed her other glove. "Thanks for telling me, I would have been worried."

A deep chuckle filled her ear. "I kinda figured. I'll see you soon. Why don't you wait 'til I get there and we'll do the chores together?"

"Good idea, I'll do that. Drive safely." Mickey smiled to herself when she tapped off the phone. *He doesn't want me going out there by myself.*

The thought warmed her heart. For the first time she began to wonder if she'd been wrong back when Christopher called from his hotel room.

After all, there were other voices, too, she thought. *Maybe what he said was true. Maybe that woman was with one of the other guys. I mean, he's never lied to me before. Why should I mistrust him now?*

Her heart suddenly burgeoned with hope. Maybe Christopher did still care. Maybe she jumped to conclusions and that woman meant nothing at all. She shed her parka and stowed the garment in the coat closet.

Mickey felt energized so, grabbing her apron, she sat down at the kitchen table and began looking through her cookbooks. She decided on peanut butter cookies and double chocolate turtle brownies.

We'll have plenty of goodies on hand if we get snowed in, she thought, feeling both happy and excited.

~ * ~

Christopher gently applied the brakes while he strained to see through the heavy snowfall. Already the old logging road down the mountain proved treacherous. He set the wiper blades on the Jeep to full speed but still had trouble keeping the road in sight.

When he finally arrived at the main road, he sighed with relief. *That was crazy,* he thought. *Thank You for protecting me, Lord. Help me to make it home to my girl in one piece.*

~ * ~

The wind picked up and snow came down in blinding swirling sheets by the time Christopher burst into the mud room. Covered with snow, he looked like a living snowman.

"Whew! That stuff is really coming down out there," he said, stamping his feet and shivering while he removed his gloves, coat, and boots. "That was crazy to drive in. I was afraid I wasn't going to get back."

He entered the kitchen and sniffed the air while reaching down to pat Kip, Kelsey, and Poncho. The dogs greeted him exuberantly, bodies squirming and tails whipping back and forth madly.

"Mmm. What is that smell?"

Mickey laughed. "You look just like them. They've been in here sniffing and begging ever since I started."

Christopher grinned when he straightened. "I'm so glad you decided to do some baking. Looks like we're going to be stuck here at the ranch for a few days. Be a shame to to starve."

"My thinking exactly. I figured we might lose power for a while, so I'm planning ahead." Mickey took a pan of cookies from the oven and set them aside to cool for a few minutes.

Christopher sat at the kitchen table, then quickly got up again and said," I think I'll get a load of firewood in here. We're going to need fuel if the power goes out. I wish I'd thought to get us a generator."

He rose and when Mickey's back was turned, grabbed a cookie from the pan. She turned just in time to see him take a huge bite. "Christopher Gordon! Eating dessert before dinner. Aren't you ashamed," she said, doing her best Miss Daisy impression.

Christopher finished his cookie, then screwed his face up into a pained expression. "I'm so very, very sorry," he drawled in an overdone syrupy sweet, yet entirely fake apology.

"Why do I not believe you?" Mickey asked sternly, yet unable hold back a grin.

Christopher winked at her, then retrieved his coat and gloves and added a thick scarf and warm cap to the ensemble. "Will you get the door for me when I come back?" he asked while he put on his boots.

"Sure thing. I'll watch for you." Mickey paused, a slight frown shadowing her face. "Don't get lost out there,

Chris."

"The wood is stacked right beside the house." He wrapped the scarf around his neck and buttoned his coat snugly around him. "Don't worry, Mick. I'll be fine. Just be ready with some more warm cookies when I'm done." He grinned at her jauntily and disappeared into the whiteness outside.

By the time he was finished, neatly stacked wood filled most of the mud room. Mickey laughed while he removed his snowy outer wraps again. "What did you do, Chris? Bring in the whole entire wood pile?" She walked over and handed him a cookie.

"Just wanted to be safe," he said, seating himself at the table. "I put what wouldn't fit in the mud room in the garage. Hey, I hope this isn't all I get." Christopher looked at the lone cookie with an aggrieved expression.

"This little guy will barely get my taste buds working again. And after all that work I did. I need to rebuild my strength, Mick." He looked at her piteously.

"Oh, poor baby," Mickey said with an exaggerated, southern accent. "I just feel so terribly sorry for you right now. Let me see what I can find. Don't want you wastin' away right before my very own 'lil eyes."

She went to the oven and peeked inside. "Lookee what just happens to be in here." She pulled out a loaded plate and placed the food in front of him. "Maybe this steak dinner will help keep body and soul together."

He laughed at her antics. "Wow. You have been busy! That looks fabulous," he said, eyeing the thick New York Strip and the steaming baked potato. "But," he looked at her with a serious expression. "I still want more than one cookie."

"Oh, you're impossible," Mickey said in mock frustration. Then she laughed and returned to the oven to retrieve another loaded plate for herself.

Mickey had never felt so happy and secure. Christopher and she had fallen right back into their old banter and easy comradeship. Maybe there really was still hope.

After dinner and several cookies each, they bundled up and headed out to care for the horses.

"Brrr," gasped Mickey when they burst into the quiet barn. "That wind is something else."

Christopher nodded. "Makes you really appreciate those calm, balmy summer days, doesn't it?"

"For sure."

The horses whinnied eagerly, heads held high, ears pricked sharply forward. Mickey and Christopher laughed when they opened the door to the feed room. "I've never seen any animals get so excited about feeding time," he commented while he gathered four buckets and set them on the small counter.

"They do love their oats," Mickey said, "But I think the dogs could give them a run for their money when it comes to dinner time antics!"

She paused for a moment. "Hey, Chris, let's give them a special treat tonight. I bought some bran and molasses the other day. We could make them some mash to add to their oats."

"Good idea." Christopher reached up and lifted the heavy winter blankets down from their racks. "They'll need something extra to keep them warm tonight. I'll go ahead and put these on while you mix up the feed."

Mickey measured out four helpings of bran and added hot water. When the mixture was soft, she mixed in some molasses. She poured a serving of oats into each bucket, dumped in a helping of mash, and stirred the mixture together. When she emerged from the room, the horses began the din again nickering, whinnying, and pacing back and forth in front of their stall doors.

Christopher grabbed Fili's bucket, walked over, and opened his stall door. He attached the bucket handle to the hook and stepped back. He smiled when the horse plunged his nose in and took a huge mouthful. He chewed powerfully a couple times, then his eyes widened when he tasted the extra treat. He took another bite eagerly, slobbering grain and mash down the side of the bucket.

Christopher laughed out loud when Chocolate did the same thing with her portion. When Mickey entered Kili's stall, he tried to sneak some feed from the bucket immediately. Mickey gently pushed his face away and hooked the bucket's handle to the wall. Kili eagerly pushed his nose in and began to eat with a contented sigh.

Gimli's manners were impeccable until his bucket was in place. Then he pushed forward, nearly knocking Mickey over. "Gimli, you behave," she said reprovingly.

The horse's only reaction was to pin his ears back and look at her as if to say, "Don't you dare even think about taking my dinner."

Mickey gave him a pat on the neck. "Now, Gimli, just chill," she said with laughter in her voice. "How quickly you've forgotten just who brought you that feed." The horse swiveled his ears around but kept munching industriously.

Christopher checked the heated automatic waterers in each stall to be sure they were working properly, while Mickey climbed to the loft and pitched down several flakes of hay for each horse. After they were satisfied that the animals were snug and comfortable for the night, they returned to the house and retired to the living room. Mickey sat watching from the recliner while Christopher knelt before the fireplace and carefully stacked some kindling around a crumpled piece of newspaper. He struck a match to the pile and blew gently. The fire soon took hold and he added a few dry logs.

He was the epitome of handsome strength. He wore a black turtleneck with a red and black plaid flannel shirt over top and black jeans. He left his heavy boots in the mud room and walked around in his gray wool socks.

Just after Christopher added another log to the fire, the light in the room went out. "There it goes," he said with a sigh.

He looked over at Mickey, whose face radiated peace and contentment. She wore a green and blue Merino wool Irish sweater with jeans and her feet were encased in leopard print slippers. Curled up in the chair, she looked completely at home. Christopher thought to himself that she seemed even more lovely than usual.

"Chris!" she suddenly gasped. "The aquarium! I can't let it get cold. All that bacteria I've been trying to cultivate will die and I'll have to start the cycle all over again from square one."

Christopher looked at the tank thoughtfully. "This room will probably stay warm with the fire going. We'll just need to make sure we don't let the wood get low."

Mickey stood. "I'll go get a couple blankets and wrap the tank, too. That will help insulate the warmth already inside. Hopefully that'll work."

After a moment, she returned with the blankets and shivered. "It's already getting cold in the house. I'm going to hold these in front of the fire for a minute."

After they cared for the aquarium, Mickey returned to the recliner. The darkness of the room and heat of the fire made a warm cozy setting. Christopher struggled with his feelings and turned to stare into the flames.

He knew he couldn't say what had to be said unless he could school his features. Finally, after breathing a quick prayer that his face wouldn't give him away, he swallowed hard and turned.

"Mick, we need to sleep in here tonight. Our rooms will be too cold." He looked at her searchingly.

Her face froze for a moment. Their relationship had slowly grown closer over the past week and more than once she wondered if perhaps they did have a chance. Their easy teasing and chatter today made Mickey's heart sing. But giving up the privacy of her bedroom, even for a night, still seemed very uncomfortable.

"I'll go up and get us a couple sleeping bags, some blankets, and a couple pillows," he said with a matter-of-fact tone, seeing the uncertainty in her eyes. "We'll also need to keep the dogs and Snippit in here, too. Let's try to keep them in between us since they're smaller. Hopefully that way we'll all stay warm." He quickly left the room.

Mickey breathed a sigh of relief once he was out of the room. "Thank You, Lord," she said softly. "This I can handle."

They bedded down in front of the fire with Kip, Kelsey, Poncho, and Snippit curled up between them. Christopher slept little through that long night. He felt keenly the weight of responsibility to protect and provide for these ones he loved so dearly.

While he dozed and prayed his way through the hours, he felt encouraged. Today was the first time since his return from the coast that Mickey had really been herself. He thought she even loosened up a little. They always got along well but he previously felt a certain sense of reserve on her part, as though she could not really let go.

Maybe we're finally getting somewhere, he thought hopefully. A little after 3:00 am, he finally fell asleep.

~ *Thirty-Two* ~

When Christopher and Mickey awakened the next morning, all was quiet except for an occasional crack and pop in the fireplace. The storm was over and the country-side glistened with a blanket of snow two feet deep. In awe, they gazed out the living room window at the beautiful sight.

After a breakfast of cold muffins and cereal, they bundled up again and went to care for the horses. While they scooped out portions of grain, the lights came on.

"All right!" exclaimed Mickey. "Boy, those power guys are fast."

"We need to get a generator, though," Christopher said. "I don't want us to be in need if they aren't able to get power restored so quickly next time."

As they carried the buckets toward the stalls, Christopher said, "Hey, Mick, since you'll have the heat on and everything, are you okay with my going out to get some pictures? I could get some awesome shots today."

"Chris, I was just fine for a whole week without you here, I think I can manage one day." Mickey laughed. "I'll be fine. Go. Why don't you take one of the horses? They can probably get through the snow more easily than the Jeep."

She looked at Fili who was practically dancing in his stall in anticipation of his grain. "Take Fili. Looks like he needs a good work out." She laughed when he gave a loud insistent nicker. "Okay, okay. Here's your breakfast." She hooked the bucket in his stall, and he munched happily. "I'd go with you this morning, but I really need to get the

249

house cleaned," Mickey said, closing the stall door firmly. "Maybe we can both go out for a ride this afternoon."

"Yeah, let's do. I always have more fun when you're along," Christopher replied with a gentle smile.

They returned to the house and after shedding their coats, gloves, scarves, and boots, Christopher hurried up-stairs to stow his gear in his photographer's backpack.

Half an hour later he was bundled up and ready. He loaded the saddlebags with the lunch Mickey and some ex-tra grain for Fili. He led the horse from the barn, mounted, and looked around with delight. Setting out into the winter wonderland made him feel like an explorer. He returned Mickey's wave from the kitchen window and headed for the north pasture, his heart brimming with happiness.

~ * ~

Mickey went to the living room and began to gather up the jumble of sleeping bags and blankets. Kip, Kelsey, and Poncho were reluctant to give up their cozy bed. They waited until she was forced to roll them off the blanket, then each playfully grabbed one end and began to play tug-o-war, growling playfully.

Mickey indulged them for a few minutes but soon the dogs went to the door, indicating their need to go out. She put on her coat, gloves, hat, and boots and opened the door.

Mickey laughed when they raced out and then stopped abruptly, nearly piling on top of each other. Kelsey sniffed the white stuff as though she had never seen such a thing before. Then she stuck her nose down and flipped the snow into the air. She and Kip began to chase each other around and around the yard like puppies.

Mickey took a show shovel which stood against the house and cleared a bathroom space for them.

"Oh, poor little baby boy," she said, looking at Pon-cho. "We really need to get you a sweater."

The small Chihuahua shivered and shook from stem to stern and begged at the door, ready to return to his warm spot before the fire.

"C'mon, now," she said gently, picking him up and placing him in the cleared-out spot. "You've got to do your business."

Seeing he had no choice, the tiny dog finally took care of his needs. Mickey let him back into the house and he made a beeline for the couch. Soon Kip and Kelsey were also ready to return.

As they raced back into the house, Mickey heard a ring. She grabbed her phone from the counter and tapped 'answer' while she closed the door behind the dogs.

"Hello," she said, expecting a neighbor to be checking on them.

"Oh, hi," said a smooth sexy female voice. "May I please speak to Chris?"

Mickey's heart nearly stopped for a moment, then began to pound wildly. *This is probably just someone with the magazine,* she thought, trying to calm herself. *But I wonder why they didn't call his cell?*

"I'm sorry, he's not in. May I take a message?"

"Where is he? I really need to speak to him." The woman sounded irritated and impatient.

"I'm sorry I don't know. He went out to get some pictures of the snow," Mickey said, a sick feeling beginning to grow in the pit of her stomach. She recognized the voice to be the same one she heard when Christopher called from the hotel.

"Look, now surely he told you where he went. Can't you just get him? He's expecting my call." The condescension in her tone made Mickey feel like the help.

"I really don't know. He's out riding somewhere," Mickey insisted.

"Okay fine." She went on in a low suggestive tone. "He said he was looking forward to talking to me. Just business of course. I'll try his cell. No message."

She hung up abruptly. Mickey numbly tapped 'end' and put the phone down. She sank to the kitchen floor, her small shoulders trembling.

I should have known. Everything I was afraid of is true. He has found someone else. She even has his cell number.

She began to sob uncontrollably, every fear and insecurity flooding through her mind, taunting her cruelly. She never thought to wonder why the woman called *her* cell if she already had Christopher's number.

Mickey got up and absently grabbed a wash rag. She began to clean the kitchen, not remembering the counters were wiped clean the night before. Her emotions swirled around and around, her mind a jumbled mass of confusion and pain.

She went upstairs to clean Christopher's room. While she dusted the dresser, she stared blankly at the picture he took on their wedding day.

How weird, she thought, *that he leaves that picture there. Maybe I should just put it away.* She started to pick up the framed piece, then shook her head. *No, that wouldn't be right. It's his stuff, he can do what he wants with it. But from now on, he can clean his own room.*
The rest of the morning passed in a fog. Christopher returned and came into the house just after 1:00 pm, ruddy faced and happy. "I got some great shots," he said excitedly. "Our place is so gorgeous. Let's go out again later, okay? I've just got to let my feet and hands thaw."

Wearily Mickey mumbled some excuse and left the room. Christopher stood still for a moment staring at the spot where she had been. Hurt and confusion overwhelmed him. Then with a sigh, he went out to work in the barn.

Mickey went about her tasks thoughtlessly, as though she were on autopilot. *So strange,* she thought several hours later while she plumped the pillows on her bed. *How I felt so badly just a little while ago. Now I feel nothing. I feel completely empty. Like I don't care at all. About anything.*

She aimlessly wandered around the kitchen that evening, knowing she should have a meal ready when Christopher returned. Listlessly she retrieved a can of soup from the pantry and warmed the liquid in the microwave. She heated up biscuits and took out strawberry jam to go with them.

When the cold finally drove Christopher back to the house, he stood in the kitchen feeling sick at the wall that had so abruptly gone up between them. She placed the soup bowl on the table and looked at him, her face expressionless.

"I'm going to bed. I didn't sleep very well last night, and I have a headache." She turned and walked from the room.

Christopher stared unseeingly out the window, feeling completely baffled. *She was so warm this morning,* he thought. *Like she was truly opening up. Now she's as cold as that snow outside.*

He sighed. *Maybe she just needs a good night's sleep,* he thought hopefully while he sat down to eat. *I know she didn't sleep very well on the floor.* But he didn't have much confidence in the idea.

~ * ~

The next morning, nothing had changed. Mickey spoke to Christopher and even smiled a few times. But the wall between them was back up and several inches thicker than before. Puzzled and hurt, Christopher avoided the house as much as possible, glad for any excuse to get away.

253

Christy R. Diachenko

As a few days went by, Mickey began to feel ashamed. *I don't really believe he'd go out and cheat on me. He isn't that kind of man. She's probably just putting the moves on him but I'm sure he would honor his vows. That doesn't mean he still loves me, though. How could he? I've been rejecting his love for years. He probably wishes he was free to pursue her.*

She sighed deeply. *Time to take a reality pill, Mick. He's just not in love with you anymore. The sooner you accept that and move on the better.*

She prayed inwardly while the tears began to form. *Lord, please give me the strength to get through this and learn what You have for me to learn. Help me to find joy and peace in You despite my sorrow.*

~ Thirty-Three ~

A few days after the storm, Christopher took another assignment from Wildlife Unlimited. He spent most of each day out in various parts of the ranch and usually returned long after the sun set behind the distant mountains. He found himself thankful the project took up so much of his time.

Mickey continued to make herself go to her Lord for comfort and strength but, while she tried to accept that Christopher no longer loved her, she unknowingly began building an even thicker wall of self-protection around her heart. Brick by brick the wall increased, and she looked for anything to distract herself. When foster horses came in, she immersed herself completely in their rehabilitation.

Another mare and a gelding were in residence at the C&M. The mare, a black and white paint, had been severely beaten. Though in relatively good health, the abuse left her extremely head shy. After the horse was at the ranch for just two days, Mickey discovered this firsthand.

Mickey ate a quick supper alone, then put on her jacket, gloves, and boots and headed for the barn. While the horses ate their evening meal, she sat at the computer in the barn office, entering information about the new mare named Kendra.

Mickey went back into the passageway twenty minutes later and decided to give the new horse a good grooming. She went to Kendra's stall and entered quietly. The mare looked at her suspiciously at first but went ahead and allowed Mickey to slip a halter over her nose. She snapped on a lead rope and led the horse out to one of the cross-tie stations.

After attaching the chains to her halter, Mickey went to the tack room for the grooming caddy. She returned, approaching quietly but talking softly so the mare would know she was there.

She took out the hoof pick and slowly ran her hand down Kendra's right foreleg. The horse lifted her leg willingly and Mickey was able to pick out her hooves without incident. The black ears swiveled back and forth, listening to Mickey's soft voice.

Next came a thorough currying. Then Mickey grabbed a soft brush, ready to start on the animal's neck. When she reached up, Kendra seemed to go mad. She jerked her head back wildly and began pulling frantically at the chains attached to her halter. Her eyes were wide with fright and panic.

Mickey gasped and dropped the brush. She quickly stepped back, knowing the danger. She stood absolutely still, talking to Kendra gently. At first her words seemed to have no effect but gradually the horse began to calm. Finally, she stopped pulling and stood still, her sides heaving.

Mickey's heart pounded while she went slowly toward the animal, holding out her hand while she walked. Kendra extended her nose and blew softly. Mickey stood close to her, rubbing the lower part of her neck.

"Wow, girl. I guess now we know where you need help."

She gradually worked her hand up the horse's neck until she was gently scratching behind her ears. Kendra remained rigid for a few moments, then finally lowered her head with a sigh. Mickey continued to calmly scratch and rub all around her ears and then down the white blaze on her face. She could see tiny white scars in the black hair around the ears.

"Somebody really hit you over the head, didn't they?" Mickey said, feeling outraged. "Poor baby. But you don't have to worry anymore. Nobody will ever hit you again, not while I'm around."

She finished grooming carefully, making sure she worked gradually up from the horse's shoulders when she needed to brush her neck and head. When she was finished, Kendra's coat shone, and Mickey surveyed her work happily.

She took a sugar cube from her pocket and slowly extended her hand. Kendra blew a little but seemed uninterested. Mickey gently pushed the cube into her mouth. The horse's eyes widened when she experienced the sweet taste, and she crunched the cube eagerly.

Mickey felt tears prick her eyes. "You've never even had treats before, have you?" she asked softly. "My dear, we're going to change that." She offered Kendra another cube and this time she lipped up the sugar immediately. "Fast learner, aren't you?" Mickey said with a grin.

She put the mare back in her stall and prepared to head for the house. When she started out the barn door, she heard Christopher's Jeep and the sound of the garage door opening. Mickey stopped abruptly, turned, and went back to the barn office.

I just can't put on a cheerful face tonight, she thought glumly. *I'll do some more work on that manuscript.*

Mickey worked for several hours via their home network until she was sure Christopher would be finished eating. With a deep sigh she saved her work, then made a final check on the horses. She turned off the lights and walked up the path to the house.

She changed into her exercise clothes and went downstairs. While she walked rapidly on the treadmill, Mickey thought dejectedly about how long it had been since she and Christopher worked out together. These days he usually did his workout in the morning, since by evening he wanted only to eat, process pictures, and fall into bed.

~ * ~

Mickey poured herself into work. Another new rescue horse, a gelding named A.J., had been neglected, abused, and hated to be ridden. Mickey went very slowly, gently re-training him with treats and lots of praise. After a few days of intense work, she was pleased to finally see tiny signs of improvement.

Chocolate was now completely restored to good health and Mickey was happy the Wilkins' daughter wanted to adopt her. She watched Jonathan and Julie load the pony into their trailer, confident Chocolate was in good hands. The young girl was already feeding her carrot pieces.

~ *Thirty-Four* ~

On the day before Thanksgiving, Christopher's family arrived. Mickey was thrilled to finally meet them. Her sister-in-law proved to be warm and friendly, and the two teenagers weren't at all embarrassed to show their enthusiasm for finally visiting the C&M.

Mickey and Christopher showed Kirsten and John to the guest room. Christopher's niece Lisa opted to sleep in the living room. When her brother Jeff was given the choice of the basement or the barn office, the teenager immediately grinned and said he would bunk down in the barn.

Satisfied everyone would be comfortable, Mickey and Christopher returned to the kitchen where Mickey was working on a batch of sourdough bread. Jeff came down a few minutes later asking if he could see the barn.

"Let's go," Christopher said, pulling his coat from the closet.

John appeared just when they were going out the door. "Hey, wait up, guys. I want to check out that barn, too."

Jeff and Christopher stepped back inside and waited while John put on his coat.

"Go for it," Mickey said, dividing the bread dough into three sections. She put each in a loaf pan, then washed her hands. She looked around at the men teasingly. "You know, you can always clean the stalls, too. I mean, you want to really experience ranch life, right?"

John laughed heartily, his eyes sparkling with good humor. "Just what I need, a working vacation. Though, I do want to keep in shape."

Jeff grinned and punched his dad's arm. "Yeah, Dad, gotta keep those muscles toned. Don't want any of those accounting books getting away from you."

John grimaced. "Hey, during tax season, I feel like I'm wrestling steers. You're more accurate than you think, son!"

"You're just lucky this ranch is no longer home to bovines. Then you'd have been out working cattle all day," Mickey said, opening a drawer and retrieving a towel.

Father, son, and Christopher laughed again and headed outdoors. Lisa entered the kitchen just when Mickey covered the bread. The girl's shiny brown hair was pulled back into a long ponytail. Her features were delicate and reminded Mickey of a China doll. Timidly Lisa asked if she could help.

"Absolutely," Mickey said. "I need some kind of salad for supper tonight."

The girl's face brightened. "I can do that. How about Watergate Salad?"

"Perfect," Mickey said with a grin. "One of my favorites! And I think I have everything you'll need."

Mickey showed here where the ingredients were stored, and Lisa started getting the salad together. The two chatted while they worked. Lisa was very inquisitive about the uncle she barely remembered, and Mickey enjoyed telling her about Christopher's many talents and his kind Godly spirit.

For a time, Mickey forgot he no longer loved her and spoke with the unfettered heart of a woman in love.
The family talked nonstop during the evening meal, catching up on all the news.

"I'm so glad you all could come for Thanksgiving this year," Christopher said with a smile, and he passed Lisa's salad.

"We usually go to my folks place but they're visiting my sister in New York this year," explained John. He took a piece of bread, then passed the serving plate to his wife.

"Lisa's been after us to come ever since you told us you were moving out here," Kirsten remarked with a laugh. "She really loves horses but doesn't get to ride much at home."

The young girl blushed, embarrassed at the attention. Noticing her discomfort, Mickey began to talk with her quietly while the rest of the family discussed other things. She asked Lisa about her riding experience and soon the two were having an animated discussion about horses.

"Lisa, I think you, your mom, and I need a trip to the barn after supper," remarked Mickey, winking at her new niece. "Since we cooked, it's the guys turn to clean up."

"That sounds great," said Lisa quietly but with enthusiasm. "I can't wait to meet Fili and Kili."

"Ladies, you have presented a valid point," John said with a grin. "We will most certainly do the dishwashing honors."

"See, I knew there was a reason I liked you. You agree with me." Mickey poked Lisa with her elbow and whispered, "Great guy, your dad." The girl giggled, enjoying the banter.

True to his word, when they finished eating, John headed up the cleanup efforts, so the ladies all bundled up and headed for the barn.

"Wow," Lisa breathed and patted Fili's nose. "They are so beautiful, Aunt Mickey. You are so lucky."

"If you're game, we'll go out for a ride before you leave. Sound good?" Mickey asked, already knowing the answer.

"Oh, yeah!" Lisa said. "I want to ride Fili."

261

"You got it," Mickey said, putting an arm around her shoulders. "Now c'mon and meet some of the rescue horses."

~ * ~

On Thanksgiving Day after the big meal, Christopher took John, Lisa, and Jeff out for a tour of part of the ranch. The day was unseasonably mild, so Mickey set up her easel in the back yard and Kirsten sat beside her with her basket of knitting materials. The conversation turned to children and Mickey decided to ask something that had long interested her.

"Kirsten, what was Chris like when he was a kid? I'd love to know."

Kirsten smiled. "He was our family's latecomer. I was seventeen when he was born." Her face clouded. "I had only been married a year when our parents were killed. Chris was seven.

"That was a terrible time for all of us but poor little Chris really suffered. He was so close to Dad. At that age, he felt like he was being a sissy if he cried and yet he was so broken up about Mom and Dad's death."

Tears glistened in Kirsten's eyes when she remembered. "Of course, he came to live with us. I couldn't find him in the house one day, so I went looking. I heard the most pitiful sobs coming from the tree house John built for him. I climbed up there and just held him for over half an hour.

"When John got home, I told him what happened and his heart broke. From that day on, he did his best to do things with Chris that Dad would have done. They went fishing and camping, built things together, and of course played numerous games of catch in the back yard."

Mickey's face reflected the sadness she felt. "Poor kid. I think having your dad for a while and then losing him would be harder. My dad died before I was born, so I never

262

knew him. He was on his way home from work one day when a drunk driver hit and killed him.

"My mom always told me about him, though, and made sure I knew he loved me." Mickey smiled at the memory. "She always told me about how, when he found out they were having a girl, he prayed every day that I would find Jesus and that I would marry a gentle Godly man.

"Mom also felt roots were important. She told me all about my relatives, most of whom have passed on, but she wanted me to know about them. She even traced our family tree all the way back to the sixteen hundreds."

Kirsten smiled. "We never could find much on our side. I guess record keeping was a little less accurate or more easily lost back in the day. After about eighteen thirty we couldn't find a thing."

"I'd like to get copies of whatever information you have," Mickey said thoughtfully, looking at her palette, then mixing two colors together. "I have a family tree program that I've entered all my information in and I'd love to have Chris' family in there, too."

Briefly and with sadness she wondered why she even bothered as there would be no children to pass the information on to.

"No problem. I'll email you scans of everything I have."

"So what was Chris like when he was a teenager?" Mickey asked, satisfied with the color she'd mixed.

"Oh, pretty typical I'd say. He's always maintained such a close relationship with the Lord. Unusually so for a child. He accepted Jesus to be his Savior when he was only five. He went through a period of rebellion in his teens but that didn't last long. I think he just couldn't stand to have his fellowship with God broken."

Kirsten put her the knitting needles in her lap and stared out at the mountains. "After he got things straightened out, he acted like an angel. I kept thinking, this is not going to last and of course, it didn't. Unfortunately, the old sinful nature still pops up now and then."

Kirsten smiled, remembering. "He used to have a terrible time with his temper. Finally, I sat down with him and said, 'Chris, you've got to try to look at things through other people's eyes. Every situation has more than one side. Getting angry and out of control because something doesn't go the way you want it to, doesn't help anybody and you grieve the Holy Spirit.' I could tell after that he was really trying to work on that area."

"He really is a good man," Mickey said wistfully. She was tempted to open up to Kirsten but quickly discarded the idea. *No good picking at a wound that's trying to heal,* she told herself firmly. *He's not in love with me anymore and that's that.*

Kirsten heard the pain and longing in her sister-in-law's tone. She thought of the separate bedrooms and felt something was amiss but knew she could not pry. *Whatever the problem is, You are able, Lord,* she prayed. *Please work in their lives. Keep them close to You and to each other.*

~ * ~

By the time they had to leave to catch their flight home, Mickey loved Christopher's family and truly felt they were her own also. Kirsten grasped Mickey's hand before climbing into the rental car.

"I'll be praying for you, Mickey," she said in a low voice. "I know things will work out. Remember, God loves you completely. You are precious to Him." Mickey felt tears prick her eyes while she hugged Kirsten tightly.

John shook Mickey's hand firmly and Lisa and Jeff each gave her a big hug. "I hope I get to come back," whispered Lisa fervently. "So, we can go riding again."

"Definitely," Mickey replied, squeezing her tight. "I hope you'll come and spend next summer with us. You could help with our rescue horses, and we can ride every day the weather's good. Chris and I both want you to come."

The girl's eyes shone while she climbed into the back seat. With one last round of good-byes, Mickey and Christopher waved until the vehicle was out of sight.

~ Thirty-Five ~

On December third, Mickey got a call from Lorrie. "Hi, Mickey," she said. "I know the weather is cold, but could I still take you up on your offer to go riding? If I don't get out of this house I'm going to scream. I got a sitter for Zoe."

"Sure thing!" Mickey said happily. "With that new snow on the ground the scenery is gorgeous. Come on over. Just be sure to dress warmly."

When Lorrie arrived, she and Mickey headed for the barn dressed in heavy sweaters, coats, warm boots, and thick gloves. They laughed while they walked down the path.

"I look like I'm pregnant again," Lorrie said. Mickey laughed. "I hope we can get up into the saddles. At least we won't have to worry if we fall off. We won't feel a thing."

As they entered the barn, the pastor's wife grew quiet. The warmer temperature in the barn soon had them both removing their coats and gloves. Mickey led Fili from his stall and put him in the cross ties. She noticed that Lorrie stayed well away from the large animal. Mickey could see that, though she loved horses, she was still a bit apprehensive now that they were up close.

Sensing her friend's fear, Mickey took her time about getting the horses ready.

"Lorrie, would you go get their bridles from the tack room?" she asked while she lifted the saddle onto Fili's back. "They're the two nearest to the door. You'll see their names above the hooks."

Lorrie nodded and hurried away. She returned with a bridle over each shoulder. "I love your barn," she said,

266

looking around appreciatively. The inside is so new and updated but the outside still looks vintage."

Mickey laughed. "I love it. Did you know the inside
renovations were a birthday present?"

"No way," Lorrie said, looking at her in amazement.
"What a wonderful gift." She handed Fili's bridle to Mickey.

"Yeah, I was ecstatic. We were also celebrating a
time-consuming project Chris completed, so it wasn't only
a birthday present.

"I couldn't believe how fast the construction company worked. They finished everything in just a few weeks.
Having things modernized has been so nice, especially when
that first big snowstorm hit."

Mickey sighed with satisfaction while she looked
around. "Yep. One of the nicest presents I've ever received, I'd say. Although that aquarium is right up there,
too. I don't think I could say one was better than the other."

Lorrie smiled. "I can imagine. That tank is beautiful.
When are you going to add fish?"

"The tank is pretty much cycled now, so I'm thinking
about going ahead and getting my cleanup crew. If all is
well after Christmas, I'll start adding fish a few at a time
when I can afford them."

"Cleanup crew?" questioned Lorrie while Mickey
deftly slipped the bit into Fili's mouth and pulled the bridle
up over his ears.

"Snails, Red-Legged Hermit Crabs, Peppermint
shrimp - critters like that," she said with a grin. "All the
little guys who clean up the gunk."

"Oh!" Lorrie laughed. "I was picturing a tiny crew of
divers with cleaning buckets and scrub brushes."

The women both got a good laugh picturing such a
thing.

"Okay, girlfriend, now why don't you buckle the throat latch on this bridle while I get Kili ready?" she asked nonchalantly.

Lorrie slowly reached up to buckle the strap, hesitating when Fili moved to put his head down. When she was finished, she stroked his nose. When she began to scratch behind his ears, he lowered his head further. She giggled and began to talk softly to the big animal.

Mickey haltered Kili and led him from his stall. She looked at both horses critically, then turned to Lorrie. "Why don't we groom them a bit first?" she said, knowing the only way her friend would feel completely comfortable would be handling the horse.

"I don't know, Mickey. He's awfully big," Lorrie said doubtfully, eyeing the tall gelding. "I feel a little silly. I really love horses but being this close makes me nervous. Petting them over the gate is a little different."

"You know, I felt intimidated when I got my first horse," Mickey said, reaching to pull a couple brushes from the grooming caddy. "I was pretty scared having to do everything by myself. I remember feeling so disappointed. After all the years of loving horses and wanting some of my own, there I was scared to death every time they moved. And they were just weanlings! You'd be surprised how strong the little guys were." Mickey smiled. "You really will get used to them. You just need some experience under your belt."

Mickey held out the brush. "Go ahead, give grooming a try," she said gently. "He won't hurt you. Just start here on his neck. He loves that."

Lorrie slowly walked forward and gingerly began to brush the shiny bay coat. Mickey stood back and watched. The petite red head went very slowly and cautiously at first. Finally seeing that Fili was not going to misbehave, she dared to work on his front legs. Mickey moved to work on Kili.

By the time Lorrie finished brushing the horse all over, she was quite pleased with herself. "You're right," she announced with a grin. "I feel better already. I just haven't been around horses in so long. Everything felt a little strange."

She went to Mickey and gave her a hug. "Thanks for understanding," she said softly.

Mickey squeezed her gently. "You're welcome." She felt so blessed to have such a wonderful friend. "C'mon." She released Lorrie and grabbed the other saddle. "Let's get him ready to go."

"That's interesting," commented Lorrie when Mickey placed the saddle on Kili's back. "What kind is that? It looks kind of like an English saddle, but the seat is deeper. And I know it's not Western, because there's no horn." She fingered the smooth dark leather.

"This is an Australian saddle." Mickey grinned. "And no comments about my trying to be the woman from Snowy River either! I don't do that down the steep hillside at a gallop thing."

Lorrie laughed and put on an innocent expression. "Would I do that?" she asked in her best Aussie accent.

Mickey grinned while she adjusted the saddle pad, then reached under Kili's tummy to grab the girth. She put the strap through the buckles and gently tightened. The horse swung his head around and glared at her.

Lorrie looked concerned but Mickey said, "Oh, don't worry. He always does that. I guess I'd be a little perturbed, too, if somebody started squeezing my stomach with something."

269

She patted the gelding soothingly on the neck. "As long as I take things slow, a little bit at a time, he doesn't get too upset."

Lorrie went to Kili's head and stroked his nose lightly. The horse blew at her gently and allowed himself to be comforted. Mickey looked at him fondly. "Big baby," she said softly.

They finished tacking up, put their coats and gloves back on, and led the horses outside. Mickey helped Lorrie mount Fili, then climbed aboard Kili. She led the way setting a slow easy pace until her friend felt sure of herself.

Lorrie acclimated to the large horse quickly and began to ride with ease. They alternated walking and cantering while they headed across the snowy north pasture. Mickey and Lorrie both enjoyed their time together, sharing spiritual insights and feasting their eyes on the winter wonderland around them.

As Mickey retired that evening, she thanked the Lord for Lorrie. She looked forward to when Jennifer would be home from school.

At least I have the company of good friends and things to keep me busy, she thought wryly. *That's got to help me forget about loving Chris.*

~ *Thirty-Six* ~

As Christmas rapidly approached, Mickey could see difficulty ahead. Knowing Greg and Lorrie would not be able to get home to Boston for the holidays, Christopher suggested they extend an invitation to them to spend Christmas Day at the C&M. He, too, did not looking forward facing more hurt and rejection on that special day.   Mickey called Lorrie and extended their invitation. She was overwhelmed and happy. Greg picked up the other phone and thanked Mickey profusely.

"Lorrie was really getting down about not being able to see her family," he said huskily. "We'll be so thankful to spend the day with our dear friends instead."

"I'll bring a bunch of goodies," put in Lorrie. "I've been baking like crazy."

~ * ~

Wednesday morning during the week before Christmas, Mickey headed down to the kitchen. *Oh crumbs*, she thought when she saw Christopher, clad in a rumpled long sleeved blue tee shirt and gray sweats, sitting at the table eating cereal.

Her heart clenched with love for him. *I was going to eat before I leave but I can't sit here with him right now,* she thought. *This is just too painful.*

Christopher looked up when she entered the room. She wore a burgundy turtleneck paired with a festive plaid cardigan, jeans, and boots. Her hair cascaded around her shoulders and small gold jingle bell earrings tinkled softly from her lobes. She grabbed her coat from the closet.

"I'm going to Great Falls for the day to do some shopping," she said quickly. "I need to get presents bought, wrapped, and mailed for Kirsten, John, and the kids. I also need gifts for Greg, Lorrie, and Zoe."

"Aren't you going to eat anything first?" he asked, pushing the opposite chair out with his foot.

"No, I'm really not hungry," she said. "I'll just stop for something on the way."

"Mickey, there's nothing between here and Great Falls. That's a long time to go without breakfast. Don't you think you'd better have something?"

"No really, I'm fine. Thanks, Chris. I'll be okay, promise." Mickey waved away his concern with her hand, then pulled on her coat and gloves and grabbed her keys from the counter. "See you when I get back," she said, making her way through the door to the garage.

She can't even stand to eat with me anymore, he thought miserably. *Oh Lord, how am I going to handle this? At least before, we were on friendly terms but now she dismisses me with a wave of her hand.*

He listlessly finished his cereal, feeling sick at heart. He looked out the window and noticed most of the snow from the previous storm had melted.

I think I'll go over to the MacGregor's place and get us a Christmas tree, he thought, while he headed upstairs to change. *Maybe that'll perk me up.*

~ * ~

Mickey felt ravenous and very shaky by the time she pulled into the city of Great Falls. She stopped at the first fast food restaurant she found and ordered a sausage biscuit, hash browns, a cherry strudel, and orange juice. She sat down at an empty table and tried to make herself eat slowly. When finished, she sighed with satisfaction feeling much improved. She headed out to the truck, ready to take on the mall.

As expected, the crowds were enormous. Apparently everyone within a ninety mile radius chose this day to shop.

She was tickled to discover the mall featured a small pet store which carried a selection of marine life and supplies.

Her reef tank was now cycled, so she decided to go ahead and get started with her cleanup crew. She purchased ten Nassarius snails, ten Cerith Snails, ten Red Legged Hermit Crabs, and ten Peppermint Shrimp. She also bought fifteen Bumblebee snails since they were on sale.

She left the store satisfied with her good selection of invertebrates to keep the tank clean and healthy. *Maybe by the time I can start adding fish, I'll have money to buy them,* she thought wryly.

By late afternoon Mickey made all the purchases she needed except for a gift for baby Zoe. She transferred her packages to her other arm taking great care with the bags containing the critters.

I really should have stopped at the pet store last, she thought, her arm aching. *These bags with water in them are getting heavier by the minute.*

As she tried to make her way through the crowd, Mickey sighed. Shopping this close to Christmas proved exhausting. People were jammed into the mall like sardines, and she constantly felt she needed to be aware of potential pickpockets.

After looking in several large department stores, she began to despair that she would ever find something suitable for her infant friend. Finally, she spotted a baby store.

Mickey veered through the shop's door and felt immediate relief from the crush of humanity. She began to look around, fingering the small garments hanging from the racks.

I wish I was buying these for my baby, she thought while pain squeezed her heart. *Now I don't even have a chance. Oh, I wish he still loved me. What an amazing life we could have had. Why did I have to wait so long? Why was I so stupid? Why couldn't I have surrendered to the Lord in time?*

Satan's lies began to trickle through her mind and redirect her thoughts. *God is punishing me now. I'm getting just what I deserve. He's going to teach me a lesson. Ask for love and you get an abuser. Don't ask for love and you get to be lonely for the rest of your life. Wait too long to trust God and then you get to be totally miserable.*

Mickey put a small lace covered bonnet back on a shelf and turned her face away from the other customers. "No," she said softly under her breath. "I will *not* think that way. My Lord loves me and wants only the best for me. He is not vindictive, and He is not punishing me. *'I know the plans I have for you saith the Lord. Plans for good and not for evil to give you a future and a hope.'*

"That's what You've said in Your word, Lord. These thoughts in my mind are *not* from You. Please defeat the spirits of satan who seek to destroy me."

She instantly felt peace settle over her soul. *Thank You, Lord,* she prayed inwardly. *Please help me not to give in to those wrong thoughts. Seems like they're always right there ready to taunt me. Thinking Your thoughts is so hard when I hurt so badly. Please, Lord. Please somehow let this situation work out for good. And please don't let me go through this without learning what You want me to learn.*

Mickey's lashes were wet when she glanced up once more and spotted the perfect gift on the other side of the store. The soft nightie the exact mauve color of Zoe's nursery even had a rose pattern.

With a sharp intake of breath, she made her way over and picked up the small item. Made of the softest flannel, the garment looked a little large, but Mickey knew the baby would grow into the nightie soon.

She took the item to the register, satisfied she found just the right thing. On her way back to the truck, Mickey

274

picked up a burger and a bottle of water to enjoy on the way home. *Don't want to take a chance of having to eat supper with Chris. Every minute I spend with him is like torture. I love him so much.*

By the time Mickey returned to the truck, she laughed at the amount of bags and parcels she carried. *My arms are going to be sore tomorrow.* She looked at the pile again and shook her head. *I'll be up all night getting this stuff wrapped,* she thought while she cranked the engine and tapped 'shuffle' on her Christmas playlist.

When she arrived home, Mickey took all the bags and shopping sacks directly upstairs. She quickly changed clothes, then went down to the living room to set up acclimation drips for her new aquarium inhabitants.

Christopher stood in one corner positioning a beautiful Frasier Fir. Mickey caught her breath when she looked at him and pain twisted her heart again.

Why does he have to be so handsome? she thought. He was wearing jeans and a teal plaid flannel shirt. His face was still rosy from the cold and his strong hands easily handled the big tree.

Oh my word. He looks like a model for L.L. Bean, she thought, clearing her throat.

"Oh, hi, Mick," Christopher said, turning to look at her. "I thought I heard you come in. Do you like the tree?"

"I do. It's perfect." She stood awkwardly for a moment, then retrieved a large bucket from the stand under the aquarium. Christopher stared at her for a moment, then went back to positioning the tree.

"Once I get these guys going, I'll go get the decorations from the attic," she said when the silence became awkward.

"Whatcha got?" he asked, attempting to sound at ease.

"My cleanup crew," she replied while she carefully placed the bags into the bucket. "I have to drip acclimate them before I put them in, so they'll sit here for a couple hours."

"What exactly does that mean?" he asked. "I'm afraid I don't know much about fishkeeping."

"The subtle differences between the tank water and the store water they're in now could shock their system. Things like differences in Ph, salinity, alkalinity, and temperature.

"I'll set up one of these siphon hoses going from the tank into each bag. Then I use this little doohickey to regulate the flow so tank water slowly drips into the bags."

She showed Chris the control mechanism on the hoses. "That helps the little guys slowly get used to the different water parameters and then they will most likely do fine when I put them in the tank."

"Wow, that is so cool," said Chris, looking in the bucket to see her selection. "I can't wait to see them in there. When can you get fish?"

"I'll need to wait a couple weeks and let the tank's biological filter get used to the new bio load these guys will add," she replied while she began a drip from each hose to each bag. "I can then add fish a few at a time when I can afford them. Since we live out here, I'll probably order them online, even though shipping costs a bunch. The store at the mall didn't have a very large section in the fish department. You have to be careful to make sure the fish you get are compatible."

Christopher nodded in understanding. "Hey, since you're getting this all set up, I'll go get the Christmas decorations, okay?"

The lack of warmth in her tone saddened him deeply. She could have been giving him a college lecture. He hoped by allowing his genuine interest in her hobby to show, she might relax and begin to act like her old self. But his efforts were to no avail.

"Sure, that's fine," Mickey replied while she turned her back to him to inspect the contents of the bucket. "I think everything is in the attic."

~ * ~

Christopher and Mickey spent the evening decorating the house and the tree, but their time together was silent and stilted, because neither knew what to say to the other.

After several hours passed, Christopher watched while Mickey carefully removed her cleanup crew critters from their bags and gently placed them in their new home. Together they watched while the snails roamed the tank walls, and the crabs and shrimp began to tour the mounds of live rock.

Mickey finally escaped to her room with a pile of cookbooks when their sad attempts at conversation regarding the aquarium became too difficult. Flipping through the pages, she tried to shake off the difficult evening, determined not to wallow in self-pity. She marked several different recipes: cookies, snack foods, and a torte.

I've always wanted to try one of those, she thought, looking at the picture of the beautiful cake with many thin layers. *I think I'll just go for it. I could use a challenge right now.*

Mickey put the books on her desk and changed into a warm flannel night shirt. Pulling on sweatpants to keep her legs warm, she crawled into bed. She patted the spot beside her and Snippit jumped up and curled her furry body close beside her. Kelsey and Kip joined her and snuggled up together on the other side of the bed.

Poncho slept with Christopher, his habit anytime his hero was home. The tiny dog joined the others in Mickey's bed only when Christopher left early or came home late.

Her heart hurt to think of Christopher alone in his bed, even though she was sure he no longer wanted her there. *I'm glad he has that little dog to be close to him,* Mickey thought.

She tried to keep the painful thoughts away by thinking of the baking she would do tomorrow. But much time passed before she finally drifted off to sleep.

~ *Thirty-Seven* ~

When Mickey awoke Christmas morning and looked outside, she gasped with delight. Snowfall during the night transformed the world into a wonderland once more. Mickey smiled and let the curtain fall.

After a hot shower, she put on a maroon wool sweater, trouser jeans, and black ankle boots. She hurried downstairs to begin preparations. Greg, Lorrie, and Zoe were to arrive around lunch time and would spend the rest of the day and evening with them.

Of course, they would all enjoy a sumptuous Christmas dinner. The aroma of the turkey, which slow roasted overnight, greeted Mickey when she entered the kitchen.

She put on her apron and prepared to get started. Christopher came in soon after her, dressed in a burgundy and green wool sweater and jeans. His throat constricted when he caught sight of his dear Mickey. He felt ready to throw caution to the wind.

I'm going to just ask her what's gone wrong with us, he thought, feeling excitement welling up within him. *When we get to the barn, I'm asking. We can't go on like this.*

Just then Mickey turned. "Chris, would you mind taking care of things at the barn by yourself this morning?" she asked matter-of-factly. "I really need every spare minute to get all this ready." She gestured to the counter filled with ingredients. "And besides, I'm already dressed for company."

His heart sank. For a few sweet moments he thought maybe things could change and they could talk. But her guarded expression told him this was not the time. Numbly he nodded and pulled his coat out of the closet.

The Norrises arrived later that morning and Lorrie helped Mickey prepare a light lunch. They all gathered around the kitchen table and Greg gave thanks for the food.

As they began to eat he said, "Now this is really sad. We have all that wonderful food and here we are eating sandwiches." He looked longingly at the laden countertop. Lorrie laughed. "Now honey, just think of how much better things will taste after you've anticipated the deliciousness all afternoon."

Greg pretended to pout. "I suppose. But I think I'd still enjoy the spread just as much if I could have just a smidgen of that cherry pie now."

Mickey put down her sandwich and placed her hands on her hips. "I don't care if you are the Pastor, Greg Norris. Nobody gets even a crumb of that pie until tonight." She looked at him sternly.

"All right, all right. I give," he said, putting his hands up in surrender. He looked at Christopher. "If there's one thing I've learned it's this: never get in a woman's way when she's in the kitchen. Not if you value your life, that is."

Christopher nodded in agreement and they both laughed heartily. *He doesn't know how right he is*, thought Christopher sadly behind the smile. *It feels like I have to walk on eggshells everywhere around here, not just in the kitchen.*

After they finished the meal, Christopher and Greg went out to the barn to putter. Mickey and Lorrie began to get preparations underway for dinner, while Zoe played in the portable playpen they set up beside the kitchen table. They made the torte together and when finished agreed that it could rival The Cake Boss's creations for perfection.

The afternoon passed easily for both Christopher and Mickey since, for most of that time, he was in the barn and she was in the house. Though Greg and Lorrie said nothing, they did wonder at the strained feeling in the air whenever their friends were in the same room together.

Lorrie never said anything to her husband about the marriage of convenience because she knew Mickey shared with her in confidence. But her concern deepened when she noticed the subtle air of aloofness Mickey put forth whenever Christopher came near. She silently petitioned the Lord for wisdom.

When Christmas dinner finally graced the dining room table, everyone gathered together once more. Christopher said the blessing this time, thanking the Lord for the birth of His Son and for the precious gift of salvation.

After consuming a goodly portion of the turkey, mashed potatoes and gravy, vegetables, and all the other dishes, they retired to the living room admire the tree and open gifts. All opted to wait an hour or two before enjoying dessert.

Each person appreciated their gifts immensely. Lorrie adored Zoe's new nightie. Greg said the iTunes gift card was just what he needed, because there were several commentary apps he wanted to utilize. Zoe immediately began to play with her exciting new toys.

Christopher sat back and admired the paintings Mickey gave him. The view of the mountains to the north was a favorite of his. She depicted the same scene on two different canvases, one during the fall leaves peak of splendor and one after snow blanketed the landscape.

He thanked her warmly, his eyes pleading with her to respond. She acknowledged his words with a nod and a small smile but quickly turned her eyes away so he would not see the pain revealed there.

281

Christopher reached into his shirt pocket and pulled out a small envelope which he handed to Mickey with a smile. "Merry Christmas, Mickey."

She slipped her finger under the flap and tore the envelope open. She pulled out a single card bearing a picture of a beautiful aquarium. She looked at Christopher, puzzled. "The tank is gorgeous, but I already have one."

"True. But you have no fish. Look at the back."
She flipped the card over to reveal a gift card to LiveAquaria.com.

"I wish it could have been more but the barn and the tank ..." Christopher trailed off awkwardly.

"No, Chris, this is wonderful." Mickey sat silent for a moment, her emotions and thoughts running wild.

I figured I'd have to save for quite a while for fish. Surely, he wouldn't do this if he didn't care, would he? I mean, this is exactly what I wanted. Then internally she sighed deeply. *Of course, he would. He's a very giving person. This present doesn't mean anything other than having an appropriate gift to give for Christmas.*

Mickey smiled but only for Greg and Lorrie's benefit. "Thank you, Chris. You're very kind and incredibly generous. Now I can get some of the fish I've been wanting. I will really enjoy this." She put the gift card on the end table and sat down on the floor to play with Zoe.

Christopher's heart sank when he heard her very polite response. *If that gift doesn't warm her up, there is nothing I can do that will.*

He prayed inwardly. *Please Lord, help me here. I don't want to put a damper on this day. Help me to look beyond my own feelings and still be blessed and be a blessing to others.*

God said his prayer and the evening indeed proved to be a wonderful time for all. The awkward feelings lessened somewhat thanks to the presence of Greg, Lorrie, and

Zoe. The baby squealed with delight at the beautiful Christmas tree. The adults were constantly on the alert since she tried to grab low hanging ornaments constantly. Her antics were impossible not to enjoy, however. Christopher took many pictures, promising to email them to the Norisses.

In spite of the good fellowship with friends and the reading of the beloved Christmas story from Luke two, Mickey cried herself to sleep that night. She always viewed Christmas as the most romantic time of the year. To be so close to the man she loved, yet to feel he no longer loved her, caused greater anguish than she thought possible. She knew the days ahead would be filled with sad loneliness.

~ Thirty-Eight ~

The next morning, Mickey's Bible reading took her to Ephesians. While she read four, verses thirty through thirty-two especially captured her attention. *And do not bring sorrow to God's Holy Spirit by the way you live. Remember, he has identified you as his own, guaranteeing that you will be saved on the day of redemption. Get rid of all bitterness, rage, anger, harsh words, and slander, as well as all types of evil behavior. Instead, be kind to each other, tenderhearted, forgiving one another, just as God through Christ has forgiven you.* NLT

Mickey sat back, deep in thought. Finally, the personal application of the verses hit her heart head on.

I haven't been pleasing to God in the way I've been acting toward Chris, she thought soberly. *I'm not acting at all like a Godly woman, being so cold to him.*

She bowed her head in prayer. "Dear Lord Jesus," she prayed aloud. "Even though I hurt like I never thought possible, please forgive me for taking my hurt out on Chris. Please work in my heart and help me to treat him with kindness, even though the fact that he no longer loves me has broken my heart."

Tears welled in her eyes while she continued. "Lord, help me to be what I need to be. I absolutely cannot do it in my own strength. Help me, Father. Please, help me."

As they ate breakfast together later, they chatted amiably and even laughed a time or two. By the time the meal was over, Mickey felt quite pleased. What started purely as a performance because she knew she needed to do the right thing, became genuine enjoyment of his company once more.

Nonetheless, being with Christopher still proved tor-
turous. She felt like a wonderful gift was dangled before
her and then yanked cruelly away.

I guess this is really what I deserve, she thought
glumly. *This is probably exactly what he went through all
those years ago.*

When the kitchen was clean, Mickey went outside.
The sun shone brightly but the temperature measured only
ten degrees. She pulled sunglasses out of her coat pocket
while she walked down to the barn. The glare off the snow
made seeing almost impossible without them.

She decided to let all the horses except A.J. out into
the pasture to stretch their legs for a bit. She went down
the row of stalls, haltering each horse, then allowing them
to leave the stall. She laughed out loud at how they raced
from the barn and began to buck and kick up their heels in
the snow.

A.J. stood looking at her forlornly through the steel
bars. "Now don't worry, boy," Mickey said, going in and
slipping a halter on his head. "You can go play soon. We
just need to have a little therapy session so you don't forget about being ridden."

Mickey loved the shiny black gelding with his four
white socks. Working through his fears and hang-ups helped
her in some ways to better understand her own. Though she
went to the Lord for healing, residual fears still cropped up
on a regular basis, sending her to her knees in prayer.

As she worked with the horse over and over to solve
each problem, she recognized the correlations in her own
life. Though God's healing covered her heart, fear and self-
doubt had become habits over the years. Time and effort
would be required to turn those negative thought patterns
around and replace them with healthy positive ones.

Mickey led A.J. to a cross tie station and snapped

the chains to his halter. She went to the tack room and returned with the saddle pad, saddle, and bridle. She let him sniff the saddle pad well before drawing the piece over his shoulders to his back.

She followed the same procedure with the saddle, grunting while she hoisted it up high in order not to knock the pad to the ground. She gradually let the full weight of the saddle rest upon him. He looked around at her but did not pin back his ears or snap.

"Good boy, A.J.," Mickey murmured, going to his head and patting him. She pulled out a sugar cube and smiled while he devoured the treat. "You see, being ridden isn't so bad. You just need to learn no one's going to hurt you anymore."

Slowly and gently she tightened and fastened the cinch, then put on the bridle. She led him outside to the mounting block. She let him gradually acclimate to her weight by stepping lightly onto the stirrup a time or two before actually mounting. He remained still and, except for a slight swish of his tail, seemed unperturbed.

Praising him again, she urged him forward and began to work him in the ring. After thirty minutes of successful riding, she brought him back to the barn. While she removed the tack, she lavished him with praise.

"You're doing great, A.J. You didn't even let the snow bother you. Now if you'll just understand that other people won't hurt you either, we'll be in business." She fondled his black ears. "You're such a sweet boy. I just love you all to pieces." The horse nuzzled the front of her coat, hoping for more sugar. Mickey obliged him before unfastening the cross-tie chains.

As the riding had been slow and easy and he did not require a cool down, she gave him a final pat on the neck. "Go on now. Go find your friends."

He took off at a fast trot, looking around and whinnying loudly until he spotted the other horses at the far end of the pasture. He took off at a gallop.

Mickey cleaned up and hung the saddle, bridle, and saddle pad in the tack room. *How sweet is that?* she thought. *A great big horse has to depend on something little like me for his safety and wellbeing.*

As she closed the door and went for the wheelbarrow, a thought struck her. *I thought that little promise of Christopher's would provide me with safety and wellbeing but now that same promise is nothing but torture.* Tears stung at her eyes. *Now I'd give anything to hear him say 'I love you'.*

Sadly, she began to clean out the stalls. Mickey was so dejected by the time she finished she could hardly stand herself.

All right, sis, she thought. *You've got to snap out of this funk. Get hold of yourself, girl.* She remembered the Christmas present from Christopher. *I think I'll go check out that site.* She brightened somewhat. *I hope they have some of the fish I've been wanting.*

Mickey walked back up to the house, pausing to quickly shed her coat, gloves, and boots in the mud room. Getting more excited by the minute, she ran lightly up the steps to her bedroom, plopped down in the desk chair, and turned on her laptop.

~ * ~

That afternoon Jennifer came over to ride. Mickey grinned while she and her friend entered the barn. "Okay, Jen, now close your eyes."

"What's going on here?" Jennifer demanded, trying to sound stern.

"Since I didn't get to see you right before Christmas, you'll have to settle for getting your present a day late."

"Oh boy!" exclaimed Jennifer. Mickey led her down the passageway. "I love surprises."

Mickey stopped in front of the tack room. "Wait right here," she instructed. "And no peeking." After a bit of shuffling around she said, "Okay. You can look now."

Jennifer slowly opened her eyes and gasped. Before her sat a brand-new barrel racing show saddle with matching bridle.

"Oh, Mickey, they're beautiful. Just beautiful." She fingered the rich dark leather lovingly. "Gimli is going to look fantastic in these."

She turned to Mickey, her green eyes damp with emotion. "Thank you, dear friend. This means a lot to me."

Mickey smiled gently. "You're welcome. I can't tell you how much I treasure your friendship." She laughed sheepishly. "I almost showed you your present early. When they were delivered, I was ready to call you right off. I knew you'd love them."

She pulled a stern face and shook her finger at Jennifer. "I expect you and Gimli to win a bunch of blue ribbons and trophies in that tack. He's been trained by the best you know."

"Aye, aye, ma'am," she said, straightening up and giving Mickey a salute. "No doubt we'll take the barrel racing world by storm," said Jennifer with an excited glint in her eye.

She paused, then said, "And now, I have a present for you." Her face clouded a bit. "I wish I could have done more but with being in school and all..."

"Oh, Jen, you didn't have to do anything. I know how it feels when money is tight," Mickey said.

"I wanted to. C'mon up to the car."

They walked back up to Jennifer's Toyota where she presented Mickey with two packages. Mickey opted to open the biggest one first. When she tore off the wrapping she found a large cork board.

Puzzled, she went on to the second gift which was in a plain manila envelope. Inside Mickey discovered a stack of photos. While she slowly looked through them, realization dawned. They were before and after pictures of each horse she rehabilitated so far at the C&M. There was a small paper placard with the horse's name behind each set.

"I thought you might like to display these in the barn," explained Jennifer with a smile. "I told Chris about my plan when you all first started taking horses, so he's been getting the pictures for me."

Mickey's eyes filled with tears, and she hugged her friend tightly. "This is wonderful, Jen. I love it. This way I'll always be able to remember them."

Mickey and Jennifer took the cork board down to the barn and mounted the piece on a wall inside the office. They positioned the pictures with the name placard over each. Both agreed the result was a wonderful tribute to the power of kindness, patience, and love.

~ *Thirty-Nine* ~

Two weeks into the New Year, Christopher got a call from *Wildlife Unlimited*. After spending almost fifteen minutes on the phone, he came slowly downstairs to the kitchen where Mickey worked on a batch of blueberry muffins.

"Mick, I just got a really great assignment," he said, trying to sound excited.

"Oh?" She continued to measure out the flour.

"Yeah. I'm going to Canada. The magazine wants a photo series on the gray wolves up there." He sat down at the kitchen table, feeling tired and beaten at her seemingly blasé response. "They're doing a documentary film that they'll be running on Nat Geo Wild, so the film guys will be going, too."

Mickey tossed the measuring cup into the dishwasher and closed the flour bin. Her emotions were so near the surface this morning. She did not know how she would hold back her sorrow.

Help me, Lord, she prayed. *Help me not to fall apart.*

"When do you leave?" she asked, trying to keep her voice bland while she put the bin back into the cupboard.

"Next week. I'll need some time to study up on the wolves' habits and try to plan a strategy for the best way to get good shots without disturbing them. I anticipate us having to shoot a lot of duds before we get what we need. That's just part of the deal shooting in the wild."

Mickey went to the refrigerator and poured some milk into a glass measuring cup, her back still to him.

I don't want him to go but at the same time I do. At least I'll have a reprieve from the pain of being near him.

She returned the milk jug and closed the door.

Just because he doesn't love me is not an excuse for me to act badly, she scolded herself. *Be kind and be interested.* Taking a deep breath, she turned and put on a smile.

"Chris, I hope you have a good time. I'm sure you'll have a fun and rewarding trip." She went back to her mixing bowl, poured in the milk, and began to measure out the rest of the ingredients.

Christopher rose. "Yeah, I think it will be. Are you sure you'll be okay here alone? A month is an awfully long time. I could always tell them I just can't do this one."

Mickey turned to him. "Chris, thank you but I'll be fine. If I need help or something, I'll just call somebody." She smiled a little too brightly. "This will be a wonderful opportunity for you. Don't give me another thought."

Yeah right, like I really could just put you out of my mind, thought Christopher. He went to the refrigerator and opened the door, looking for a snack to take up to the office.

"Okay, then. I'll tell them I'm in." He opened the fruit drawer and took out a large red apple. "I'm going to get started on my research."

He entered the office and turned on his computer. While he searched Google, he sighed deeply and shook his head.

At least I'll have a little break. Maybe if I get really immersed in this project, I can forget for a while.

~ * ~

The day before he was to leave, Christopher called Andrew and Greg and asked if they would be on call if Mickey needed anything while he was away. They agreed willingly and Greg offered to help him get several loads of shavings before he left.

Early the next morning, Christopher prepared to set out. Mickey heard him rattling around, taking his things downstairs. The kitchen door opened and closed several times while he loaded the Jeep®.

Reluctantly Mickey rose and put on a warm robe. She bolstered her spirit and forced a smile while she went downstairs to say good-bye and wish him a safe trip. She stood in the driveway bundled in her parka and waved while he climbed into the Jeep and started off down the drive.

~ * ~

Mickey tried to look forward to this time alone, feeling the solitude might offer some peace at last. But the days proved to be miserable for her. She missed him terribly but knew she really missed how things used to be, when their relationship was easy and friendly.

One milder day Lorrie came to visit again and she and Mickey went on a two hour ride. This time baby Zoe accompanied them, comfortably stowed in a sling on her mother's back. The women enjoyed her excited outbursts while she saw new things.

Though Mickey's time was filled with caring for the horses, enjoying the new additions to her aquarium, and time with friends, she felt a weight pressing on her soul.

Never in her life had she been forced to rely on the Lord so completely. She continually went to the scripture, desperate for God's nearness and comfort.

"Please, Lord," she prayed daily. "I don't want to go through this and miss what You have for me." Though the tears streamed down her cheeks every time, she doggedly asked, "Teach me what You want me to learn, Lord. And help me not to let my pain cause me to be unkind to Chris."

Whenever she felt especially down, she would spend extra time with the black gelding A.J. and so had developed a special bond with him. She decided to tell Christopher when he returned she wanted to adopt the horse herself. She did not think she would be able to stand seeing A.J. leave the ranch. When Christopher returned five weeks later, he wholeheartedly supported her decision and took care of the paperwork immediately.

~ * ~

As the remainder of the winter passed, Christopher and Mickey continued to have their individual quiet times but evening worship together became a thing of the past. Mickey found herself increasingly thankful Christopher spend most of his time either outdoors or working on his computer.

She no longer used her desktop computer in the office much, opting more often to retire to her bedroom with her laptop. Though she resolved to be kind and Christ like in her behavior and demeanor, her heart was in agony and she found life easier to handle by avoiding Christopher whenever possible.

Every time she saw him, thoughts of self-doubt plagued her. Remembering something Pastor Thompson once told her, each time the negative thoughts surfaced, she dismissed them with scripture and resolved to steadfastly put her trust in the Lord.

"Satan will run if you pepper him with scripture," Pastor Thompson had said. "Pretty soon, you'll find he doesn't come after you with those thoughts anymore. He hates God's Word!"

Mickey kept her ammunition verses on index cards beside her bed and read them each morning and evening to impress them constantly on her heart and her mind.

When thoughts of a bleak future crossed her mind, she recited Psalm 31:19 and Jeremiah 29:11. *How great is the goodness you have stored up for those who fear you.*

You lavish it on those who come to you for protection, blessing them before the watching world. 'For I know the plans I have for you," says the Lord. 'They are plans for good and not for disaster, to give you a future and a hope.'

When whispers filled her thoughts that she was fat and ugly, she brought out Psalm 139:13-14. *You made all the delicate, inner parts of my body and knit me together in my mother's womb. Thank You for making me so wonderfully complex! Your workmanship is marvelous - how well I know it.* She also clung to Psalm 139:17-18. *How precious are your thoughts about me, O God. They cannot be numbered! I can't even count them; they outnumber the grains of sand! And when I wake up, you are still with me!*

When she was tempted to despair because of the length of time she held onto the sins of bitterness and unforgiveness, she quoted Psalm 145:8-9. *The Lord is merciful and compassionate, slow to get angry and filled with unfailing love. The Lord is good to everyone. He showers compassion on all his creation.*

She also included First John 1:8-9. *If we claim we have no sin, we are only fooling ourselves and not living in the truth. But if we confess our sins to him, He is faithful and just to forgive us our sins and to cleanse us from all wickedness.*

Lord, I know You are not a vindictive God, she prayed one night while she lay in bed. *I will no longer allow myself to think that. But I also know the consequences of sin can't necessarily be erased. Maybe I did take too long to surrender all to You. Maybe the chance for Chris and me to be happy together has passed. If so, help me to find my peace and joy in You alone and to live a victorious life for You.* A tear trickled down her cheek. She turned on her side and tried to sleep.

~ *Forty* ~

Mickey put on the loafers she left by the door, then went to the refrigerator and got a few carrots. She cut them up into small pieces and stuffed them into her jeans pockets. She shrugged into a light jacket before leaving the house. The warmer temperatures of late April hinted that winter's hold was loosening.

As she walked down the path, she looked up. A full moon shone and the blanket of stars twinkled brightly. She walked slowly, head back, enjoying the splendor and vastness of the night sky. Finally, she bumped into the gate, bringing her reverie to an end.

She slid the large barn door open and reached to the side to flip the light switch. All was quiet except for a gentle welcoming nicker from Gimli's stall. Though Jennifer finally completed her degree, she decided to keep the gelding at the C&M and come there to work him. Mickey embraced the idea, thankful she would have opportunities to see her friend more often.

Mickey walked slowly down the row of stalls, greeting the horses and reaching in to give each a gentle pat. When she approached the last occupied stall, she felt faint warning signals go off in her brain.

Fili usually waited with his nose close to the steel bars in hopes of getting a treat. He would make such a fuss nickering and whinnying that she was forced to talk to him first.

He hasn't made a peep tonight, she thought, and her heart quickened a beat. She walked over quickly and looked into the stall.

The horse stood in the center staring blindly at the wall. Every few seconds he would kick at his belly with his hind leg and swing his head around to bite at his side. He moved stiffly around the stall in a circle and swished his tail in frustration. Then he returned to his stance in the middle. His flanks glistened with sweat.

Mickey gasped softly. "Oh no! No, not you, Fili." She grabbed her iPhone® from her pocket and with shaking fingers tapped contacts and found the veterinarian's number.

"Andrew, this is Mickey Sterling. Can you please come? We need help," she said. "Fili has colic." Her voice was strained while she tried to hold back her fear and panic.

"Okay. I'll be there as fast as I can," Andrew replied.

"Thank you. Bye." Mickey's voice wobbled. She looked back in Fili's stall. He walked around in a continuous circle now and she knew soon he would lie down and try to roll.

Taking a deep breath, she attempted to calm herself. *I don't want to make him any more stressed.* She lifted his halter and lead off the hook on the stall door. *They can always sense when their people are upset.*

Quietly she entered the stall and went to the gelding's head. She slipped on the halter and buckled the strap gently. With words of encouragement and reassurance, she coaxed the suffering horse out into the passageway where she began to walk him slowly up and down the length of the barn.

Christopher came striding through the door. "Andrew just called. He said for you to, oh. Looks like you're already doing what he said. Just keep him walking so he doesn't roll."

Mickey nodded and said nothing, concentrating solely on the animal beside her. Christopher sat down in a nearby chair and leaned his head back against the stall door behind him. The only sounds to be heard were the slight grunting breaths Fili took and the sound of his hooves clopping back and forth. Twice Mickey felt him pull against her trying to lie down but she tugged at his halter gently and managed to keep him moving.

After what felt like hours, Andrew arrived. He immediately went to the horse and began to check him over. "What did he get into?" he asked while he looked at Fili's eyes.

"Nothing that I know of," Mickey said in a frustrated tone. "I always try to be extra careful to lock the feed room. I'm sure he didn't get into the grain. I don't know what else he could have eaten. I try to be so careful of them and ..." Her voice broke and a sob escaped her throat.

Andrew began rummaging through his bag. "Mickey, I wasn't blaming you," he said gently. "It could have just been the new grass that's starting to grow when he's been used to hay all winter. I know you all are careful but these things sometimes just happen anyway. Don't feel badly."

"Yeah, Mick," put in Christopher when he came up behind them. "This is not your fault. I've never known anyone who was more conscientious about their animals."

Mickey appreciated his attempt to comfort her and gave him a quick smile. "Thanks, Chris."

She continued to watch while Andrew gave Fili a shot, then stood back.

"That's about all we can do," he said. "Now we wait. Mickey, keep walking him."

She tugged Fili's lead and began to walk him up and down the passageway once more. Agonizing minute after agonizing minute passed.

Finally, Fili caught his breath and swallowed. For the first time that evening, his eyes showed a spark of their usual brightness. He nosed Mickey's red sweatshirt gently, looking for treats.

"You big goon. You want to eat already." Mickey took his face in her hands and caressed him gently. "After all you've just been through and you want food." She shook her head and pressed a kiss on his nose.

"Walk him around a bit more," instructed Andrew. "He needs to eliminate."

Mickey tugged Fili's halter again and he followed her willingly. When they started their second trip up the hall, he cocked his tail and deposited a huge pile on the floor. Mickey breathed a sigh of relief and laughed when he began to prance beside her, obviously feeling much improved and ready for action.

"That's it, then," Andrew said with a smile while he put the syringe away. "Don't feed him anymore tonight and take away anything he didn't eat from his evening feeding. He can have a little warm water but not more than two or three swallows an hour."

Mickey nodded and handed the lead to Christopher. She removed the uneaten oats from Fili's stall and put the bucket in the feed room. She also gathered up the un-touched hay and placed the flake outside the stall to use in the morning.

She laughed when Fili made a grab for the hay when Christopher led him back into the stall. The horse looked out from behind the steel bars pitifully and gave a little nicker.

"No way, bud," Mickey said firmly. "We're following doctor's orders. I want to keep you around for many years to come."

Christopher and Mickey walked Andrew back to his Blazer. "Thanks for coming so quickly, Andrew," Christopher said, shaking his hand. "We really appreciate you."

"Yeah. Thanks so much." Mickey also squeezed the veterinarian's hand with gratitude. "I would have been absolutely heartbroken if I'd lost him."

"Hey, no problem. That's what I'm here for. You all were fortunate you caught the colic so early. The longer the horse suffers, the worse the prognosis, especially if they start rolling.

Andrew started to climb into the driver's seat, then stopped. "Mickey, are you comfortable giving injections?" he asked.

"I think I would be. Just need a little training," she said thoughtfully.

"Okay. Next time I'm out this way, I'll stop by and give you a lesson. I'm thinking if you keep a bottle of the medication I used tonight on hand, you might be able to avert a full-blown issue if one of your other horses should colic. I'd hate to be too far away to help in time."

"Wow, thanks, Andrew. That would be wonderful," Mickey said gratefully. "I'm sure I can learn."

Andrew climbed into the Blazer and started the engine. "Call me if he has any more trouble." They waved while he drove off down the driveway.

Mickey turned to head back to the barn. "Where are you going?" Christopher asked.

"I'll just check on him one more time before I go to bed," she said over her shoulder.

Christopher walked back up to the house feeling his heart was being torn out slowly, piece by piece. He sat down in the living room and flicked on the TV. He allowed himself to be engrossed in a documentary about lions in Africa.

He did not realize until the programming changed an hour later that Mickey had not returned. With a heavy sigh, he clicked off the TV and headed back to the barn.

Mickey sat on the floor in Fili's stall, the horse curled up beside her like a big dog. She scratched him gently behind the ears, talking to him in a low voice. Christopher looked down at them, his heart full at how tenderly she cared for those she loved.

"Mick, it's after midnight. You'd better get some rest," he whispered after several moments.

Mickey looked up, startled, and then replied, "Actually, I think I'll stay here with him. I want to be sure he's okay."

"Mickey, I have to insist. You'll have another migraine after all this upheaval if you don't get some sleep." He opened the stall door. "I'll stay here with him."

"But, Chris—"

He interrupted firmly. "You need your rest. I'm perfectly capable of looking after Fili. Now go. Or I'll carry you up myself."

Mickey could see by the look in his eyes he meant what he said. She sighed with a bit of frustration at being bossed about, even though his command was for her own good.

"Oh, all right, fine." She rose slowly so she would not alarm the horse, then stalked out of the stall and up the hallway. "But I'll bet I won't sleep."

Christopher settled in beside Fili. "I'll bet she will too sleep, don't you think?" he asked. The horse nickered softly. "Yep. I knew you'd agree with me."

Christopher nodded in satisfaction and leaned his head back against the wall. He began to pray again for the Lord's guidance and wisdom in his relationship with his wife.

~ * ~

Mickey climbed the stairs to her bedroom and pulled off her clothes. She shrugged into a long tee shirt and bounced into bed with a frustrated grunt.

300

Lord, his feeling responsible for my well-being makes this even harder, she thought. *Even though Chris is not in love with me anymore, he still feels his duty is to look after me. I'm having a really hard time with that. Please help me to respond in a Godly way because honestly, Lord, right now being someone's 'duty' just makes me mad.*

She awoke the next morning and remembered her last words to Christopher the night before. *Oh well, so much for not sleeping,* she thought wryly while she climbed out from under the warm covers. She hurriedly dressed and ran down the stairs, intent on making a beeline to the barn.

Christopher stood in the kitchen, dressed for the day, with a pan of bacon on the stove. "He's fine," he commented matter-of-factly when Mickey burst into the room. "I gave him a light feeding instead of his usual ration, though. And we should probably keep him inside today except for maybe a little hand walking."

Mickey glared at his back, her frustration of the night before rising again.

Oh, and who died and made you the expert? Don't you tell me how to take care of my own animals. With effort she kept her angry thoughts to herself and exited the house quickly.

Halfway down the path, her conscience smote her. *I'm sorry, Lord. Forgive me for feeling so hateful. This whole thing of feeling like I'm just his responsibility or something has given me such a bad attitude. Please help me to react in a Godly way.*

Fili welcomed her with an eager whinny, and she grinned while she patted his head through the bars. "Looks like you're back up to snuff," she said. "You're going to need a good grooming after that sweat bath last night."

Seeing the horse back in a normal state of health improved her mood greatly. Ignoring her growing hunger pains, she haltered the horse and led him to the cross ties.

An hour later Fili was gleaming like a show horse. Mickey put him back in his stall, promising she would give him some exercise that afternoon. She left the barn slowly, but her steps quickened when she saw Christopher's Jeep® was gone. She latched the gate behind her and ran to the house, eager for breakfast.

~ *Forty-One* ~

Christopher pulled out his phone and called Greg Norris. "Hey there, Greg. Chris Gordon here. You feel like going on an overnight fishing and camping trip up on our mountain this Friday and Saturday? I know it's still a bit cool but the forecast doesn't predict any rain or snow."

"That sounds fantastic, Chris. I could really use some time away. This has been a long winter." The Pastor's voice conveyed his excitement. "I just need to get back early enough Saturday to polish my Sunday sermon."

"Great. I'll pick you up around one, Friday afternoon."

"Perfect. Thanks a lot, Chris."

By early afternoon Christopher and Greg packed their gear and headed up the mountain in the Jeep. While they made their way up the rough unpaved logging road, Greg sighed.

"This is the life. It's awesome to go camping again. My dad used to take us kids all the time. The ministry seems to take up so much of my time that I'm rarely able to get away." He laughed. "And camping just isn't Lorrie's thing. I found that out the hard way."

Christopher grinned. "Glad you could come, man. I needed some time away, too." He carefully negotiated the Jeep over a protruding root. "We're going to a little lake I found on the other side of the mountain. The temperature will be a bit chilly but these mountains are so breathtaking you won't even notice."

"I believe you. I feel so blessed to live in this part of the country." Greg smiled tenderly. "Lorrie has been a trooper about living out here. She's really a city girl but she's done her best to adapt to country life. She felt God's calling us here just like I did. At least she truly does love the horses! I'm glad she and Mickey have grown so close."

The men continued to chat amiably during the drive. They stopped several times so Christopher could get out to take pictures. After about an hour they began the descent down the other side of the mountain.

When they reached their destination, they made camp a short distance from the lake in the spot where Christopher and Mickey discussed building a cabin. Greg agreed the spot would be a perfect retreat area, but Christopher told him the plans were on hold indefinitely.
The small blue lake was surrounded by last year's dry grass dotted here and there with Lupine and other early spring wildflowers. Pine, fir, and spruce trees made a dense forest further in with clusters of Aspens also. Mountains stretched up on every side, creating a sense of seclusion and peace.

Christopher and Greg fetched the small rowboat from the top of the Jeep and carried the craft to the lake shore. While they started to push off into the smooth calm water, they heard the sharp distinctive cry of a hawk. They looked up, watching the bird fly gracefully overhead, then disappeared over the mountain. Close by, they could hear the chattering of squirrels. A male Mallard patrolled an area on the far edge of the water and a small flock of Canadian Geese swam here and there in search of food.

Each man took an oar. When they reached the middle of the lake, Greg tossed the small anchor over the side. Christopher dug around in the bait pail and pulled out a worm. He pulled back his arm and cast the line in a wide arc. The hook settled into the water with a 'plop' and he sat back to begin the wait.

Greg grabbed the other pole and did likewise on the opposite side of the boat. Within minutes, Christopher felt a good tug on his line.

"All right," Christopher said with glee. "Got one!" He slowly began to reel in his line. He was tremendously pleased when he landed the fish safely in the boat. He looked proudly at the large Mackinaw. "We eat fish to-night!"

"Amen, brother," Greg said with a deep chuckle.

The rest of the day proceeded in a relaxed manner. Both men caught several fish by the time night began to fall. They rowed back to shore and prepared several of the trout.

While they sat by the fire, relaxed and rested by a satisfying day in the great outdoors, Greg spoke. "So, Chris, are you going to tell me what's on your mind?"

"Now, how did you know anything was up?" Christopher asked with a grin, wrapping the fillets in foil and burying them in the ashes.

"I'm not a pastor for nothing, my friend. I'm pretty good at reading people. C'mon. Spill it."

Christopher sobered and leaned back against a tree. "Greg, I just don't know what to do about Mickey. You probably don't know but our marriage is not exactly traditional. She had nowhere to turn when her mother died. She would have had to give up everything she loved just to survive and she'd already lost so much."

He leaned back, crossing his arms in front of him, and stared up into the night sky. "I remember so well how I felt when my mom and dad died. But at least I had a sister. Mickey had nobody." He sighed deeply. "Plus, I've been in love with that girl since I first met her. I thought for sure I could win her love in college but she made me promise not to ever mention my feelings again."

"Wow," Greg said. "Are you serious? Ouch."

A look of intense pain crossed Christopher's face and his voice dropped low while he remembered. "She said our friendship could not continue unless I made that promise. So, I did. Hurt more than anything but I just couldn't stand being without her."

His voice broke and for several minutes he could not continue. "Better just friends than lose her completely, right?" He looked at Greg. "You probably think I'm nuts."

"Absolutely not," Greg said firmly. "I love my Lorrie more than anyone else on this earth. I'd gladly lay down my life for her. I know how it feels to love someone that way."

Christopher sighed deeply and ran a hand through his hair. "When I went to visit Mickey after her mom's funeral, I felt sure the Lord wanted me to propose to her. Convincing her was tough going but when she saw I wasn't going to press her for romance or try to trick her into something, she agreed. I know she did a lot of praying of her own before she made up her mind. I really thought we made the right decision. We've always hit it off and the whole business partnership thing has been a great set up."

Greg looked thoughtful. "I don't have a lot of experience with this sort of thing. As you can imagine, people don't marry for convenience much anymore."

After a moment of silence he said, "But she still hasn't come to love you, even though you've been together for a while now?"

Christopher shook his head. "Nope. Our one-year anniversary is coming up in a couple weeks, but she seems so distant now. So strange. During that first big snowstorm this past winter we seemed close. I mean, man, I really thought she was opening up and it was all going to happen.

"But the next day, she was cold like ice. She warmed up slightly a while later and she is always kind but it's like her heart and soul are completely closed to me. She's there but she's not there. Does that make sense?"

"It does," Greg said nodding.

Christopher sighed deeply, then moved the ashes from the foil packets to check the fish. The meat flaked easily, so he divvied up the portions. They paused for a moment to thank the Lord for the food, then began to eat.

"Mickey was in a really emotionally and verbally abusive relationship in college and I know that affected her a lot in how she related to men later."

Christopher continued after several bites. "I just don't know what to do now. We hardly ever see each other. She seems so uncomfortable around me. Everything is so awkward. I have to admit, I'm uncomfortable around her, too. And I've never felt that way before."

He finished his trout and looked thoughtful. "I know I've been wrong. I've tried to avoid her but I just couldn't take the cold shoulder anymore. Now so much time has passed since we're really talked, I wouldn't know how to begin. Or where."

Greg ate the last forkful of fish and put the plate aside. "I probably don't have an answer you want to hear. I know you've already been patient. Pat answer though it be, keep it up. Keep yourself close to the Lord, Chris. Pray for Mickey and continue to love her. Do your best to make her feel secure and show her that she can trust you."

He reached for a chocolate bar and began to unwrap the candy. "Dr. Charles Stanley has a saying that I love: 'God acts on behalf of those who wait for Him'. Personally, I think she'll come around.

"You're a good man, Chris," he said earnestly. "Honest, trustworthy, a gentleman. Don't give up. I know you have already but commit the situation daily to the Lord and seek His will. He won't let you down. And you can take to the bank the fact that He has a reason for this time in your life. Be open to learning what He has for you to learn. Remember Isaiah 41:10."

307

Christopher nodded. "Fear thou not; for I am with thee: be not dismayed; for I am thy God: I will strengthen thee; yea, I will help thee; yea, I will uphold thee with the right hand of my righteousness," he quoted. "I memorized that in the King James Version when I was a kid. I love some of the newer translations but there is still such beauty to the old English."

Greg nodded. "Sometimes remembering that God's ways are not our ways is very difficult. But whatever His way is, He still loves us, even when we don't understand what's going on. I can promise you this: God is working, even when we can't see any sign."

He smiled tenderly. "Lorrie loves the illustration of God weaving a tapestry. Here in this life, we can only see the back side, full of hanging threads, tangles, and knots. But God sees the beautiful work of art on the top that He is weaving with our lives."

"Wow, that's a great thought," said Chris.

"I know the Lord has a definite plan for you and Mickey, Chris. I know this waiting on Him can be so hard."

"That's for sure. One good thing about all this, I'm learning how to watch, wait, and pray. I've never been in a situation like this where I absolutely cannot see a light at the end of the tunnel. Or figure out a solution."

"You can be assured that the Lord won't let you fall, even when you feel like you're stumbling in the dark. He really is there, leading you step by step. And I know for a fact that He has a plan."

The pastor took a long drink from his water bottle. "One thing, Chris. Whatever happens from day to day, be kind to her. After the abuse she suffered you absolutely cannot be harsh, even when you get frustrated. To do that might mean you'd lose her forever."

Christopher nodded thoughtfully. After praying together, he put out the fire and the men crawled inside the tent and into their sleeping bags.

They spent Saturday morning hiking, enjoying the physical exertion and the beauty of God's creation. When they reached the mountain peak, they held a small impromptu praise service. Singing at the top of their voices and praying on the mountain top made them feel even closer to God. Somehow in that wild, untamed place, Christopher felt his heart burgeon with hope and with the knowledge that God had complete control of his life and of Mickey's.

As the men explored the mountainside and woods, Christopher took shot after shot and Greg began to laugh.

"How many pictures have you taken," he asked.

Christopher checked his camera. "Uh, about 1200."

"Dude! Are you serious?"

"Greg, this is a slow day for me. Usually by now, I'd have at least 2500." He grinned.

"Oh, right. I forgot this is your profession." Greg shook his head and grinned. "The ultimate shutterbug. You won't mind sharing some of those, will you?"

"No problem," said Chris with a smile. "I'll get them to you on a flash drive."

~ * ~

After dropping Greg off at his house late that afternoon, Christopher reflected on their time together while he drove back to the C&M. His spirit was refreshed by the Godly fellowship and found himself encouraged. *Your will be done, Lord*, he prayed. *Please help me to be patient and to trust in Your goodness and in Your timing.*

~ Forty-Two ~

Hungry and ready for supper, Mickey set out the makings of a peanut butter and honey sandwich when the plaintive notes of one of her favorite love songs began to pour out from the iPod speaker dock in the kitchen.

Numbly she listened while she stared out the window. The words felt like a knife in her chest. The feeling that she would never have the loving tender marriage she dreamed of cause anger to surge through her, gaining force and strength like a tidal wave. She let herself, Kip, and Kelsey out before slamming the door behind her. With quick steps she headed for the barn.

~ * ~

Christopher drove into the garage about twenty minutes later. He felt relaxed and in tune with the Lord after his trip with Greg. Though much of the pain remained, peace once again settled his over his mind and soul. Seeing the wisdom of the pastor's advice, he vowed to keep on waiting, praying, and trusting the Lord for answers no matter how long that might take.

After putting his gear in the kitchen, he headed for the barn to see if any new horses came in while he was away. When he neared the door, he heard Mickey's voice. "It's not fair," she said furiously. "These men don't know what true love really means. It's despicable."

Christopher peeked around the barn door and saw Mickey sitting on a bale of hay, shaking a finger in Kip's face. Kelsey sat beside her looking stern and Kip looked properly chastened.

Mickey went on. "Don't you ever stop loving someone just because the situation seems impossible." Her

310

voice broke while her anger gave way to sorrow and began to weep uncontrollably.

Kip came to her then and she hugged both dogs close. "I knew this would happen," she whispered. "I knew this would never work. If I hadn't held on to my sins and to my stupid fear, he might still love me. Now it's too late."

She buried her face in Kip's silky hair while gut wrenching sobs overtook her. "Oh, Lord, help me to keep trusting You and believing in Your goodness," she choked out. "This is so hard right now. So very hard."

Christopher ducked into the office, grabbed a tissue, and silently walked to her with his hand outstretched. Mickey jumped when she saw him and tried valiantly to re-gain her composure but to no avail. She took the tissue but looked up at him helplessly, unable to stop the torrent of tears streaming down her face.

He knelt beside her and gently took her hand. "Mickey, honey, what's wrong?" he asked tenderly, his voice low and deep. His heart ached to ease her sorrow. She looked down and shook her head. "Oh, Chris, I was afraid this would happen," she said sadly. "I knew from the very beginning that this whole thing wasn't fair to you."

Christopher put his hand under her chin and lifted her face. She tried to avoid meeting his gaze, but he wait-ed until her eyes met his. "What's going on?" he asked, wanting desperately to understand. "What are you talking about? What's happened to upset you so? What's happened to us?"

Christopher moved to sit beside Mickey on the bale of hay and took her firmly in his arms, hugging her tightly despite the way she stiffened. "Mickey, please."

He sighed and pulled back slightly to look deeply in-to her eyes. "I know I promised not to pressure you or tell you how I feel but I have to break my promise. Mickey, I have to tell you one more time."

He paused, then took a deep breath. "I love you, Mickey. I've loved you since the day we met. I wanted to marry you even after the promise, because at least I'd get to be with you for the rest of my life."

Mickey relaxed immediately but began to sob again and he dropped his hands.

"I'm sorry, Mick, really I am," he said dejectedly. "I knew you wouldn't want to hear that. I think I've been a good friend and up 'til now, I've kept my promise. I just felt so strongly that I should tell you once more how I really feel. I guess I was wrong. I'm so sorry."

Overwhelmed with joy, Mickey marveled at the fact that Christopher did still love her. She could scarcely believe her ears.

He knows me completely, she thought. *He's seen me at my best and my worst; my prettiest and my ugliest; when I'm self-reliant and when I'm totally helpless. When I act in a manner becoming of a Christian and when I show out like a rebel. And he still loves me. Thank You, Lord.*

She sat in amazement. *Not too late! Not too late! He loves me! He loves me!* The words rang in her head like a beautiful melody. Her beloved Christopher loved her the same as always, even after all this time, even after all the pain.

Her heart twisted when she remembered all the wonderful things he did for her. How he wanted to be with her, all the while never knowing if she would ever return his feelings.

Christopher slowly rose, brushed the hay from his jeans, and turned away in misery. He knew his speech caused her further unhappiness and his heart sank.

Have my hasty words ruined everything now? he thought while he slowly walked toward the barn door. *Oh,*

*dear Lord, please help me. I really felt this was of You but
I can see she doesn't love me. Please Lord, don't let her
leave me. I'll never do anything to hurt her. I can't stand
the thought of losing her. Please let her stay in my life,
even if we just continue on as friends.*

Mickey looked up and stared after him, wondering
why he was walking away at a time like this. Suddenly she
realized how her reaction must have looked to him.

*I am acting like an idiot! He thinks I'm angry with
him!* She jumped off the bale of hay and ran up behind
him.

"Chris," she said, speaking as firmly as her shaky
voice would allow. He stopped and stood still, dreading the
words she was sure to speak. Mickey came around and took
his hands in hers, looking into his eyes.

"I love you, too, Chris," she said with a smile. Then
in one bold move, she put her hand gently on his face and
kissed him firmly on the lips.

Christopher stood completely still, stunned. He felt
like an electric shock jolted through him. *Lord, did I hear
her right?* he thought. *Is it possible that she really does return my love? After all this time, after all my prayers, is
this Your answer, Lord?*

After she drew away, he cleared his throat and said
huskily, "Did I hear you right? Are you sure, Mickey? I don't
want you to do something you don't really want."

Mickey framed his face with her hands and said fervently, "I'm sure. I love you, Chris. And what's weird is
that I feel like I always have."

She stepped back from him and reached a hand to
push a curl behind one ear.

"The whole time we've been married, I've never
been able to surrender to God the matter of love or the
pain Lee caused me," she continued. "The Lord's been af-

313

ter me for a long time but I guess I have a stubborn streak or a blind eye. That and my faith was just too weak. I couldn't bring myself to really trust that He could change and heal me. And it never dawned on me that I needed to forgive Lee or that I was drowning in my bitterness."

Mickey looked down, clasping her small hands together. "I was scared to ask God to let me love you. That one time I prayed to have a specific person, I got what I wanted and it was awful. After that, I decided I would never ask for love again. I was afraid if I did, that request would backfire on me."

She looked into Christopher's kind brown eyes, willing him to understand. "I knew you weren't anything like Lee. Please believe that. But I was just so afraid. I realized back while you were on that trip to the coast, I'd never asked the Lord to heal my pain. I hadn't known how much what Lee did was still overshadowing every aspect of my life. That baggage kept me from realizing I really did love you."

Christopher nodded and Mickey went on. "The day before you got back from that trip, I was listening to my praise playlist and "Hello My Name Is" came on. I seriously have probably heard that song a hundred times and knew all the words but for some reason that day, they got my attention.

"I realized how I was still allowing shame and defeat to color my life and I'd never even asked God to heal me. Plus, there was the bitterness that came from not forgiving Lee."

Christopher sighed. "I know what you mean. I still haven't quite gotten there. The forgiving part, I mean. I need to ask God to help me with that. Every time I think of what he did to you I want to pound him good."

Mickey looked at him shyly. "I have to admit, I kind of like your protective side. But anyway, during that song, when I realized the freedom I have in Christ to ask that His will be accomplished in my life, suddenly I knew. I love you. In every possible way I love you."

Then she sobered. "I thought of how I'd feel if you never came home. Then after you called and I heard that woman in the background, I was sure I was losing you. After that first snowstorm, she called here. At first I thought you'd found someone else but after I had time to think, realistically I knew that you'd be faithful to me. But I really thought you didn't love me anymore and felt you probably wished you could pursue her."

Christopher grimaced at the pain Gillian Fitzgerald caused. He put his hand tenderly on Mickey's face. "You know, don't you, that she was nothing to me? She was just interested in playing games with people's lives. I never dreamed she would go so far, especially after I made it quite clear that I am a happily married man."

Tears glistened in Mickey's eyes once more. "I know that now. I realize she just made up the whole thing about you expecting her call. I feel so badly about that misunderstanding and about all the time I've wasted being afraid.

"I realize now that with Lee, I demanded my own way and I didn't care about God's will. I wanted what I asked for, period. If I had asked God to work out His will about loving you and if I had acknowledged my unforgiving spirit toward Lee, things might have come together for us a long time ago."

Mickey smiled sheepishly and bit her lip. "The Lord kept showing me that verse 'Ask and ye shall receive' but there was just too much fear in my heart. And hating Lee was easier than forgiving him."

Christopher held out his arms and Mickey snuggled close. He hugged her tightly and she hugged him right back.

"The Lord is so good, Mick. So faithful," he said, smiling while tears welled up in his own eyes. "I knew when I proposed to you back after your mom died that I was doing the right thing even though you didn't love me. But believe me, I've prayed every day since then that you would come to love me. I've learned a lot about patience and trust. I knew you were hurting but I also knew only the Lord could heal you."

He ran his hand gently up and down her back. "Don't feel badly about the time lost," he whispered, pressing a kiss on her head. "Besides if I had addressed the Gillian issue right off we might have avoided some of this. That was my fault. But the Lord's timing is perfect despite our weaknesses. Remember Romans 8:28? 'All things work together for good to them that love God'."

"That is so true. You know, God taught me so much during this time of pain and sorrow," she said, her eyes moist. "I see that now. He said my prayer in such an amazing way. I begged Him not to let me come out of this without learning what He had for me to learn. I believe He wanted me to know how to lean on Him and how to act in a Godly way, even when my emotions didn't cooperate. I have never felt closer to God than I do now."

"Like the song says, Our God is an Awesome God," Christopher said with a smile.

Mickey leaned back with her arms still around his waist. "Now we can have a real marriage," she said shyly.

"That's right," he said with a roughish glint in his eye. "No more of this his and hers bedrooms. From now on, we will have our room."

"Absolutely," she said with a giggle. "Unless you snore, that is."

Christopher smiled and reached to bury his hand in her hair. "I don't think that will be a problem," he murmured huskily, drawing her face to his. His lips met hers joyfully. The kiss deepened and intensified when they realized they were finally free to express the love they kept hidden for so long.

Several minutes later flushed, happy, and completely in love, Christopher and Mickey made their way to the house, barn chores forgotten. They walked up the path hand in hand while the dogs ran excitedly beside them barking happily sensing that all was finally completely right with their world.

When they reached the porch, Christopher suddenly stopped. "Wait right here," he said and dashed into the house.

Mickey looked after him quizzically but did as he bade her.

In a moment, he returned with two small boxes. "I've been saving these since last May," he said a bit sheepishly. "I know you didn't want wedding rings before. Am I right in thinking you might have changed your mind?"

"You are," Mickey said with a grin.

He opened the first box to reveal a beautiful diamond in a vintage setting. "This was my mom's," he said, getting a bit misty eyed. "She would have loved you, Mick. Kirsten and I both want you to have her engagement ring."

Mickey's eyes welled up with tears and she held out her left hand. He placed the diamond on her ring finger and kissed her gently.

"Now, this one is for both of us," Christopher said, opening the second box. Inside nestled on blue velvet lay a beautiful gold wedding set with tiny inset marquise cut diamonds.

"I bought these before you made the comment that you didn't want us to wear wedding rings. I was afraid you would feel I was pressuring you for romance if I showed them to you." He looked at Mickey, his heart in his eyes.

317

"Would you do me the honor of placing my wedding ring on my left hand?"

Tears rolled down Mickey's cheeks when she realized again the depth of Christopher's love for her and his trust that one day God would bring her to love him in return. She placed the wedding band on his hand and he did likewise for her.

Then he scooped Mickey up easily into his arms. He looked at her lovingly with teasing in his brown eyes. "I just realized, I really must apologize, you know. I broke my promise. I hope you can forgive me."

Mickey pretended to consider his apology for a moment. "I think," she said, kissing him softly, "that these were extenuating circumstances. That particular promise needed breaking."

Christopher kissed her again, then she laid her head on his shoulder. "You know what, Chris?" she asked. "My daddy prayed for me before I was born. He prayed that I would find Jesus and that God would bring me a gentle loving husband." She sighed with contentment. "Daddy's prayer has been said."

As they crossed the threshold of their home, they smiled when they thought of that long ago prayer of a loving father and of their new life together which would be filled with love and be blessed by a loving Heavenly Father.

~ END ~

Broken Promise

Dear Reader,

Domestic violence is the plague of our age. Every day, thousands of victims fall prey to this travesty. Domestic violence often starts with verbal abuse and escalates into physical violence. I would present, however, the theory that verbal and emotional violence do just as much damage, even though the harm done is not always outwardly visible.

Broken Promise is a story of hurt, restoration, and abiding love. My most fervent wish is that through this story you would see not only the lasting effects of abuse but the freedom and healing available through Jesus Christ.

If you're suffering from the effects of an abusive relationship, please go to Jesus. His gift of salvation is free to all. His healing will make you stronger. I speak from experience when I say that only God can take a person from feeling lower than dirt, to feeling completely confident and restored. He did that for me. He can do that for you as well.

If you are currently in an abusive relationship, I implore you to get out and find a supportive environment. Abuse is never okay. Violence is never okay. If you are considering a relationship with someone and this story raised some red flags, heed them. You cannot be too careful. If you are in danger, please call the National Domestic Violence Abuse Hotline at 1-800-799-7233 or escape to a shelter near you.

In Christ's love,
Christy Diachenko

Christy R. Diachenko

Broken Promise

Christy R. Diachenko

Made in the USA
Columbia, SC
26 November 2023

26703095R00176